CRY OF THE WHIPPOORWILL

BY

KELVIN POORE

Kelvin Poore
16 Buttermilk Pike
Ft. Mitchell, Kentucky 41017
(859) 866-3862

TABLE OF CONTENTS

CRY OF THE WHIPPOORWILL

BY

KELVIN POORE

CHAPTER ONE

It was time. Time to open the doors and let the day begin, a day of light and promise, a day to build dreams or conquer nightmares. It was a fine day for murder.

Robert Glen Pierce had spent his entire life anticipating a day such as this. His earliest dreams and aspirations had directed him toward this day. Today, Bobby Pierce planned to change his station in life. He wished to be more than a victim. Today was to be the day Bobby Pierce gets his.

Vernon Price had made life a living hell for Bobby. As long as Bobby could remember, Vernon had been a thorn in his side. Since kindergarten, Vernon had tormented him. Vernon was not the only person to have victimized Bobby. There were many others. Today they would all pay and that price would be high.

Bobby could still remember the day his Uncle Jimmy came back from the "Gulf." Jimmy had been away fourteen months. The last six had been spent on the border between the Iraq and Kuwait front line. Jimmy had been a good soldier. He loved everything about the military. He loved the uniforms, discipline, the tough physicality of the life, but most of all he loved the weapons.

Jimmy had fulfilled his fondest dreams in the Gulf War. He had killed people. He had killed with machines that made the entire experience seem like a video game. He had also killed face to face and this he much preferred.

Jimmy Pierce had brought home a lot of things from his military experience. He brought home his training, his hate, his love for violence and his arsenal of illegal collected items of war. These "souvenirs" were the key to Bobby's plan. Uncle Jimmy had shown Bobby all of his toys soon upon his return from the war. Jimmy could sense within Bobby a kindred spirit.

Jimmy had lived most of his life scared and hunted just waiting for his chance to exact payment upon a world that he felt owed him plenty. He had waited twenty-three years for a chance to make someone else feel the pain and anger that had been part of him since birth. Jimmy was such a good uncle that he was going to make damn sure that his nephew Bobby did not have to wait that long.

Bobby's fear of Vernon Price was a conditioned response beat into him. Every morning when Bobby stepped out of his front door, he could see Vernon at the end of the quarter mile stretch that connected his parents' home to the highway. Bobby's family, along with Vernon's family and the Gatz family all shared a common bus stop.

They lived in a rural area and the bus ride to school was forty-five minutes each way. These were the worst ninety minutes of Bobby's daily hell.

Vernon's uncle, Hobe Wells, drove the bus. Hobe was a large, mean spirited man who encouraged his nephew in his endeavors on the school bus. Vernon's routine usually started with a little verbal abuse and escalated from that point. A typical encounter would go…. "Hey fuckface, you better hurry or Uncle Hobe'll leave yer dead ass a standin' in the road, you little shit fer brains."

"I'm coming. I'm coming"

"Hey Bobby, why are you always so slow gettin' out here in the morning? If I didn't know better, it'd seem like you maybe didn't wanna be here. But we know that ain't so, because everybody knows little shitface Bobby loves school and can't wait to go see Miss Dumphreys and kiss her ass like the little punkass sissy faggot that he is. Ain't that right?"

"If you say so."

"Yeah, well I say so. You're goddamned right I say so and you better quit gettin' mouthy."

This little interchange is usually followed by a couple of slaps on the side of the head. Vernon refers to these slaps as "bitch smacks" and to Bobby as his "little bitch."

Smack! Smack! "Hey little bitch, you gettin' mouthy with your ol' buddy Vern?" Smack! "Gettin a little too smart for your own good, huh?"

"Vernon, here comes the bus." "Yeah Vern, let him go, you proved your point."

"Ah fuck you too Marnie. You like the little fucker. You probably want to suck his little dick like you do Arnell's."

"You better watch your mouth or I'll tell Arnell and you'll be the one getting smacked."

"Yeah, well tell him and I'll tell dad I seen you and him and we'll see what pop thinks about you sucking your own cousin's dick."

"Oh, fuck you Vernon!"

"Oh, fuck me, Marnie. I mean hey, you're already doin' your first cousin, why not your little brother?"

"Right there's why, little brother, with the emphasis on little."

"Oh, fuck you, get on the bus."

"Mornin' Marnie, Gail, Francie, Jack, Vern, Bobby. Vern what'd I tell you about hittin' Bobby with your hands?"

"I know. I know, Uncle Hobe. You said get a stick because these are the only hands I got. Hah, hah, hah."

"That's right now, settle down, all of you"

Vern sits in the rear while Bobby tries to sit midway. Vernon tells him to come to the back because he needs to talk with him.

"I don't wanna, you ass."

"You get back here or I'll knock the dog shit out of you boy."

"Okay, I'm coming. I'm coming."

"Oh, I'm sorry, I didn't mean to insult your precious sister. I mean I know she has problems and I should be more sensitive. That's why me and Freddie Wilbanks are coming over this afternoon. We are gonna help her with her problems. When we get done, her biggest problem's gonna be swallowing all the jizz we gonna slam down her neck. Hah, hah."

"Little Bobby wanna watch me screw his big sister again? I know you peek when I slam it up her ass and put it in her face. Don't get mad little bitchie boy. I'll let you lick the shit off my dick when I pull it out of your sister's ass. All right?"

At this little interchange, everyone laughs except Bobby. Bobby hates Vernon. He is everything Bobby wants to be. He is tall, good looking, has money, and he has indeed, fucked Bobby's sister.

These are all the things Bobby wants, but cannot have. He may get his sister, but the rest are things that are definitely not going to happen. Bobby's life has been this way up until now. This day was going to bring something different. It began two weeks before, quite innocently.

CHAPTER TWO

Bobby and his Uncle Jimmy were riding around the farm in Bobby's old truck. An old "72" GMC truck with a 350 in it, but it had no fenders or grill. The truck was not licensed or insured, so Bobby wasn't allowed to drive it on the road unless he was sent to the store or some such.

Jimmy was driving and that was fine with Bobby because he became self-conscious whenever he had to do anything such as driving around anyone whose opinion he cared about.

Bobby's life had become a series of trials in which the whole world stood in judgment, and he, the sole defendant in a case he felt he could never win. He had no idea that almost every sixteen-year-old felt this way and they were probably correct.

This same group will find out later, that the people sitting in judgment lost their cases also, and the appeals afterward, still life proceeds. It doesn't get easier, it just mutates into something so wretched that the opinions of others have no meaning.

Jimmy was relating a story to Bobby. "Hot damn son! You ain't seen no shit like that in your entire miserable God forsaken life. I mean man, these fellers are all a settin' on this hilltop a lookin' at these little ol' blips and bleeps on them there radar screens an all's we gotta do is push a button and the blips get a little bigger then they's gone. It ain't even real killin' like that. Don't mean nothin' a'tal. Pussy mother fucker ain't never throwed a punch killin' all hell outta people they ain't never seen. The next day these

-6-

same mother fuckers is puking they damn guts out looking at that damn convoy. It finally struck home that they wasn't playing no damn videos and that them little blips was real."

"Real as hell! Real men dying and dying real bad, real hard. Personally, I preferred looking at what I was killing. That way I could make sure warn't nuthin' left to kill me, if you know what I mean? Hah, hah, hah! Cough, cough…. They's a few ol' boys aroun' here I wouldn't mind hanging their guts on a limb given the chance. What about you son? You ever feel like stickin' anybody? I mean with something asides that thang you packing ye britches?"

"Oh yeah! Hell yeah! Everyday, all day. I'd like to kill half this town fast and the rest slow, real slow!"

The words had no sooner come out of his mouth than Bobby realized they were true. He did indeed want to kill people, a lot of people.

Jimmy Pierce had never taken his nephew very seriously. He felt Bobby was somewhat of a sissy. He liked him well enough, but had never noticed anything special in the boy. When Bobby had made his outburst about killing, Jimmy took notice. He finally found some common ground with his nephew.

Jimmy was a man who detested weakness. He was somewhat of a cruel man. He had always felt Bobby weak, but had tried to be fair with the boy. Jim now saw something strong in the boy, *hate*.

Bobby had hate in him like Jimmy had hate. A strong, powerful hate, which if directed right, could change Bobby into something more than the sniveling little shit that Jimmy had always felt him to be.

"You mean that, don't you boy! Why shore you do! Well, son, I know a little about that sorta thing if 'n you serious."

Bobby didn't reply for a full minute. He let the words sink in. Bobby Pierce had resigned himself to a life of being a loser. The low man on the totem pole, someone lost in the crowd. He never felt he could be anything else.

Uncle Jimmy's offer brought something forward in Bobby that he had feared to even dream about. It offered an opportunity to strike back, to be noticed, to step forth and grab a little of the life he had always felt out of reach. Bobby mouthed his answer silently, then with force. "Yes, I'm serious. I don't care what happens. I'm serious. I'll do anything."

The journey began. Bobby's transformation from sniveling shit into homicidal fiend began that day.

CHAPTER THREE

Jimmy had some ideas about training killers and most were not to be found in

manuals. Jimmy Pierce pulled the truck into the side yard. Maxwell or "Maxi" Pierce"

was Bobby's father. He didn't give two shits for any of his three children. His two girls,

Ellen and Maxine were both sluts and knew to stay out of his way and his youngest,

Bobby, was a major disappointment, to say the least.

Maxi was in a hurry. He noticed the duo pulling into the yard. "Bobby, feed the

dogs." Maxi got into his car and pulled out of the driveway. Maxi loved one thing on

God's green earth, and that was his dogs. He had fifteen in all. Most were mongrels or

mixed breeds, but he had three prize AKC registered "Blue Tick Hunters." One a bitch,

and the other two males. He made upward of six thousand dollars a year just selling

pups. The care and feeding of these dogs fell to Bobby.

Bobby proceeded to feed and water the dogs while Jimmy hooked up the high-

pressure hose, which he used to clean the dog run and kennels. Jimmy didn't care about

cleaning, but he did like aggravating the dogs. "Hah, hah, hah, watch that bitch roll.

Dem blues ain't got a lick a sense. Hup, hup, hup, here Rex, does puppy want a drink?

Hah, Hah, wasn't near as thirsty as you thought, was you?"

Jimmy sprays the dog a second time. He enjoys the mild torture. There is something

slightly sick and twisted about Jimmy.

"Bobby, hey Bob, git out here. I got an idea." Bobby stepped out into the pen. He threw the dogs handfuls of a mixture of chopped beef, hamburger and dried dog food. The meat was raw and almost rancid, but the dogs ate every shred.

Maxi preferred to keep his hunters hungry. It wasn't unheard of to throw injured game into the pens and let the dogs kill and feed.

Jimmy began Bobby's training at the dog pens. "Boy you wanna get back at the whole world, don't you?"

"Yeah, I guess I do, why?"

"Well, I's just a sitting here a studyin'. Now who do you s'pose you are most mad at? I mean who deserves the shit you got to give out the most?"

"I don't know! Everybody, I guess."

"Nah," Jimmy said, "the way I figure it is, you the way you are because that worthless asshole of a brother of mine didn't take the time to learn you to be no other way. So, I's got it figured, you need to start your rehabilitation with your daddy, cuz he's the one put you in this shit as deep as you is anyhow."

"Huh? Yeah, I guess. But how? I don't wanna kill my father."

"Bullshit! Of course you do. Every man worth his salt wants to kill his daddy one time or another. It's natural as breathin' but that ain't what I'm talking about anyhow. Killing ain't easy. I ain't even sure you got it in you. Killin's a hard row to hoe, for anybody. Killing something you hate, well that ain't so tough, but for the type full scale get even with the world type shit you got in you boy, you gonna need to be the type a killer that can kill anything. You gotta be able to wipe out anything and everything that gets in your way. Now a 'fore we go any further, I want you to kill everyone. I mean every single damn one of those dogs in that cage. I'll be back about dark and if them dogs ain't dead, I'll know you boy and I'll know you ain't got what it takes. It's about three o'clock now. You study on it awhile and you do what your heart tells you. Don't make no never mind to me. I gets mine and I'll take whoever's including you, if you start fucking wit me boy. Later."

Jimmy finished his speech and jumped into the pickup and took off across the yard. Bobby stood stunned for about five minutes, as if slapped.

Jimmy knew, as did anyone who knew Bobby that the dogs were the only thing Bobby looked forward to each day. Bobby felt betrayed. He felt his uncle had played some cruel joke and was laughing at him. His uncle had gotten him all excited talking about strength, hate and getting even. He had given him hope where there had been none. He told him of murder and how good it felt to rip the life out of those you despised then he had asked the impossible. He wanted Bobby to kill the only creatures in the world he loved. The only creatures that loved him back.

Bobby sat down on a sack of feed and started crying deep sobs that shook his entire body. He cried soundless, pitiful, soulful squalls of grief. A speckled pup came up and licked his face. It sensed his pain and tried to make it better. Bobby tried not to, but could not help it and began to laugh.

Seven o' clock came and with it, Jimmy Pierce returned to the dog kennel. Jimmy was in a great mood. He had driven down the road to Earl Parker's place and drank a few with Earl and his brother Clyde.

Earl and Clyde were a couple of pretty good ol' boys. They were not too bright, but free with their beer and dope. Clyde's ol' lady was even more free than her husband. She'd get right down and slurp that thing if you got her in the right mood. Clyde didn't mind being a punk. He just didn't want to look like one.

Jimmy was chuckling to himself. He figured Bobby wasn't ready to kill, not yet. He would be, but first, he had to get him thinking like a killer. (He had to get the boy's mind right for the job.) Hell! Jimmy was so sure of Bobby when he made his request; he hadn't even left a gun.

Jimmy got out of the truck whistling the Marine Hymn. (He hadn't been in the corps but he liked the tune.) Jimmy was Army all the way, but he felt Marines were all right.

He didn't notice the quiet at first, but then it stuck him. The dog run, usually a bustling center of activity was eerily still and silent. He could hear a soft scraping noise followed by a splashing sound. He heard this along with snatches of a whispered song, mixed with intermittent giggles. He rounded the corner of the building into the dog pen yard proper. He stopped in mid-stride. He couldn't believe the scene before him, not at first, but it sunk in! "Damn boy! I'll be God-double-dee-damned! I didn't think you could! I mean, how?"

Before Jimmy's eyes, Bobby stood in nothing but his underwear. He was covered from head to toe with blood, feces, brains and innards. Strewn around the yard were the remains of what a few hours before had been his healthy dogs. The dogs had been killed, each and every one.

Bobby stared at his uncle and smirked. He had found out something about himself. He knew the answers and no longer cared about the questions. The killing had begun in a frenzied attack. Bobby had grabbed an ax from off the wall inside the shed. It was a double bit, used to split stove lengths in cold weather. He had run out into the yard and slashed at the first dog he saw. It had been a mixed, black and tan with some terrier.

The dog had approached in a friendly manner. It had stopped five feet from Bobby and started whining. The dog could sense the tension and smell the fear. It started to growl. Several dogs began to bark, growl, and howl. Bobby could not stand the noise. The terror of the dogs acted as a trigger. It released the anger and hate within the boy. Bobby began swinging. He connected with the first dog, hitting the animal in the right front leg. Bones splintered, blood flew, and the dog screamed a very un-dog like howl.

The other dogs could smell the scent and the fear. The dogs reverted to pack instinct and turned on their comrade. Bobby continued to flail wildly with the ax connecting over and over with the various animals. The melee continued for over an hour. Bobby extracted himself and ran back into the shed. He was covered with blood and feces. He removed his pants, shoes and shirt. The animals continued to bark and snap at each other.

Bobby's first confrontation with the dogs had resulted in four animals dead and three more injured beyond repair. Bobby was experiencing shock and a mixture of other emotions. He felt fear, anger, disgust and a vague stirring of exhilaration.

Uncle Jimmy had said all the dogs were to be dead when he returned. Bobby's initial assault had been effective, but he could not try another attack in the same manner. The animals had become unapproachable. Bobby had sustained various bites and scratches.

Two were serious and needed attention. They would have to wait. Bobby had a job to complete.

Bobby searched the shed looking for a means to kill the rest of the animals. He no longer worried about the consequences of his actions or the dogs themselves. He had become obsessed with finishing the job.

Bobby had listened to the stories his Uncle Jimmy had told him. Jimmy had told him a lot of bullshit, but he had also conveyed some very useful information. Jimmy Pierce had told his nephew many stories of war and weapons; most were useless.

Jimmy had seen fighting in the Gulf. The weapons the enemy had used ranged from the most sophisticated anti-tank rockets available to rocks.

Bobby found a metal pesticide container. Into this, he poured a mixture of motor oil, gasoline, and detergent. The mixture was thick and soupy. It would not flow through the sprayer at first. Bobby thinned the mixture by adding more gasoline.

He mixed and re-mixed until the sprayer would emit a fine steady mist that sprayed about a five to six feet area from right to left. The gasoline mixed with the motor oil and detergent would stick to anything it struck. With one match, Bobby had made a very effective homemade flame-thrower.

Bobby found a big problem in using his "flame thrower." He only wanted to kill the dogs. He did not want to burn down the shed or destroy anything on the farm. He took the pressure washer that Jimmy had used to wash the dogs and sprayed the entire building. He soaked it thoroughly and then left it turned on, just in case.

Bobby herded all the dogs into one pen – the one furthest from the building. He closed this pen off from the rest. He sprayed the dogs with his mixture, trying to get some on each animal. Bobby then ignited his homemade flame-thrower.

Bobby did not attend church often, but he had been to Sunday service enough to have his own version of hellfire and damnation. Nothing had prepared him for the screaming, agonized images that confronted him. The dogs that had loved him and depended upon him were writhing and howling in pain. Here they were, with their tortured limbs clawing at the side of the pen with some rolling themselves out only to be doused again. Bobby laughed and danced maniacally, spraying his deadly mist. Lucifer torturing the damned. He had never felt so alive or so in power. Each animal's death became a conquest for the scared, little victim. Each spray of fire killed more than its canine target. The fire also burned away shreds of compassion and empathy that a victimized sixteen year-old boy had within him.

The slaughter of Maxi Pierce's dogs had taken almost three hours. Bobby Pierce sprayed each corpse over and over until his homemade flame-thrower was empty. He surveyed the carnage before him with dazed, unfeeling eyes.

He was removed from his actions, walking around half-naked, not feeling the burns and bites that covered his body in various places. Bobby did not hear his Uncle Jimmy return. He was listening intently for any signs of life within the dogs' pen. He finally heard a faint, scratching followed by a faint whimpering. He followed this noise until he tracked it back into the shed proper. Under the lawn tractor, Bobby found two pups. One a speckled bitch, the other a little blue. He grabbed both pups, one in each hand. He stepped back into the yard and finally noticed his Uncle Jimmy.

Jimmy had a look on his face that Bobby had never seen. His face showed awe, doubt, respect and fear. Yes! His own Uncle Jimmy was scared and even shocked by him, *Bobby Pierce*!

Bobby looked at his uncle and held out a pup. "Want one?"

"What?"

"Do you want a pup? I got two left, one for me. One for you."

"Huh? What do I want one for?"

"To show me how to kill, of course!"

Jimmy Pierce was a brutal man who had received an unexpected shock. A person that he had categorized one way in his head had turned out to be something totally unexpected. He could not help but be surprised, but he would not let his brother's punk of a son make an ass of him. He reached out and grabbed a pup with his left hand and smacked Bobby backhanded with his right.

"Don't get smart with me, you little shit! You think you're hard boy? You kill a few mangy mutts and you think you know something about death? I'll show you death." Upon making this statement, he took the pup and raised it to Bobby's face. Using his left fist, he squeezed slowly while looking Bobby in the eye. He squeezed the life out of the innocent little pup. Its pitiful cries ineffective upon the two.

Bobby met his uncle's gaze and squeezed also. Both pups died within seconds of each other. Bobby and Jimmy stared into each other's eyes and committed homicide upon the harmless creatures. They both were so caught up in the act of killing the dogs, that when they were done, they both started laughing. They were a little embarrassed at the intensity of the moment. They both also felt something had forever changed within their relationship. They were not equals, but Bobby had indeed upped his status within his uncle's eyes.

CHAPTER FOUR

The murder of the dogs was not finished. Maxwell Pierce was going to be *very* pissed at the sight of his prized hunting dogs charred, dead bodies. He would not accept this fate lightly. He would hunt down the perpetrators of such a deed and most likely kill them in such a way as to make the murder of the dogs look humane.

Maxwell would have to be dealt with. He would need to be convinced the dogs were killed accidentally or that some third party had done the deed. The fact that Bobby was his son would not make the least bit of difference in the wrath of Maxwell Pierce.

Bobby and Jimmy struck upon a plan to cover the incident and have a few laughs as well. There was no love lost between Maxi Pierce and his brother and the relationship with his son was even worse.

Inside the shed there were two tanks of acetylene. They were used for welding. Maxwell Pierce had traded a speckled pup for these tanks. The pup was not sired from his prized hounds, but he had not bothered to tell that little fact to the man who traded with him.

The Pierce's lived next door to a family of four, the Smith's. The Smith's were farmers and not very good ones. Randall Smith had inherited his farm from his father and didn't give least concern about its upkeep. He much preferred to sit in the shade of his front yard and drink Falls City beer everyday and let life take care of itself.

Eliza Smith, Randall's oldest daughter, did all the farming that went on at the Smith farm. She was not concerned with traditional crops such as corn, soybeans or hay.

Instead, her taste ran more toward crops that had a higher return on their yield. She grew some of the finest marijuana in the nation. Last year she harvested over six hundred-pound of high-grade pot. This was very, very profitable and not an easy task. In order to do so, she had to grow year round and constantly patrol her farm to keep the law and theirs from her crops. Eliza also harvested mushrooms after each rain. She was very skilled and no one had ever gotten sick from getting the wrong species from her.

Jimmy and Bobby's plan to cover up the dog incident depended upon Randall Smith and his daughter. Eliza Smith could perhaps be the best pot farmer in the entire region, but she was in no way a great beauty. Miss Eliza tops out at five feet, eleven inches in her stocking feet. She weighs somewhere in the neighborhood of two hundred and forty pounds and has a face that could, at its best, be considered homely. She has had a crush on Jimmy Pierce for years. Jimmy knew this and milked it for everything he could. He borrowed money and never paid it back. He never paid for his smoke. He let her blow him and never returned the favor. She was not allowed to talk to him in public. She would do anything for him and he knew it.

Jimmy Pierce and Randall sat drinking in the Smith's front yard. They were both drunk and more than a little high. Bobby Pierce was waiting down by the dog pen. He was waiting for a signal. He was scared. He knew what his father would do to him if this plan didn't work. He felt alive.

Jimmy had been at the Pierce's for about three hours. He considered this a great sacrifice upon his part and planned on making sure his nephew became well aware just how great a favor his uncle was performing. The visit had not been entirely unpleasant. He had to be nice to Eliza upon arrival.

He had kissed and fondled her until she had blown him. He then let her cook him some ham and potatoes. Eliza's sister Mary Ann came home from school at three o'clock. Jimmy flirted shamelessly with the thirteen-year-old. He even felt her up when her sister wasn't looking. He told the young girl to touch him and she would not. He told her to go into the next room and watch and she would see what she was missing. Jimmy's desire for her sister provided Eliza her dream come true. Jimmy proceeded to make love to Eliza so her little sister could watch. He pulled her sweat pants off and rubbed her mound. He spoke into her ear as he rubbed himself on her generous ass. Mary Ann watched intently as her sister answered these caresses. She could not help but be aroused. She could smell their scent. She could feel their heat. Jimmy kissed and fondled Eliza's huge tits. She removed her top. He made her leave her bra on and pulled it under her breast making them stand up and out. She was a large, ugly woman, but she was hot, burning hot! She had lived this moment a hundred times alone in her bed, and at last it was happening. Jimmy, her Jimmy, was making love to her. Jimmy was indeed making love to Eliza. Jimmy had never been big on foreplay, but the thought of Mary Ann watching him was inspiring him to some very creative foreplay, at least by his standards. His dick was like stone and he was stroking it between Eliza's butt cheeks as he rubbed her tits. He was licking and kissing her neck and ears. His hand roamed over her gut shamelessly. Her very ugliness was turning him on. She was emitting a stench unlike any woman he had ever been with. Fluids streamed down her thighs. Eliza was cumming harder than she had ever came in her life and Jimmy hadn't even entered her. She rubbed herself and placed her fingers under his nose. He got the scent and it did its job. He had to taste her. Jimmy had never performed oral sex on a woman before in his life. Eliza Smith, the ugly bitch next door, had him so hot, he had to taste her, devour her. He had to take her essence and suck it inside him.

He got on his knees. He could still see Mary Ann at the door. Her hand was in her pants. She was leaning on the door, "weak" from the intensity of her orgasms. Eliza grabbed him by the hair and pulled his hand into her hairy gush. She ground his head between herself and the sink. He couldn't breathe. He didn't care. He didn't try to pull away, indeed he dove deeper his tongue driving, lips slurping. He was in, but couldn't get enough. He sucked her twat until she pulled him off and even then he tried to go back.

Eliza was breathless. This was better than she had ever dreamed, but she needed him inside her. She pleaded. "Fuck me, Jimmy! Oh, Jimmy please give it to me! Come on baby, fuck me. Hurry! Hurry! I need you so bad, baby!" Jimmy grabbed her ass, one cheek in each hand, came up off his knees and slammed up and into her wet cunt. God, it was good! So fucking good! This fat, ugly bitch was giving him the fuck of his life. He drove her into the hard linoleum and she grabbed him and pulled him deeper. His feet were tangled because his pants were bunched around his ankles. He pushed both feet against the sink and bucked into her. Their sweating, writhing bodies slid and bucked against each other. The entire struggle lasted less than three minutes, but it was the most powerful sex either had experienced. When it ended, both lovers were more than a little stunned. They laughed a little self-consciously and got up and arranged themselves.

Eliza told Jimmy to wait outside ant that she would bring him his food on the porch. She turned and resumed cooking, whistling all the while.

Jimmy started outside and spied Mary Ann. He approached her. "Next time, it'll be you, little girl." Mary Ann looked Jimmy in the eye and told him pick her up the following afternoon at five o'clock if he meant it. He said he would.

This had truly been a good day for Jimmy, but he had a reason for being on the Smith farm that had nothing to do with pussy or dope. His plan was to direct the blame for the dog murder in another direction. If everything worked out to plan, this would indeed be a banner day for Jimmy Pierce.

"Randall, what kind of guns you got for trade?"

"Well all I's got a couple a ol two two's and a thirty-thirty I might figger to swap, 'n you got something worth trad'n fer."

"Well, I got an ol' goose gun ten gauge and a twelve bor like new. I figure you might be needin' something a little fancier with all you got to protect here on the farm n' all.

'H'mm, full auto, huh? Must cost plenty to keep ammo for. Where's I'm from, we usually aims first and don't need all's that bullshit."

Jimmy Pierce had been trading all his life in these hills and he knew no surer sign that a man was hooked when he talked something down.

"Randall, I guess us younguns just ain't got what it takes like you old timers. But ifn't you ain't never fired full auto, you probably wouldn't appreciate it anyway. You probably should stick with what you know. Wouldn't want nothin' to happen to you."

"Fuck you, boy! Go get that piece a shit weapon. I'll show you who should stick to what and who should shut his hole."

"Hah! Hah! Hah! Calm down, you old fuck. I'll let you play. Just be careful this ain't no squirrel gun. This is the real shit."

Jimmy goes to the truck and retrieves a short ugly gun with a folding stock. He grabs a green can that holds seven hundred and fifty rounds of mercury tipped shells. "These shells I got up at the flea market off Rafe McDaniels. He said they was took outta the armory down Cookville. Beats the hell outta store bought cept'n they play hell on your gun. Takes twice as long to clean, they blow so much."

"How you load it? On a belt?"

"Naw, you gotta use magazines. I got three, thirty rounders, which are all right, but I had Early Harp down to Greenville to make me a drum that fits onto a magazine and it'll hold a hunnert. Onliest in the world, I reckon."

Randall Smith had done a fair amount of trading his own self and he wasn't too keen on specialty items. It was usually bullshit or too overrated. "You'll have to convince me. I'd still like to try one a them regular ones though."

"Why shor, Randall, here you go. Here's a thirty rounder. Let go on that ol' locust down there."

Randall Smith had been around guns his entire life, and it didn't take but a couple of seconds for him to figure out how to fit the magazine into the receiver and throw the bolt forward. He sighted on the old stump and pulled the trigger. The weapon leaped skyward letting loose half a magazine before Randall got it back under control.

Jimmy's plan was working fine. Randall Smith was blind drunk and having a good ol' time. He had already fired about three hundred rounds through the thirty round clips and he was getting more aggressive the more drunk he got.

"Well Randall, this shor has been fun, but we're losing light. I might ought to put this ol' gun up afor we hit something we shouldn't."

"Bullshit, boy. Let me fire off one more clip."

The men had moved out of the yard and were on a small rise between the two farms. Jimmy Pierce had just fired an entire thirty round clip into an old Vega station wagon sitting on the Pierce property. This car was fifty yards in front of the dog pen and was the key to his and Bobby's plan for deferring blame for the dog murders onto someone else, specifically, Randall Smith.

Bobby Pierce had been waiting for Jimmy to shoot the Vega. It was a signal for him. Bob was placed one hundred and fifty yard on the other side of the shed with a 30-06 deer rifle with a scope. He had a clear field of fire through the open top half of the shed door. His targets were the two acetylene tanks inside. "Well Randall, I'll tell ya what, we ain't tried this ol' drum out yet. It's never been tested. I got it loaded, but I been saving it. You wanna try 'er out?"

Randall Smith took this statement as a direct challenge on his manhood. He grabbed the weapon that was a lot heavier with the extra rounds. He looked around and finally sighted in on the same target that Jimmy Pierce had just shot at. He let loose and about halfway through the 100 round clip, the building that lay about fifty yards further down the pasture erupted with a deafening explosion. Randall Smith at first thought he was being raided by the ATF and he kept firing in the direction of the explosion until the weapon discharged the last round. Randall Smith laid down the weapon and surveyed the damage and came to the conclusion that Jimmy Pierce wanted. "Oh, shit! I done fucked up!"

Jimmy Pierce smiled. "What the fuck have you done? You done killed Maxi's dogs. You killed the dogs." Yep, it shor was a banner day for ol' Jimmy Pierce, a banner day indeed.

CHAPTER FIVE

"Dead! Every last damned one dead as a fucking doornail. Finest bunch of dogs in three counties. Shot to hell and blown to smithereens. That drunk sum bitch is going to pay! I'll see to that. You better by God believe that."

"All right, Daddy. Calm down. Mr. Smith has already promised to pay. He didn't mean any harm. It was just an accident. A couple of drunks playing with guns is all. Didn't nobody mean no harm."

"Bullshit! Bullshit! Bullshit! Any goddamned son of a bitch ever picked up a gun oughta have more sense than to shoot a whole goddamned shed full a dogs. "

"Randall Smith has never liked those dogs. He always accused them of messing with his livestock. Hell the only stock he owns is that horse faced daughter Eliza."

"Them Smiths just better make damned shore they do pay. I mean every last dime. I got a mind to go over there and show that bunch some real shooting. That stupid brother of mine would be right smack dab in the middle of all this horse shit. Truth be known he's probably more responsible than ol' Randall."

"Aw shit! I don't even want to talk about it no more. I'm going over to Sam Eckert's in Booneville. He's got two pups I sold him last year. He said he might sell me one back. Probably going to charge twice what he paid. Randall Smith better be ready to spend all of Eliza's money because I shore am."

Having said all this, Maxi Pierce stormed out the door letting it slam behind him.

Maxine Pierce remained sitting upon the couch in her father's living room. She didn't care about the dogs, Randall Smith or her father for that matter. Maxine hated yelling and fights. It seemed that was all anyone around this house ever did was yell and fight.

Maxine had always been a very pretty girl. At nineteen, she was one of the most beautiful girls in the country. She was a fairly smart girl. No one seemed to notice or care so she had learned to hide it fairly well.

Maxine had three things she liked to do. Get high, fuck and ride motorcycles. She did not ride behind someone else. She had her own bike. It was an '84 Sportster and it would fly. She had worked two summers and saved her money and paid cash for it.

Maxine knew a lot more about what went on than people gave her credit for. She knew who really killed her daddy's dogs. She was keeping the information to herself until such a time that she could use it to benefit herself. Maxine Pierce was nobody's fool and someday everyone would know.

Two days after "Randall Smith" blew up the dogshed, Bobby got to speak to his Uncle Jimmy. Jimmy had hung low because he knew Maxi would be mad at him as well as Randall Smith. He also knew Maxi would place most of the blame upon Randall because that would be the only way he could hope to get anything back from his loss.

"Where have you been? Pa was mad as I've ever seen him. Mr. Smith says he's gonna pay for the shed and equipment. Pa's out right now trying to find some new breeders."

"I know. I know. Hold up a minute, hoss. Now take a breath or two. I've been over to the valley shacking up with some ol' long hauler's ol' lady. I got a couple of questions my own self. Who you been talking to?"

"Nobody! I swear."

"Wait up! I ain't finished. Where did you say you was at when the shed blew?

"I was down in the second field spreading hay. I know all that. Nobody's even asked."

"I know that, but if they do. What's your story, boy? Let's hear it."

"I was in the bottom field pasture laying down hay and tobacco stakes. I was supposed to have done it Saturday, but I couldn't get the truck started. I heard the explosion and came over to see what had happened."

"That's pretty good. What did you do with that rifle? I don't want nobody coming up saying they seen you with no deer rifle walking on the ridge line."

"I rolled it in that ol' tarp and hid it in them big roll up bails of straw. It's the third from the barn door."

"Okay. I'll get it and clean it tonight. You will never see that gun again. Man down Halsey way wants to buy it. Far as you know, nobody round these parts even owns an ought six."

"Sure, Jimmy, no problem. I can handle it. What's next? I mean what are we doing tonight? I mean can I come?"

"We'll see Bobby. We'll see. I need you to run down to Matheson's and pick up a couple of twelve packs for tonight and I think I will take you with me.

CHAPTER SIX

Mary Ann Smith was pissed off at the world. She had watched her sister and Jimmy Pierce "fuck" in the kitchen. Jimmy Pierce had made a date with her and had not shown up. Mary Ann was not the kind of girl to forget such an incident. She was plotting a proper punishment but she still wanted to get with Jimmy and soon. She had a boyfriend. In fact, she was with him now. The couple were watching a basketball game in progress. The game involved two pick-up teams from the junior high where Mary Ann attended school.

Boyd Thomas was a nineteen-year-old dropout. He had met Mary Ann in this same parking lot. Boyd's father owned half of the town, so Boyd didn't worry much about appearances. Boyd had been trying to join the marines. The biggest obstacle in the path of Boyd's military career was his inability to pass his General Equivalency Exam.

Boyd was not happy. He had arrived at the school at three o'clock, like always. Mary Ann had walked out and started her shit. He didn't know why she was in such a pissy mood. He did not care. He was, at the moment, wondering whey he put up with it all. There was no shortage of little freaks that would kill to be with him. This little cunt was really pushing it.

"Don't you have to go home early? I mean yesterday you could hardly wait. What, some big after school special on? 'How to Land a Man and be a Twat at the Same Time?'"

"Oh hush! Sometimes people need private time. Besides, this brooding stud routine of yours is wearing awful thin. Teenage angst and Elvis sneers are both out of date."

"Bullshit. Teenage angst will always be cool and Elvis had one of the deadliest sneers on the planet."

"Yeah, well. His parents weren't rich. He didn't have everything given to him. Plus he made it in the military. You do have one thing in common, though. You both like molesting little girls."

This little interchange was starting to upset Boyd. He had liked the "brooding stud" remark and welcomed any comparison to Elvis. The molesting little girls comment was out of line. Boyd dating a thirteen-year-old was not strange; in fact, it was fairly common practice in the community.

Pineville was like many small towns across the country. There was a courthouse, a drive-in restaurant, some shops and a couple of gas stations. There were convenience stores and truck stops out on the interstate and several "General Stores" spread out through the community. Dating in a town this size required a vehicle. Older boys had access to cars therefore they were able to date. A pretty girl would usually start dating at about twelve. She would usually be sent along on dates with her older sister or cousin. The idea was the younger girl would chaperone the couple. This very seldom worked out this way. The older couple would usually prearrange an escort for the younger girl, as well. This date would be picked up last. Many times the new couple would be as involved as the primary pairing. Couples sometimes dated as long as two years without the girl's parents having met the boy. People say it's impossible to keep a secret in a small town. It is also true that people hate to be the bearer of bad news. People also notice what they want to notice.

Boyd had no idea that Mary Ann had wanted to get home early the day before in order to meet Jimmy Pierce. He also didn't know she was mad because Jimmy hadn't shown up. He did know if she didn't shut her smart mouth she would be walking home.

"Let's go out to the old mine and shoot some." Jimmy was referring to an abandoned strip-mining site that was used as a swimming hole and parking spot. Boyd and Mary Ann liked to go out and target practice. They usually wound up in the back of Boyd's pick-up. This was Boyd's plan. It had been four days since Mary Ann had hooked him up. If she didn't come across soon Boyd was gonna pop.

"I know what you want to shoot. Wait a little while. We got all night. My dad's so fucked up lately he doesn't have a clue what I'm up to."

"Yeah? I heard that he blew up Maxi Pierce's dog run and killed all his dogs. I shore woulda liked to have seen ol' Maxi's face when they told him. How'd he keep that crazy sumbitch from killing him? Ain't a jury in the country would blamed him. He shore had some good hunters."

"Dogs! Dogs! Dogs! That's all I've heard about for two damn days. Who the fuck cares? Dad's paying for everything. He feels like a murderer or something. He's ashamed to leave the house. He called the bank and had Ronald Yates mortgage one hundred and forty acres. Ronald told him he couldn't lend that much so he's selling the whole section. We never used it anyhow. He kept the mineral rights so they'll most likely log it off. All over a bunch of big old ugly dogs. "

"Let's ride by the Deuce and see who's spending their old ladies' paychecks."

"All right! I can deal with that."

"Might as well get something to sip on. You want to shoot some pool?"

"Sure."

The Deuce was an old barn that had been remodeled and turned into a roadhouse. It featured live music on Thursday, Friday and Saturday nights. There were two pool tables, a jukebox, two pinball machines, a bowling machine and hot food served from eleven o'clock til whenever the cook decided he was through. Anyone could come inside until ten o'clock. Everyone under twenty-one was supposed to leave at that time. This rule was not strictly enforced. Business was pretty good. A lot of people from Pineville, along with neighboring Prestonville and Jacksboro Crossing all came in. It was a long ride but the trip itself was something to do.

Boyd and Mary Ann made the trip in just under twenty minutes. Pretty good, considering it was thirty-one miles on secondary roads and they were smoking a joint. Boyd was an excellent driver and knew the route well. Driving made him come alive. He knew the road and felt fairly safe driving it; still, you never knew when you went around the curve at eighty, whether or not some hay wagon or combine was gonna be blocking two-thirds of the path. This didn't worry Boyd. He figured he could handle it.

"Wanna play some eight ball?"

"Sure, let me get a Coke."

"Coke? Don't you want something a little stronger?"

"Not right now; maybe later. You can if you want."

"I can? Gee, thanks. That's mighty nice of you to give permission."

"Boyd really, you don't have to be an asshole all the time. Let somebody else put out some shit once in awhile."

"Hah, hah! I'll rack."

Boyd headed toward the pool tables, Mary Ann toward the bar. She ordered a Coke. The barmaid, an older woman with stringy blond hair gave her a twelve-ounce can and a styrofoam cup full of ice. "Thanks Dottie. Here's a dollar. Keep it."

"Sure hon. Thanks."

Mary Ann turned back toward the poolroom. The front door opened at the same time. She had to hold her hand to block the sunlight. When she did, a hand reached out and took the drink from her hand. The hand belonged to Jimmy Pierce.

"Thanks. Don't mind if I do. I usually drink Bud, but this'll do for now, Little Girl."

"Give it back! Now! Or..."

"Or what? Huh? You gonna sic handsome on me? Oooh, I'm so scared. Fuck it. Dottie, give me another Coke. You really should watch who you let in here. The riff raff are starting to take over." Jimmy tried to hand back the Coke. Mary Ann ignored him. "I was just playing. Come on. Give me a break."

"Playing? You mean like yesterday when you didn't show up. That was real funny."

"Oh shit. I'm sorry. Damn! Look babe, I just thought after the fire'n all, things might be a little hectic around your house is all."

"Oh! You mean you were scared to show your face after you and daddy shot up and burnt Maxi's dog shed."

-33-

"Well... Yeah! If you wanna look at it that way. I figured ol' Randall might be in a bad way and might need his little girl more than I did."

Hearing this, Mary Ann stepped close to Jimmy and whispered, "You don't feel any need? Not even a little?" She then turned and walked to the pool tables.

Boyd was busy picking a stick. He had seen Jimmy Pierce walk in and take the Coke. He figured it was just the case of some old guy having a little fun. It never occurred to him that Jimmy was only four years older than he. "What was that all about? That old dude bothering you?"

"No. He's just another turd in a world full of shit."

"Okay. You wanna break?"

"Sure."

Mary Ann bent over the table and with considerable skill launched the cue ball at the triangle of balls. The ball connected solidly and scattered the others all over the table. A seven rolled into the left-hand corner pocket. Mary Ann gave a little cry of triumph. "Yes! I'm solids." She then proceeded to line up her next shot.

The couple shot pool for about two hours. The bar/restaurant started to fill up with people coming from work.

Jimmy Pierce was deeply involved in a conversation about Ford versus Chevy. He being a Ford man. The man he was talking with had very strong feelings toward Chevy. They were close to blows.

"Never been a motor made equal to a Ford. The 351 Cleveland or Windsor will shut a 350 down every time."

"You are a moron. I got me a little ol' 350 in my pick'em up out there and I'll put it up against any Ford in the county."

"Well, all I'm running is a 300 six banger, so I ain't gonna race you right now. But I got a little ol' Ranger out on the farm. I'll put it up against you any time farm boy."

"I'll show you farm boy when I plow your ass into the pavement. "

"What you want to race for? Pink slips? Fuck no! Why would I wanna own a piece of shit Chevy anyway? No. Let's race for something worth something. What say we race for two hundred dollars?

"All right. When and Where?"

"Friday night. Plank Road cut off to Old Curry Road. Eleven o'clock."

"I'll be there. I'll see you there, in my rearview mirror, of course."

During this interchange Mary Ann and Boyd had finished playing pool. They were talking with another couple and planning their night's activities.

"We were thinking about heading out to Prestonville and catching a movie. Wanna come?"

"Naw, fuck those P-ville asswipes. We were gonna grab some booze, pick up a couple of joints and head out for some target practice. If you know what I mean."

"Hell yes! I wouldn't mind doing some shooting my own self. What you say, girl?"

"Well…. Okay, if we stop and get a couple grams off your brother."

"Done. I picked up three eight balls this afternoon about one o-clock. I took that shit over to Jacksboro for Levi and you know I whacked the fuck outta that shit. I got at least two grams; and the shit is kill."

"All right. Let's do a bump. You want to hit one Mary Ann?"

"Sure. It's about the only way I can stand Boyd sometimes."

"Let's hit the shitter."

"Let's do it."

"All right."

"Okay."

Jimmy Pierce had finished his little discussion about cars and had overheard the kids' plans. He found these plans very interesting. He decided that the little gathering that the two couples were planning needed something. He felt that the presence of one dashing, charming and unbelievably handsome Jimmy Pierce would make the event spectacular. Hell it would be the height of the social season.

CHAPTER SEVEN

Jimmy Pierce left the bar rather quickly. No one paid any attention. Jimmy was not known for his social grace. He had a very important date.

Bobby Pierce's week had been very eventful. He was a mixture of emotions. He felt exhilaration at the successful cover-up of the dog murders. He felt powerful, yet sad at his killing of the dogs. He felt confused about his Uncle Jimmy's role in his life. Jimmy had always been his hero. His word was law. He could not believe Jimmy even felt the need to cover up anything. He could not understand why Jimmy just didn't walk up to his brother (Bobby's father) and tell him, "I told the boy to kill them dogs and that's what he did. You don't like it, I might just kill you."

In Bobby's mind, Jimmy Pierce could be anybody or do anything he wanted. Bobby believed everything Jimmy said. He did not understand why Jimmy felt the need to explain his actions to anyone.

Bobby's life at school was much the same as always. Vernon Price still tortured him daily. Bobby could not do anything about Vernon, yet. His Uncle Jimmy was going to show him how to deal with people like Vernon. Jimmy was going to show him how to deal with everyone.

The only problem was Jimmy hadn't spoken to Bobby since the day he told him to get rid of the thirty ought-six. He had hidden the gun in the haystack like he told Jimmy except he had gone back and moved the gun. He didn't know why he had done this.

He was starting to have doubts about his Uncle Jimmy. He was beginning to believe that his Uncle Jimmy had lied about some of his wartime exploits and that maybe, just maybe he wasn't the great killing machine he claimed to be. Bobby was sitting on the front porch of his father's house when Jimmy pulled into the yard. He needed to confront some of his feelings.

"What you doing, boy? You got yourself a little spare time on your hands now, hoss? Don't have to feed and water them dogs anymore? Hah, hah, hah!"

"No I guess not. Jimmy, were you telling me the truth about the war? Did you ever actually kill anyone? Are you really gonna help me? Can you teach me how to kill?"

"Will you listen to this shit? Who the fuck you think you are talking to? You little slimy piece of shit. You want to know about killing? Do you? You really want to know. I'll show you, you little fuck. I'll show you some about death."

Jimmy grabs Bobby by his hair and pitches him into the yard. He kicks him over and over. Bobby gets up and is knocked down again. Jimmy goes into the house. He returns with a pistol in; his hand and a shoe box in the other. He puts the pistol between Bobby's eyes and pulls the trigger. The hammer on the pistol fell on an empty chamber. Jimmy points the weapon up into the air and pulls the trigger again. The chamber turns this time and an explosion comes from the barrel followed by two more. He throws the box at Bobby's feet.

"I'm going to take a shower. You look through this box. When I get out we'll talk. You want to know about death. I'm going to teach you about death and few other things as well."

Bobby picked himself up. He dusted himself off and gingerly picked up the box. He sat down on the porch steps and opened the box. Inside the box were various items. There were some pictures and objects that were not instantly identifiable. Bobby removed the pictures from the box. He gathered them together and began to leaf through them. The first pictures were fairly ordinary. His uncle and some buddies were standing in front of an armored personnel carrier. The next one showed his uncle and a very pretty girl (a prostitute). The next showed the girl naked. The next one showed her tied up. The next one showed her again. This picture displayed the girl tied to the bed again but this time she looked scared and there was a gag in her mouth. The next one showed her corpse. The body was slashed repeatedly across the breast and face. The person in the picture had to be dead. There was blood everywhere.

If Bobby had any doubts about his Uncle Jimmy being a killer, they were gone. The final picture showed his Uncle Jimmy sticking his tongue into the lifeless head. The head was not connected to the body. It was a hideous parody of a tongue kiss. There were other pictures. Some were of girls, all dead at the end. Some pictures showed twisted burnt piles of flesh – war casualties. These were images from the war. Precious to Jimmy Pierce because all were of people he had personally executed.

Included in the box were other mementos, dried copper pieces of skin that Bobby did not recognize. He realized with dawning horror what they were. They were body parts, three were nipples torn from young females, two were ears and one dried worm-like objects was the dried shrunken penis from a man who had tried to kill Jimmy Pierce.

All the items were Jimmy Pierce's. They were his greatest treasure and secret. He had shown them to no one else before Bobby. Bobby knew this without being told. He felt ashamed forever having doubted his uncle. His hero was back. Bobby still didn't understand everything, but he knew that his uncle was indeed a great man. No weakling or coward could accomplish such deeds. A man with treasures such as these was a person unconcerned with what others felt or thought. His uncle chose his own path in this world and he, Bobby Pierce, would do the same. He didn't understand why his uncle did some things that he did, but he would not doubt nor question him again.

Jimmy Pierce had been furious. He could not believe the nerve of his punkass little nephew. He had almost lost it. He had come close to killing the little shit. Jimmy Pierce was a killer. He was not, however, brave or foolish. Every murder Jimmy had ever committed had been in a situation that placed very little chance for him to be caught or hurt by his actions. For all his talk of daring, Jimmy Pierce's wartime "victories" had all been hapless captives. He had shot all the enemy soldiers he could draw a bead on. They had all given up and were unarmed. The only people that Jimmy had killed that were not tied up prostitutes or captured enemy soldiers were two privates from his own company. They had threatened to expose his actions and Jimmy had shot them in the dark, from behind.

Jimmy was scared because he could sense something in Bobby that he did not have. Bobby, unlike Jimmy, was not afraid of the consequences of his actions. Where Jimmy Pierce was a skulking, little, murdering coward, Bobby was a truly deranged individual seeking his first victim. Jimmy didn't know what to do. He did know that Bobby

-40-

worshipped him and would do whatever he wanted. He had the perfect weapon. He just needed to know where to point it. Jimmy finished dressing and went back outside where Bobby sat.

The mood had changed. Jimmy was no longer mad. Bobby was no longer questioning.

"You ready? Really ready?"

"Yes."

"Let's go. Get the truck. It's time to go to school."

CHAPTER EIGHT

The two couples were partying hard. They had left the Deuce one car behind the other. Boyd was driving fast but not recklessly. The other couple was right on their tail. They were headed out to the strip pit.

The weather was still warm this time of year. Cars were scattered around the field above the pit. The couples parked side by side. Mary Ann exited the truck with a joint in one hand and a Jack and Coke in the other. She passed the joint to Cheryl, the girl from the other couple. The other guy's name was Glen Sparks. He was a small time hood in the area with aspirations to be a big time hood. He was well on his way.

"Glen, you going in?

"Not right away. I want to get that real good feeling first. Anybody need a beer?"

"Sure," all three people yelled.

Glen handed all three members of the group an ice, cold Budweiser. The makeshift party toasted itself and headed toward the cliff where they could observe and trade banter with the people already in the water.

Jimmy Pierce had his "babies" displayed on the workbench before him. They glistened, dark sinister, wicked and deadly. A light coating of oil covered their surface. "I always wrap 'em up like this when I'm gonna store 'em for awhile. Grab a cloth and start wiping 'em down. I got somewhere to be right after dark. I may need you to go with me. If we do this, there ain't no coming back. Once we start, we go all the way. You best make damn shore this is what you want! I mean, really want!"

"It is. I have always wanted this. I never knew how much till now. I think I was always meant for this."

"Maybe. May very well be, but we gotta be careful. This is a small town and ain't nothing goes unnoticed. We gonna have our fun but we don't want to wind up in Marion on no life sentence. We keep our mouths shut and we cover our tracks."

The would-be killers cleaned their weapons, loaded them onto the truck and drove out away from prying eyes to test them.

Jimmy's private arsenal consisted of a small but deadly assortment of stolen and "souvenir" weapons that he had acquired while in the service. Most were automatic of at least fired bursts of fire. He had a Colt AR-15II, which he had replaced the M-16AI. He also had one of those for regular service. The Colt was not fully auto. It fired semi-automatic or three round burst. The military had switched to this arrangement in order to control fire and conserve ammunition. The M-16 was a fully auto and fairly dependable weapon if cleaned and handled properly. He had a Kalishnakov AK-47, a Russian made weapon that had been taken from a fallen enemy. The enemy had tried to surrender but was shot point blank in the face. It had been one of Jimmy's proudest moments of the war. He had actually been facing the man at the time he killed him.

The crowning glory of Jimmy's arsenal was an M-60 machine-gun that he had purchased from "a friend" who was still in the service. His friend was a supply sergeant at Fort Hood and had access to all sorts of goodies. This was also the source of Jimmy's ammunition. Along with these weapons he had also owned a M248 grenade launcher that fit onto the M-16 or Colt assault rifle. He had about forty live rounds for this weapon.

Jimmy was loath to use this device because he was the only person around "as far as he knew" who owned one. There were several men in the county who could claim to owning weapons not unlike Jimmy's but the grenade launcher was special.

Two crates of grenades were stacked in the shed. One crate was all fragmentation grenades and the other contained C-2 or tear gas as it is more commonly known and smoke of various colors and three white phosphorous grenades. The white phosphorous were meant to destroy equipment left behind in war. This is done to keep the enemy from making use of abandoned equipment. The grenades were capable of melting right through an engine block of an automobile.

Jimmy also had the SKS that he and Randall Smith had used to destroy the dog shed. It, with its custom drum magazine, had done quite well on its trial run. Jimmy had other toys but these were the heart of the arsenal. All the weapons were untraceable to any one individual. They were all either reported as stolen or lost. The weapons were ideal for Jimmy and Bobby's needs.

It was around eleven o'clock by the time Jimmy and Bobby had returned from "test-firing" all the weapons. Jimmy gave Bobby some instructions he wanted him to follow. Jimmy had decided to pursue his penchant for murder and to include his nephew.

Jimmy had listened to the conversation of the couple's at the Deuce. He knew their plans for the rest of the evening and had decided that he would crash their little party.

The party in question was winding down. The couples had gotten that "real good feeling" and then went swimming.

The people who had been at the pit had left gradually until only four remained. They were drunk, stoned and very coked up. The couples had paired off around nine o'clock. They had had sex and returned to the fire.

Cheryl needed to get home or her parents would giver her a bunch of shit. She was fourteen, but her father was not a drunk and did notice when she came and went. If Mary Ann didn't go home it would probably go unnoticed. She could stay gone for two or three days as long as she went to school. The school had a policy of calling the homes of the absentee students in order to find out why they were not in school. Boyd sometimes stayed away from home for weeks. He made infrequent stops for cash and clothes. This was a fine arrangement for everyone involved.

The fire was getting low and the cooler was getting lighter. Glen and Cheryl finished their beers and threw their cans into the fire.

"I'm baked, hoss. It's been sweet but think it's time I hit the street."

"Yeah, Hon. We better go. My daddy's gonna whup my ass if I ain't home by twelve. Ever since my sister Lyla got knocked up, he don't give me a break. I mean it ain't like she didn't mean too. She done and took herself off the pill and all. It was the only way that low-life Albert was gonna marry her. Big laugh on her when he ran off with Carrie Lee. Now Pa's madder 'n a hornet having to raise Albert's bastard 'n all

"Shut up, Cheryl. Man, that coke gets you so wound up a man can't get a word in edgewise. If 'n it didn't get you so damned horny, I wouldn't even let you look at the shit."

"Hush! You don't need to be talking like that in mixed company and all. You shore as hell didn't mind about an hour ago. I didn't hear one complaint."

"That's because your mouth was full. Hah, hah, hah, hah."

"If 'n you ever want to fill it again, you better shut up and let's get."

"Okay Baby, just playing. You know I love you. Later people. Don't sit out here too long, Sasquash'll get you. No, the boogieman."

"Come on, boogieman."

They got in the car and drove off. They didn't even notice the old battered Ford pick-up truck pulled off onto the clearing where the high-tension electric wires are run. These wires are spread all over the country. They have clear-cut areas beneath them that is ideal for driving on.

Jimmy Pierce sat smoking a cigarette watching the car pull out and leave. He was not worried about being spotted. He had sat in this very same spot many nights watching couples and beating his meat.

The remaining couple sat perfectly still by the fire. They were silent and content. Both were lost within their own heads. The weed, beer and cocaine had combined to create a soft, cloudy, tension inside them. Neither heard the soft scrape of boot soles on gravel. Mary Ann felt the weight of a shadow on her back. She turned her head and gave a little yelp. Boyd jumped and reached for a limb that was sticking out of the fire.

"Who's there? Come on out so I can see you."

"Calm down, boy. Don't wet your panties. It's just me." Jimmy Pierce walked into the light. "How ya'll doing? Little late for you to be out on a school night?"

"Fuck you!"

"Why shore. Your little boyfriend don't mind."

"Yeah buddy, I mind. Watch your mouth."

"Or what?"

"Or I'll bust it. You're old enough to know how to talk to a lady."

"Hah, a lady, huh? That wasn't the impression I got. I figured her for full grown the way she keeps trying to get me to take some of that little butt off her hands."

"Buddy, I done and told you to watch your mouth. I don't know what you are blabbing off at the mouth about but I think you better leave afore I gets to stomping the shit out of you."

"Is that right?" Jimmy reaches behind his back and pulls out a short black pistol. It is not the one that he pulled on Bobby earlier in the evening. This was an automatic and clean. The registration numbers had been erased and the weapon could be thrown away and never traced back to Jimmy Pierce.

"Maybe you better watch your mouth, Sonny boy. Me and your little girlie there got us a bit of history that maybe you ain't so wise to. You see little darlin' here has been watching me pork her butt ugly sister and she's just itching to straddle me her ownself. Now I ain't gonna keep it and you can't hurt it. So, little girl, you can come on over and step up to what you been needing and ol' loverboy ain't been a providing. You might want to want to wait awhile boy, this here girl might need a ride home. Could be needing a little help a walking after I gets done."

"You son of a bitch! What's he talking about Mary Ann?"

"Tell him Mary Ann. Tell ol' pretty boy how you was supposed to meet me yestiddy and how you rubbed my nuts at Deuce. Tell him how you watched me fuck the dog-shit outta your butt ugly sister while you rubbed your little box till it rang like a bell. Tell him how you want to eat, suck, fuck and shit this hard dick. Tell him you little bitch!"

"Shut up! Leave us alone. He's lying Boyd. He's just a dirty, lying piece of white trash."

"Tell him, girl. Tell that boy how you want this fat dick."

"Mary Ann, is he the reason you wanted to go home early yesterday?"

"Why, shore boy. I's supposed to pick up Mary Poppins yesterday and let her ride the old Baloney Pony here."

"You little bitch! You been acting like a little cunt all day and treating me like shit over this old fucking hillbilly. I oughta beat the living shit out of you."

"Hold up there, Junior! You the one better be watching his mouth now. You can beat the shit outta her all you want, later. Right now, the little lady has a few unkept promises to take care of. You can stay and watch or you can leave. You best make up your mind. This here little automatic is a might touchy and I shore would hate to shoot a pretty boy like you. I might find myself down state one of these days and need a little honey like you pass a little time. If you know what I mean?"

"Mother fucker! You calling me a punk?"

"Yeah, I'm calling you a punk. In fact, I'm sure of it. You are a punk." Saying this Jimmy Pierce places the automatic between Boyd's eyes. "In fact, little punk boy, I think

-48-

I'm gonna let you make it hard for me and then your little girlie can take it up the ass. Unless you want it the other way around?"

"Bullshit! I ain't sucking no man's dick. I'll die first."

Jimmy smacks the pistol into the side of Boyd's head. He hits him three more times. The young man falls down. Jimmy hits him again. He kicks him onto his back. He straddles his chest and sticks the gun into the boy's mouth. "You just might! Get your pants off, you little bitch. Now! Take off your damn pants or loverboy here is gonna lose the back of his head from the front."

Jimmy resumes hitting Boyd until he is sure that he is unconscious. He then turns his attention to the girl. Mary Ann has sat huddled, shaking, her arms encircling her legs, rocking to and fro during this exchange. She is terrified and sobbing hysterically.

"What's wrong, little girl? Get a little more than you bargained for? Grown men don't play like little boys. You hush that bawling and shuck them drawers. When I get back you better be nekkid as the day you were born. I mean it!"

Upon saying this Jimmy turns and walks away. He goes to his truck and gets some rope from the back. He gathers up about twenty feet of barbed wire that lies tangled in the bed of the truck.

He returns to the fire. Mary Ann is crouched over the limp, unconscious form of Boyd. Jimmy Pierce grabs her from behind by the hair on her head. He smacks her twice and throws her to the ground. "Get you goddamn clothes off, you fucking little whore. If you ain't naked in about ten seconds, I swear to God I will beat your breath out of your body. You hear me bitch!!!?"

"Yes. Yes." The girl/woman stammered. The would-be temptress had reverted to the thirteen-year-old girl. She starts undressing.

Jimmy quickly ties Boyd's hands and feet. He takes the length of the barbed wire and wraps it around the boy's neck. He runs the wire between the boy's hands, which are tied, behind his back, wrapping the wire twice around the rope, binding Boyd's wrists. Jimmy connects the barbed wire to the bound feet of his hostage. This effectively makes Boyd helpless and any sudden movement would put pressure upon the barbed wire around his neck. Jimmy then cuts the belt off Boyd's pants. Jimmy yanked the trousers around the knees of the helpless victim. The sudden movement caused the wire to cut into the wrists and neck of the boy.

Mary Ann started screaming. She had taken off all her clothes except a flannel shirt. Jimmy screams back into the girl's face. His scream is much louder.

"Ain't no one to hear you, bitch! Nobody here 'cept us chickens."

He grabs the front of the girl's garment and rips the front out. Her breasts tumble free.

"Get on your knees." Mary Ann complies. Suddenly a light shines on the scene. Mary Ann suddenly starts to stand up sensing salvation near at hand. The girl yells out.

"Help! Help! He's got us. He has killed Boyd and is trying to rape me! Help! Please!"

Jimmy Pierce burst out laughing. "Come here, boy. Help the little damsel in distress."

Laughing, Bobby steps into the firelight. In his hand he is holding the Colt Ar-15 rifle. The flush of adrenaline is upon his face. He is loving every minute of the action.

"Hot damn! Ain't she something? Lord Mercy! Look at that butt. You gonna let me have some of that, Uncle Jimmy?"

"Sure! We got all night. First things first. I made ol' Boyd here a little promise. I told him he was gonna suck my dick or I was gonna stick it up his ass after I made his little girlfriend get it hard. Come here, Mary Ann. You don't wanna make a liar out of old Jimmy now, do you?"

Grabbing the young girl by the hair he drags her up to her knees. Unzipping his trousers he pulls out his engorged penis.

"You suck this good, little girl, and if I feel one tooth, I'm gonna make you pay."

"Hell yes, Uncle Jimmy! Fuck her. Fuck that little cunt's face. Make her like it."

"Damn right, she's gonna like it. Before we get done she's gonna beg for it. Don't just stand there boy, she ain't doing a damn thing with that other end. You enjoying the show, Boyd? Look close cause you are next."

Bobby can hardly contain himself. He had spent many nights alone in his bed dreaming of little Mary Ann. He could not resist the delicious sight before him.

Bobby got down on his knees. He loosened his pants and pulled out his member. He stroked it a few times then bent down and parted the lips of the young girl's vagina. It looked so hot and wet. There was still a trace of the girl's earlier sexual adventure of the night to be smelt. Bobby knelt closer and took a deep breath. He inhaled the sweet, musky scent of the girl's sex. He leaned his head forward and started licking at first tentatively, then more assertively. In moments he was licking furiously. In spite of what was happening to her, Mary Ann's body began to respond. She got wetter and began to writhe.

Jimmy, meanwhile, was occupied on the other end. He put his prick in her mouth and grabbed the girl behind her head. She at first began to gag then finally her throat accepted the intrusion. He started fucking her face at first slowly then with more force, bucking his hips in a mad rhythm.

Bobby got off his knees and placed his hands upon Mary Ann's hips. With a sudden movement he thrust himself up and into the girl's inner folds. Bobby was in heaven. The girl's thoughts were a blur. She was terrified for her life. Bruised and battered she shut off her mind. She became an automaton, responding to the twin assaults upon her person. The attackers neared their climax. Jimmy Pierce jerked the girl's head up dislodging himself from her mouth.

"A promise is a promise, little lady. You keep her occupied Nephew Mine. I got a mouthy, little punk to take care of."

Jimmy Pierce kicked Boyd Thomas awake. He pushed and prodded the supine form until Boyd and Mary Ann were facing each other. He made Boyd watch as Bobby continued the assault upon the girl. Mary Ann was oblivious. She was lost in a world of pain and misery, yet here was a building heat in the girl that Boyd recognized. She was responding. A low moan escaped her throat. Boyd was shocked and angered. He felt degraded by what had been done to him and betrayed by Mary Ann.

Jimmy pushed Boyd closer. "She likes it, boy. You can look at her and see it. That girl was made for it, boy. You ain't been doing nothing but warming that thing up. You get done, she probably has to go home and frig herself for two, three hours just to get some sleep. Well don't worry. She's gonna rest easy after this night. Now what was it you was saying about you'd die before you'd suck another man's dick?"

Jimmy grabbed the boy's pants and pulled them further down until his entire ass was sticking out. He pushed Boyd's shirt up and wrestled him on his knees. He placed his penis about a foot in front of Boyd's nose. His dick was covered with blood from the forced entry into Mary Ann's mouth. Jimmy had not even noticed. The blood was from the girl's nose that was bleeding heavily from the repeated smacks and blows to her head.

"Lick it clean, pretty boy." Jimmy whispered like a lover. "Lick it clean and make it shine. One false nibble and I'll kill you." His voice was soft and this scared Boyd more than anything had before.

Boyd started begging. "Please don't. Don't make me do this. Let us go. We won't say anything. I swear."

"Get started. I like it slow."

Boyd started shaking. He could barely breath the wire was cutting into his throat. "Don't. Please, don't."

Jimmy guided his penis into the young man's face. He was not particularly gay; he just wanted to show the little faggot who owned this situation. Jimmy By God Pierce that's who.

Bobby was nearing the point of no return. He grabbed Mary Ann's hair and twisted

cruelly. She screamed. He started whipping her and bucking in a frenzy. He pulled out.

She yelped. She was hot now and close to orgasm. Bobby did not want her enjoying this.

He wanted her to hurt. He slammed his prick up her ass. The flesh at first would not

give. He persisted and the anal ring gave in a tearing, ripping motion. Mary Ann yelled

in agony. Bobby climaxed in her hot little shitter. He let loose with a rebel yell oblivious

to the damage he had done to his own sex in the rape. Thrusting harder and harder Bobby

started pounding on the girl's back and skull. Mary Ann became unconscious long before

Bobby's shrunken, bloody member fell out of her ass. She did not see Jimmy's assault on

Boyd.

Jimmy watched impassively as Bobby raped Mary Ann's ass. For the first time in his

life he felt pride in his nephew. He would twist the wire anytime Boyd displeased him,

either by not sucking or sucking too rough. The boy was catching on quick. Hard to

believe this was his first time.

Boyd stared in horror at Mary Ann's plight. He could not believe this was happening

to him! He was cool. He was rich. His father owned half the town. He whimpered like

a puppy and gasped for breath. He wished the stinking hillbilly would come and leave

him alone. He began to retch and literally puked around the dick in his throat.

The feeling of the boy's vomit running down his nuts at first disgusted then amused

Jimmy Pierce. He almost lost control. It felt so good. The boy was a natural. He hadn't

bit him even once. The forced oral sex was feeling too good. He pulled his penis out of

Boyd's mouth. He twisted the wire until the blood ran freely. The boy could barely breath. He released the wire and leaned close.

"You like that didn't you, boy? You don't have to say nothing. Jimmy can always tell when a little bitch likes what he's doing. You like that so much. You're gonna love this. Hell, you'll die laughing."

Jimmy dragged the boy forward. Boyd's face was in the dirt on its side. He was on his knees with his hands behind his back. The wire connecting his feet and hands to his neck was taut. Jimmy held the boy's head to the ground. If Jimmy moved at all the wire cut off his breath. Jimmy pulled the wire to one side. He wrapped the shreds of Boyd's shirt around it so it would not rub against him. This made the wire tighter.

"All right pretty boy. Here comes the real deal. I'm gonna show you what kind of bitch you really are."

Jimmy forced his dick into the virgin recesses of Boyd's ass. He twisted the wire savagely at the same time. Boyd could not breathe at all. Jimmy continued to thrust and twist with savage joy. Jimmy Pierce raped Boyd's ass until he literally fucked the life out of the boy.

Upon his death Boyd Thomas took one small measure of revenge. His bowels released farting and shitting the attacker from his body.

Jimmy Pierce started cussing and laughing. "This little mother fucker done shit his pants. I done fucked the shit outta him. Hot damn. I gotta get some more of that."

Jimmy had not yet climaxed. He resumed his assault on the blood splattered, shit covered corpse of Boyd Thomas. He was not in the least put off by the smell or mess. In fact, he came harder than he could ever remember.

Bobby stood and watched the rape and murder of Boyd Thomas. He was not repulsed by the unnatural display before him. In fact, he was becoming aroused.

When Jimmy Pierce had finished, Bobby asked if he could fuck the corpse as well. Jimmy told him if he wanted to fuck a dead body he had better make his own. He pointed at Mary Ann and handed Bobby a hunting knife off his belt.

"Let her clean the shit off my dick first and then we can see if you got what it takes to play with the big boys."

Bobby stood and watches silently as Jimmy made the girl suck the shit and blood of her dead boyfriend off his uncle's dick. Jimmy finished, stepped out of his clothes, walked to the edge of the pit, turned to Bobby and said, "I'm gonna clean up some. You know what to do."

He did know and by the time his uncle had returned, Bobby needed to clean up also. He did indeed have "what it takes."

CHAPTER NINE

Regardless of the events from the previous evening, Bobby still had to go to school. No one knew about his and his uncle's actions.

The world still knew Bobby Pierce as a non-entity, a person of the shadows. Bobby, the geek, picked on, pushed around, ignored, despised, unnoticed and unwanted.

Bobby could not believe that after what he had done people still treated him the same way they always had. He could not understand how they could ignore the greatness inside him. He wanted them to pay but mostly he wanted them to notice him. He was determined to make people see him. His uncle had shown him the way and is was a path that he was more than willing to follow.

"Hey dipshit! What are you so quiet for?"

Bobby had been so busy that Vernon's booming voice startled him. Years and years of conditioning had failed. Bobby had become so caught up in his own thoughts that his knack for self-preservation had suffered, his biggest enemy, Vernon.

Vernon was in a very good mood. He felt good and here was his best friend, Bobby to brighten his day.

"Hey Bobbo. Where have you been? I been looking for you all day. I hardly ever see you since I got my car fixed. You still bussing it? Why sure you are. I hear it smells like burnt wieners over your way. Hah, hah. Maybe it'll cover up the pussy smell that reeks off you. All bullshit aside, you got my book report? It's due today and I know you have done your usual bang up job. The whole school is counting on you, boy. I need a B to stay on the team.

Panic set in. Bobby had completely forgotten the book report of which Vernon had spoken. If the report was late the best grade he could get would be a B. Bobby for one moment gathered some of the ferocity that had helped him rape and kill the night before.

"Fuck you, Vernon! I don't have it. I didn't do it. I'm not going to either."

"What!?!" Vernon stood as if struck. He could not believe his ears. Bobby Pierce had just done two things that Vernon would have thought impossible. He had defied him, Vernon Price, and fucked him over at the same time.

Vernon was going to be in deep shit if he got kicked off the football team. He had counted on Bobby and Bobby had let him down. Bobby always came through. Bobby was his ace in the hole. Unknown to Bobby Pierce, Vernon considered Bobby his only friend because he trusted him. To Vernon, Bobby was not a threat and would do as he was told. Vernon felt betrayed and truly pissed.

Bobby viewed their relationship differently from Vernon. To Bobby, Vernon was not a surrogate, older brother. He saw Vernon's tirades as threats and abuse not friendly guidance.

Bobby was freaking out. He had just told Vernon that he didn't have his homework and to go fuck himself. The reason he was freaking was because he was still standing in one piece. All that was about to change.

"Fuck me? Did you just say fuck me? Fuck me. Fuck you."

Vernon hit Bobby in the mouth, hard. His mouth split open and he landed on his ass. Vernon started warming his head. He would smack one ear and then the next. All the while Vernon was kicking Bobby's ass, he kept up a steady dialogue. Each punch and kick was punctuated with an epitaph. A right to the cheek may sound something like this: Smack! "You little punk, piece of shit." Smack! "I'm gonna beat some respect into your little geek ass!" Punch. Kick. Punch. "You hearing me, boy!?!" Smack! "Come on. Let's hear it. You sure were running your mouth before." Kick. Punch. Kick. "What's wrong? Cat got your tongue or could it be?" Smack. "You done turned back into the pussy you are."

"Hold up there. What the hell is going on here? I said hold up! Vernon Price, you release that boy this second or I will suspend the both of you." The principal, George Harvis, stood about ten feet from where the boys were "fighting."

Vernon stood up reluctantly. He was just starting to get into the beating. There was a fine sheen of sweat on his brow. The blood was pumping freely. He was now in a very good mood.

"Yes sir, Mr. Harvis! Sorry, Sir. We were just having a slight disagreement. Technically we aren't even on school property, Sir. I'm not being a smartass but we are on a private drive and school hasn't started today. It's still at least ten minutes before first bell."

"What are you boy, a fucking lawyer? If you want to play it that way, why don't I just call the police. They can arrest you for trespassing, assault and by then I'm sure you'll be truant and then I can suspend your ass anyway. Anymore bullshit, Clarence Darrow or

should I say, Johnny Cochran?"

"Huh? What are you talking about?"

"Lawyers, peabrain. You think you're a lawyer. I called you some famous lawyers.

Oh, forget it. Get you and your little 'friend' here and meet me in the Vice Principal's

office. Now! Get going."

Bobby sat in the corner. He was placed between a large leafy tree-like plant and a

very pissed off Vernon Price. Across from the two boys sat an equally pissed off Truman

Coats, Vice Principal and resident disciplinarian of Pineville High. (He's always pissed.)

"Mr. Harvis sent you here and you will remain here until he gets here. I don't wish to

hear your side or your side of anything. There can only be one side to this issue and that

will be Mr. Harvis' side. Do you understand?"

"Yes. Yes. I understand."

"Is there a problem here? Do you have a problem, son?" Mr. Harvis leaned forward

placing his nose within two feet of Bobby's face. Bobby could see two long gray hairs

growing out the man's nostrils. Also present were crusts of dried snot and flakes of a

half-eaten Danish, the rest which sat upon the man's desk.

"No problem, sir," Bobby replied, almost gagging from the boogerific image.

"Really? No problem, huh? Well I'm glad. I am glad that you do not have a

problem. You sit there dripping snot and blood onto the remains of your soiled t-shirt.

Greasy, unwashed, uncaring, disrespectful and filthy but you have no problem."

"What about you, Price? You got any problems?"

"I guess not."

"Wrong answer. You got a problem right there. You are indecisive. You don't even know whether you have a problem or not. I would think if I were in your shoes, sitting with my bloodied comrade, in the Vice-Principal's office at eight a.m. in the morning, I would think I very definitely had a problem. Perhaps I might even consider the possibility that I had more than one problem."

"Indeed. I believe you may have a very valid point here Mr. Coats. I think these boys have numerous problems."

"Good morning, Principal Harvis. I was just explaining some basic points of procedure for being in this office."

"Yes. I think these two fellows are acquainted with the procedures involved, but it never hurts to reinforce information. We are educators."

"Mr. Price. Mr. Pierce. What was with the crap I witnessed a few moments ago?" Mr. Price, please be brief and tell me your version. Let me warn you I have already been briefed by a group of your peers. Three points stand out. Number one, there was mention of a book report. Number two, Mr. Pierce told you to 'get fucked,' which seems to have had a big impression upon the student body as a whole. Third, you, Mr. Price, threw the first punch. Now, I would like you to tell me after hearing these three points. I am anxiously awaiting the story you have for me. By the way, I am waiting to hear why I shouldn't suspend you."

"Well. Let's hear it."

Vernon, for all his brutish ways, had a very well developed sense of self-preservation .
He used this now.

"Well, Sir, it was like this. I had asked Bobby to type my book report for me. I'm not
a very good typist and I didn't want to turn in the work handwritten, it being so important
and all. So, I gave Bobby here ten dollars to type my work for me. Bobby said the work
would be ready this morning."

"I asked him if he had my book report typed and ready as we had agreed. He told me
no he hadn't typed it. I was very mad but I stayed calm. I asked him for my untyped
report back as it was due today and Mrs. Dumphreys docks one letter grade if you're late.
I explained that I needed a B to stay on the football team and that was the reason I had
wanted the paper typed in the first place. Bobby not only hadn't typed my paper, he said
he had lost it completely and that's when he told me to 'get fucked.'"

"What were the exact words he used, Mr. Price?"

"I believe they were, 'I don't have your damn book report. I threw it away and if you
don't like it, well fuck you! Fuck you! Fuck your book report! Fuck Mrs. Dumphreys!
Fuck football! Fuck this school and fuck the world.'"

"Well, I could handle his bad mouthing me. I could even handle the loss of my book
report. I could even handle the knowledge that I would be benched for not having my
report. But when he badmouthed the school, something in me snapped. This school is
everything to me, Sir. You know that. I mean everybody knows how much I love this
school."

"Yeah. Yeah, you love this school. You love your mother and you're a great American. I know and you know that what you just told me is bullshit. I'll talk to Mrs. Dumphreys. Don't worry about that."

"Here is a late pass. You get yourself to class. No stopping at the restroom for a smoke. No going to the auditorium to look at little freshman girls in gym class. I will speak with Coach Williams and together we will devise an appropriate punishment for you. Now get out of here!"

"Yes Sir!" Vernon rose hulkingly from the metal folding chair. He towered over everyone in the room. He took the late pass from Principal Harvis. They both smiled a little secretive grin, the grin of co-conspirators everywhere.

Vernon turned to exit the room. Before leaving he sent Bobby a happy, little thought to get him through the day. "I'll see you later."

"Oh joy!" Bobby replied sarcastically.

"That will be enough out of you, young man! I would think after all the trouble that smart mouth of yours has caused this mourning you would be content."

"You are in deep trouble, young man. I think it is high time you take a good look at your life and where you want to be in five or ten years from now."

"You probably think this is a big joke. It's probably funny to you that Mr. Price may fail English and get kicked off the football team. You think it's funny that without Mr. Price on the team that our school stands little or no chance at regionals much less the state."

"For the first time in your miserable little existence, you think you are important. You think that fucking this up for Vernon Price and the entire student body gives you some kind of power. You think that finally you matter. I'm going to let you in on a little secret. I'm going to tell you the real deal, the facts of life, you might say. I'm going to tell you how life really works and if you repeat what I say, I'll deny it."

"You, Mr. Pierce and all the little mousy shits like you do not matter! You are nothing! You are a waste! You do nothing. You give nothing. You have no dreams or aspirations. You spend your entire life trying to disappear. You and all like you should be expunged from the planet."

"Mr. Price is a moron, but he at least gives something back to the world. He does not live life as a rock, trying to be scenery. You and people like you have no commitment to anything. You cannot possibly understand the pressures and responsibilities an athlete like Vernon Price feels. He represents everyone in this school when he is on that playing field and, I might add, he does one hell of a job. Mr. Price is a team player. He understands the concept of going beyond one's individual wants and needs."

"You think you have disrupted Mr. Price's life by destroying his book report?"

"I didn't destroy nothing. There was nothing to destroy."

"Shut up, you little shit! Shut up! You spend your entire life trying to sink into the background and not be heard. Well I'm giving you your wish. I'm ignoring your lying little mouth. I don't give a shit what you have to say. I don't care what the facts are. I don't care because you don't care. You don't care about anyone or anything. I'm going to give you a real learning experience."

-64-

"This is how the real world works. Vernon Price is an important person to this school and this community. His actions have an effect on others. He is a giver. You don't exist. You do nothing for no one."

"I owe Vernon Price for his contributions to this school and this community. One hand washes the other. You have dirty hands and you have washed nothing."

" I am going to let Mr. Price remain in class. I am, in fact, going to convince Mrs. Dumphreys to give him an extension without her usual late penalties. I will, of course, have the Coach make his life at practice a living hell. This will in all likelihood result in a learning experience for Vernon and result in a better performance on his part at game time. There will be two positive results from this negative situation that you have created."

"Now, here's the real lesson I want you to learn. Vernon Price takes care of me, so I'm taking care of him. You spend your time causing me grief, so I'm going to cause you some grief, as well. You are suspended for one week, effective immediately. You will also be required to bring your father to school to be re-admitted. Upon re-admittance, you will be placed on probation. Any further bullshit from you will result in expulsion. Do you understand?"

"Yes. I understand."

"Any questions?"

"One. Why don't you get him to wipe his fucking nose?" Bobby points at Mr. Coats, turns and walks from the room. He will not be seen at school again for nine days. Bobby vows to himself that when he returns he will no longer be a nothing.

CHAPTER TEN

Vernon Price leaves the Vice-Principal's office with his late pass in hand. Vernon has an intuitive knowledge of the value of such an item. He stops by the boy's restroom and smokes a Marlboro while he reads and corrects any new graffiti on the walls. He then proceeds to the gymnasium where he idles away fifteen more minutes watching the morning Physical Education class. The new crop of freshman girls were developing nicely. He would have to check into some private tutoring with Ms. Wilcox, the girl's coach and see about a muscle or two that needed pulling as well. Vernon's world was in its proper orbit and life was good.

Vernon finally loitered into class. Fifteen minutes remained. He took his usual seat at the rear of the class next to the windows.

Mrs. Lola Dumphreys taught English at Pineville High. She liked her job very much. Mrs. Dumphreys, a very statuesque and attractive, auburn-haired, green-eyed woman in her early thirties, remained somewhat intimidated by students such as Vernon. She had experienced a handful of lovers but was in no means what would be considered an experienced woman. She did; however, live a very rich and full fantasy life. Vernon was a key figure in several of these fantasies.

Mrs. Dumphreys very attraction toward Vernon often led to her having a stern, somewhat brusque attitude toward the young man. She was over compensating. It worked quite well. Vernon felt the "old bitch" hated him and would do anything to make his life a living hell.

"Vernon, why are you late? Do you have a pass? If not, you will need to go to the Principal's office."

"I've got a pass and I just came from the Principal's office. Thank you."

"May I see it?"

"Sure. Here, check it out." Vernon walks to the front of the room. He leans over the young teacher's desk, places one hand on the surface and hands the late pass over with the other. This position enables him to look directly down the woman's dress providing an excellent view of the treasures within. Vernon stares intently. He in no way tries to hide his actions or intent.

Mrs. Dumphreys turns bright red under the gaze of the young man. Her breathing pattern becomes faster and her dress is suddenly much too tight. Her nipples pop out boldly. Vernon is quite impressed and his clothes become a little tighter as well.

"Okay. Everything seems to be in order. Do you have your book report? It is due today and I am looking forward to your interpretation of Mr. Faulkner's work."

"Well, that's sorta the reason I'm late. I did do my report and I was having it typed up but the guy I got to type it, lost it and uh, Mr. Harvis said he would talk to you about the entire thing."

"Uh, huh. Are you sure your dog didn't eat it? Maybe aliens swooped down and took it as representative of earth culture and are at this very moment setting up temples to commemorate the great work."

"No. No. I'm serious. Just call down to Mr. Harvis' office. He'll explain the whole thing."

"I really don't care to hear his explanation. I would like to hear your book report, though."

"I told you. I don't have it. Bobby Pierce was supposed to type it for me and he lost it."

"I heard all that. Regardless of whether Bobby lost your written report, if you read the book and wrote a report about what you read, you shouldn't have any problem giving an oral report on the material. I'm waiting."

Vernon's good mood had vanished. He was in a mild panic. "I told you I don't have it and I told you why. You just call down to the office. Mr. Harvis can straighten out everything."

"I know that. I heard you the first time. Now you listen to me. If you want full credit for this assignment, you will give your report orally, right now. I don't believe you deserve it, but I am giving you the benefit of the doubt and offering you the opportunity to give your report orally. Otherwise, you will be penalized. You are a Senior in high school and it is time you learned your actions have consequences. You need to learn not to shirk your responsibilities. There are thirty-one people in this class. You are the only one who hasn't turned in his assignment. If you wish credit, you will give that report orally now or not at all."

"You bitch! I got your damn report for you. Why don't you get oral on this, you floppy titted old cunt!" Vernon grabs his crotch and shakes it in the woman's face.

Mrs. Dumphreys is taken aback and somewhat shocked by the outburst. She sits stunned. The bell rings ending the period. No one moves at first. Everyone sits transfixed waiting for Mrs. Dumphrey's reaction to Vernon's vulgar display of power.

Mrs. Dumphrey's gathers her composure quickly.

"You, young man, are going to regret this little episode very much. The rest of you may leave. You, Mr. Football Star need to return to Mr. Harvis' office. I will accompany you and I do believe Mr. Harvis is not going to be very happy with this morning's events."

"Suck me, bitch! I ain't going anywhere with you and if you know what's good for you, you'll sit back down and shut up."

"What? Are you threatening me? I'll have you expelled. You cannot talk to me like this."

Vernon leans close to the woman and whispers. "I got a secret, baby. I know who you're fucking. I know your home phone number also. I bet Mr. Dumphreys would like to know just what you been doing in the afternoons. I even got about thirty-five minutes of videotape taken at the boat dock last year. Maybe you remember? Frank and Leonard Wilson? August? You, them, a bottle of bourbon, little blue Calvin Klein panties? You are quite the little actress. What about it? You still want to make a big deal about this?

"I don't know what you are talking about! Everyone may leave except Mr. Price."

The class slowly empties until only Vernon and Lola Dumphreys remain.

"What are you talking about? Vernon, I would really like to know what you are trying to accomplish with these accusations?"

Lola Dumphreys was a happily married woman. She was currently involved in an extra-marital affair with an Assistant Coach. They would meet three times a week after school. She did not know how Vernon could know this. She was totally confused about the videotape remark and truly wished to know what the boy was talking about.

"They ain't accusations. They is fact. I know you and Coach Tweed been getting it on since August. Hell, half the varsity has seen you. I bet your sweet, little hubby would like to hear about it. Don't you?"

Lola sat down. She knew the boy told the truth and that if her husband, Robert, found out he would divorce her.

"Whatever Coach Tweed has told you, I will deny. As for the rest of your statements, I don't believe I have ever been to any boat house with a Frank or Leonard."

"Hah, hah! I know you don't. You were so fucking loaded you couldn't possibly remember. You were at Carl Mathers' party and Frank Wilson dosed you with three Valiums and a couple a Vicodin. His brother got you to suck his dick at the party and then Marvin Watkins drove you home. Frank and Leonard waited until Marvin left and went in the house and got you. They drove you down to the lake and took turns all night. I took the video myself. Everybody got scared you would turn us in but you never did."

Lola knew the boy was telling the truth. She could remember flashes from that night. She had thought that she had dreamt the entire thing. She felt nauseous. She sat down.

"Get out! Get out of here, you pig! You swine! You helped drug and rape me and then you film the whole thing to blackmail me with. Oh God! I can't believe this is happening. How could you? What did I ever do to you, to any of you?"

"Nothing. At least not to me. I wanted to, but you were waking up so we got you back home safe and sound. Nobody planned on blackmailing you and only a few people know about his. Half the school knows about you and Coach Tweed but there's no proof. You and he can deny that as rumors. You can't deny what's on that tape and what it's worth, you look like you were having a really good time. Nobody, and I mean nobody is gonna believe you was forced."

"I have never hated anyone as much as I hate you right now, you smug little shit."

"Yeah, whatever. I don't really care. You just make sure I don't get anything less than a B on anything for the rest of the year."

"I want the tape."

"Really? People in hell want ice water. What's it worth?"

"I'll give you your grades."

"Oh, I know you will. I want more."

"How much?"

"Oh, no, not money. I want what Frank and Leonard and Coach Tweed been getting. I want you and not just once either.

"No way in hell. I'll rot in hell first."

"Sure you will. If you want that tape, you will give me that pussy and just to make sure, I think you better show some good faith and start right now."

"Bullshit! I'm not going to do that here. Anyone could walk in."

"Lock the door. I mean it. I want it now. Just lock the door and come over here. I don't care if I come or not. I just want you to lick it and let me put it in you."

The young teacher smiles to herself. The big, dumb piece of meat had a crush on her. He was trying to blackmail her though. Shit! No time to worry about it now.

She locks the door and slowly approaches Vernon. His breathing has quickened. There is a bulge in his pants. She rubs him through the material. Slowly she slides to her knees. She quickly unzips and unbuttons his trousers.

Vernon's penis is a bright red color turning purplish. She takes him into her mouth, at first briefly. She engulfs him and swirls her tongue very slowly. Cupping his testicles, she looks Vernon in the eye. "Is this what you want? Tell me what you want. I'll do anything, just hurry."

"I told you I want in your pussy. This is the best head I've ever had but I want to be in you!"

Lola had hoped to make the boy squirt quickly into her mouth or hands. She did not want to remove any clothing. She was very conscious of the time they had before being interrupted.

"Okay, just hurry. We don't have much time."

She quickly stands and bends over her desk. She bunches her skirt around her waist after stepping out of her underwear.

Vernon steps behind her. He is harder than he can ever remember. This situation was better than anything he had ever dared dream. He placed the tip of his penis at her opening. She was soaked and her smell permeated the room.

"Put it in, come on." The teacher, no longer concerned about the time, begged the student to fuck her. She was in a place beyond this room. She was in heat.

The young man thrust himself into her in one swift movement. He began pumping wildly. The young teacher returned the favor hump for hump. They found a rhythm, a sweet powerful rhythm.

Sex with her husband had never been good. She began coming. Her entire body shivered. It was so good.

Vernon pushed forward hard, much harder than before. He growled like an animal and jerked himself free from the encounter. Mrs. Dumphreys gave a little yelp. She could not believe that he had pulled out.

"What's wrong? Put it back. Come on, baby. Fuck me…. Oh shit!"

She realized why Vernon had stopped. Someone was banging on the door. It was time for her next class. She stood and smoothed her skirt. Vernon was buckling his trousers.

"Just a minute. I'm counseling a student. Here, take this." She handed Vernon another pass. "Meet me in the bookstore storage room in ten minutes."

"No. I gotta go to class. I told you I just wanted to put it in you. We can finish later. You better clean yourself up. I'll give you my version of an oral report later. I gotta go. Later." Vernon exits the room.

The next class pours in. A few girls and a couple of boys recognize the scent of sex. The boys smirk and the girls giggle.

A tall, gangly, pimple-faced lad bends down and retrieves something from in front of the teacher's desk.

Lola realized what the teenager is holding before he does. She quickly grabs her panties from the dumbstruck boy's hand and throws them in the garbage.

"Please find your seat and we'll get started."

A young, overly wise, pretty girl snickers. "Don't you mean get finished?" Only a couple of students gather the meaning of the remark. They laugh.

Mrs. Dumphreys, a bit visibly shaken, blushes a bright crimson. Somehow she retains her composure and recovers her authority. She feels a bit flustered and something else. She is a bit surprised to find herself humming a few minutes later. The entire episode should have left her humiliated and shaken. She felt better than she could remember.

The entire class noticed the teacher's good mood. The rest of the day passed uneventfully.

CHAPTER ELEVEN

Brandon Stuart had attended six separate high schools in four states. He was used to being the new kid. His father had a good job that required him to move a lot. He was in charge of cutting away the fat in business. His arrival to a town or company meant only one thing. Somebody was going to lose their jobs. Sometimes Daniel Stuart's presence signaled the closing of a town's major source of income. Brandon did not expect to be very popular at this school. He was a realist.

Brandon arrived at his second period English class to find a small group of perhaps six students standing in the hall outside the classroom. One boy was steadily pounding on the door. A brown nose if Brandon had ever met one.

Brandon could read people at a glance. His judgment was excellent. He was seldom wrong. Brandon had developed this skill as a way to survive. He had avoided many precarious situations and events by following this hard won intuition.

He could tell something wasn't right about this situation. He was not overly concerned because he could not sense any immediate threat to himself. He was content to sit back and let a moment make itself. This talent enabled him to observe and learn about the people around him. It also provided many hours of prime entertainment.

"Dad's right. This group is better than the last. These hillbilly's act like trained apes. The little brown nose nerd boy is about to shit his corduroys just because he can't get into his little English class.

The teacher in this class was fine. He expected to breeze through if only because he had covered ninety percent of the material two years before when he had placed in a magnet program at a school in Las Vegas. His father had gotten the red carpet treatment in that town. No danger of closing the plant in a place that produced nothing but empty wallets. His recommendations had actually resulted in sixteen people being hired and a renovation to a very large hotel. Brandon had loved Vegas. Pineville, he did not like near as much.

Brandon could find only one point of redemption in the entire, sordid mess that his life had become. Hicksville, the name he had given Pineville, had an extraordinary amount of attractive, horny, dumb and easy to approach females. There were drawbacks, of course. The stalwart young morons who were laughingly referred to as his peers closely guarded this group of femininity.

Every girl Brandon had talked to had been very friendly He could tell that most were very interested. The problem was that after he talked to someone, he would be told, in no polite manner, that the object of his affections was invariably spoken for. These little "reminders" were often accompanied with curses and epitaphs of a most brutal nature. Twice, he had been held and punched after talking to a particular pretty, young lass. These hillbillies guarded pussy harder than gold. Guess they were more happier to make "deposits" and couldn't stand those penalties for early withdrawals.

The door finally opened. Before the teacher's pet could squeeze inside, one of the larger cornbread fed, milk grown Cro-magnum beasts of inbred genetics appeared at the door. He pushed through the crowd with a strange look on his face. He was tucking in his shirt and zipping his pants as he went.

Brandon was one of the last to enter the classroom. His foot got tangled in a stray piece of cloth in front of the teacher's desk. He bent to retrieve the stray fabric. He realized that he was holding a pair of slightly damp, French cut, powder blue, satin ladies undergarment. Mrs. Dumphreys snatched the snatch covers from his hand. She wadded them up and threw them into here wastebasket. She turned as if everything was normal and started talking about the talent and vices of the great American writers focusing on William Faulkner.

Brandon sniffed his fingers and tuned out the lecture. His opinion of Faulkner differed greatly from Lola Dumphreys. He felt the reason Faulkner could convey a moron so realistically in his writings was because it took a retard to write like a retard. No wonder he was so convincing.

It did not take Brandon's cynical mind to interpret the obvious. Most people in the class had reached the conclusion that Vernon Price was fucking Lola Dumphreys. A few thought he had been doing so for quite awhile.

Ellen Pierce sat two rows back and to the right of Brandon Stuart. She had taken in the situation and came to the correct conclusion. She figured Vernon had scored on Mrs. Dumphreys and then dismissed the whole thing as boring. She was much more interested in Brandon. He wasn't the most attractive boy in school. He didn't even look like he shaved yet. Several girls had tried to get with the new guy but no one had met with any success. Ellen liked a challenge.

Most guys in the school and surrounding county were a little intimidated by Ellen. She was very pretty and had her pick of "boyfriends." She was far from being a virgin. She had done the deed with Vernon even. (She wasn't sure, but she had a suspicion that her little brother may have gotten the goods while she was passed out.) No big surprise. He watched her constantly. The little shit was definitely perverted.

The new guy was a bit nerdy but he definitely tweaked something inside her. She didn't give two shits for anyone around this town and this guy was so different. He should probably be put on the endangered species list.

Ellen was smart as well as pretty. Very few people knew this about her. Fewer people cared. A smart girl was not necessarily a good thing. They got to expecting too much and became high tone. Women might be able to do anything a man can do and they may be as smart as any man, but just as soon as a woman started acting like she was as good as any man, she would get a response that a man would give another man in the same situation — resistance. Men do not like smart, able men coming into their world and trying to take over and when a woman tried it, it was even more insulting. People do not like to feel threatened, not by anyone.

Ellen did not care how threatened anyone felt. She realized that if she gave people the impression of herself that they already had, life was a breeze. If people wanted a dumb, pretty girl that's what they got. This gave her the advantage in almost every situation. Ellen herself had a problem with underestimating people. The entire community expected the worst from people and they were seldom disappointed.

Ellen decided that after class she would introduce herself to the new kid. She spent the remaining time writing their names in little hearts. Ellen and Brandon forever. Ellen Stuart. Mr. and Mrs. Brandon Stuart and so on. Ellen hated this practice but she found herself guilty of it quite often. Girls were trained from infancy to be wives and mothers. Ellen did not want to be either, but seventeen years of training was seventeen years of training.

Third period bell rang. The class rose en masse and headed for the door. Ellen made sure to be right behind her target. They reached the door together and Brandon stepped aside to let Ellen through first. She had anticipated this move and was ready. She sprang her assault.

"Why thank you. You couldn't possibly be from around here. What is your name? Here, walk me to class. I really must talk to you. Glenda Wells told me you had been all over the country. I've never been anywhere myself. You've got to tell me all about it. By the way, I'm Ellen. Ellen Pierce. Not Ellie. I can't stand that. People think they can call you Ellie; they invariably call you Ellie Mae, next. I never could stand that show."

Brandon Stuart arrived at his third period class just as the final bell was finishing its clamor. Mr. Waddle was closing the door.

"You better get on in here Mr. Stuart. I would send you to get a late pass, except that would give you twenty more minutes of loafing around the halls. I figure you to be one of the few bodies around here that can appreciate the high level of bullshit that I am delivering every day and it would be a pity for you to be denied that privilege."

"Thank you, sir. I really appreciate it."

"Ah! Isn't that nice and so automatic. You really got a future lad. Anybody who kisses ass so sincerely will go far in this world."

"Huh?"

"Oh, never mind. Just take a seat and prepare to be dazzled by the brilliance that is Theodore Waddle the third. History and Civics teacher, supreme."

"This is Sociology."

"Indeed. Yes it is. I am also a most passable Sociology teacher and Girl's Softball Coach, as well. I guess you could say I am an all around educator."

"Yeah, that's one thing you say. Big round masturbator would be another."

"Who said that? Oh! Oh! Oh! A voice from the void and it used a word with four syllables. Please, I must know. Who said that? Which of you little devils has the audacity and panache to attack the sovereignty of Theodore Waddell, educator supreme."

By this time the entire class was rolling. Brandon was still standing at the door. He did not know if he was in trouble or not. Mr. Waddell noticed his plight.

"Please take a seat. It is time to begin my oratory."

"Yes sir."

Brandon took a seat halfway back against the wall. He liked this class. Mr. Waddell was a bit wordy but he usually managed to keep his class entertaining. This was naptime for most of the students. The class was not very demanding and anyone with any intelligence could pass with a minimum amount of effort.

Brandon settled in and tried to listen but he kept going back to his encounter with the good-looking girl in the hallway. He had noticed her his first day in class but had never approached her. He had learned enough about small towns to know sixteen-year-old boys

did not date seventeen-year-old girls because they were all probably married or dating

guys in their mid-twenties. The girl, Ellen was quite stunning and obviously interested in

him. He was a bit wary though. He expected some big goon to come up and tell him she

was spoken for or some such. He needed more information before proceeding. He just

did not know where to get the information.

"Hey, dude." Brandon felt a tap on his shoulder. He turned and was greeted by a

weasel-faced boy of about sixteen years who had very prominent buckteeth and red hair

with freckles. "Did you hear what happened in Dumphrey's English class second

period?"

"What? Hey, I'm in that class."

"Well, Gerald Powell is too and he said that he walked in and seen Vernon Pierce and

Mrs. Dumphreys knocking nasties right on her desk. He also said her panties were laying

on the floor and some jerkoff picked 'em up and was sniffing 'em for like ten minutes.

He said you could smell it. Oh man, I'd give my left nut to nail that bitch."

"Who is Gerald Powell? Did he really say jerkoff?"

"What? Oh, I don't know. Did you see the panties? I mean, were they really her

panties?"

"Yeah, I saw 'em. I didn't see anybody fucking but you could smell something. The

panties were there though."

"You seen them! You really seen them!"

"Mr. Harvis, would you mind letting the rest of us in on the conversation. Mr. Stuart you are really trying to irk me this morning. You show up when you want and then you spend the time you are here talking with Mr. Harvis. Time well spent, I'm sure."

"Fuck you!" Jarrod Harvis mumbles.

"Excuse me, Mr. Harvis, did you have a comment?"

"No sir. I didn't say nuthin'.

"What about you Mr. Stuart?"

"Uh, no. I didn't say anything, sir."

"Well okay then. Let's get back to the sociological ramifications of "Barbie" versus "G.I. Joe." Please pay attention."

The remaining time in class passed uneventfully. Brandon sat and daydreamed about Ellen.

Between third and fourth periods Mr. Harvis (Jarrod) approached Brandon in the hall. "That fucker needs to leave me alone. I'd a busted him one but my dad told me he would rip me a new asshole if I got in any more trouble. I guess he'd have to make bail to do it but he probably would too. What class you got now?"

"Study Hall, Mr. Grant."

"Yeah. I got Industrial Arts with Blaine. We're making toolboxes. Mine's twelve by three. When he asks what kind of tool I'm putting in it, I'm gonna show it to him."

"That's funny. Do you know that girl?"

"Yeah. That's Ellen Pierce. She's fine. She is a little weird though."

"She seeing anyone?

"No. I don't think so. At least nobody with any sense."

"Why? Something wrong with her?"

"No. I don't reckon. Her little brother is a tad off center but I guess she's all right. She's one of them girls you always think is laughing at some joke nobody else gets. You wonder if she is laughing at you. You know what I mean?"

"Yeah, I think so."

"Well, I gotta go. My box awaits."

"Yeah, catch you later."

Brandon reached class a little early. He failed to notice the irony involved. He could get to Study Hall on time but had been late for class. He settled in and within moments was fast asleep. A slight breeze awakened him on his neck. The breeze was a steady stream of air being blown on his neck by a bright-eyed, pretty girl of about fourteen.

"Hi. I'm Sara. You can call me Tea. Ellen Pierce wanted me to give you this. She thinks you're cute. So do I. I gotta go. My boyfriend's goofy friends will tell him I was flirting with you.

"I'm Brandon. Nice meeting you."

"I know and yeah, nice. Later."

The girl had placed in his hand a tiny square of paper. He unfolded it and read the message within.

Brandon

Hey it's me, Ellen. I wanted to talk some more with

you. I would like to meet by the basketball courts after

school, if you can make it. I can get you a ride home if

that's a problem.

Kisses,

Ellen

P.S. I think you're cute. Sniff. Sniff. What did you do

with the panties? Hah! Hah!

Brandon was blushing. He hadn't realized how many people had seen him pick up the panties, much less sniff them. He was becoming somewhat of a celebrity. He always tried to go unnoticed, Mr. Cool, inconspicuous as white socks. The spotlight for some reason was on him today. It felt good for right now but Brandon realized there was a bad side to all this attention as well. People put others in categories and once you got labeled something in someone's mind, it took a lot to discourage their ideas. He did not want to be placed in a situation where he would have to live up to an image he never wished for in the first place.

He could hardly wait to meet her after school! He could walk home easily from here but he needed a car if he intended to get anywhere dating. He had a motorcycle but it was a Honda 250 Rebel and he was a little embarrassed to ride it to school. He had been walking home and having his father drop him off in the mornings.

Ellen was pretty sure that Brandon would show up. She needed her good friend, Sarah Wheaton, to double with them this afternoon. She actually needed her boyfriend's car. Ellen hadn't been on a walking date since she was thirteen. Brandon was cute but she was not going to date anyone for long who didn't have the means to get her out of this shithole occasionally. Brandon would definitely need to get some wheels. Oh well, first things first. Gotta see if the dude has anything going on or if he's another turd like the rest.

The rest of the day dragged by. The stories of the morning had escalated to the point that Bobby and Vernon had gotten into a fight so bad that Bobby had to be taken away in an ambulance. Another version had Bobby winning the fight and that was why he got expelled. Another, that Bobby and Vernon were fighting over Lola Dumphreys. Vernon had won and she had rewarded him.

Bobby Pierce was a rare individual. He was one of the few people in the world that others actually liked more than he realized. Most students at Pineville liked Bobby and many felt that Vernon Price was a royal pain in the ass. Bobby was under the impression that Vernon was very popular and well liked. Bobby didn't understand that Vernon victimized many others besides Bobby. Vernon himself liked Bobby and would be shocked to find out the intensity and depth of Bobby's fear and loathing.

-85-

Bobby, being a quiet person by nature, had a way of listening to others and people were drawn to him for this reason. He felt, like many teenagers, everyone was laughing at him and that no one took him seriously. He felt if he could just get Vernon to leave him alone, he would be all right.

Bobby did not realize that the other kids had problems of their own. They had to deal with the Vernons of the world also. They did not have time or inclination to obsess over his personal trials and tribulations. Many of Bobby's classmates felt Bobby had it going on. They felt his timidity was a quiet, self-assurance and envied him this personal strength and courage. This latest flare-up with Vernon gave the other kids more respect for Bobby. Bobby thought they were laughing and sneering at his plight. Instead, many looked to him as somewhat of a hero — the under dog fighting the bully and lending hope to others.

Bobby was not worried about his being suspended from school. His father would not care and his grades were no problem to keep up. Bobby did know that most of his teachers did like him. Unlike most students within the system, Bobby knew how to really think. He could make use of the knowledge he gathered at school. Analogies and parables became instantly applicable for Bobby to everyday life. He did not learn for grades but took in knowledge as an end.

Bobby Pierce, like many adolescents and teens, lived in a fantasy world. Empathy not being his strong suit, Bobby was becoming totally self-absorbed and on his way to being a true sociopath. The couple his uncle and he had killed were not really people. They were diversions and Bobby had not felt anything but exhilaration and joy from the event. The entire point of Mary Ann's and Boyd's lives had been to live long enough to provide one night's entertainment for a semi-moronic, dyed in the wool, low down, skulking, cowardly, psychopathic hillbilly and his punkass, little, self-pitying nephew. It never occurred to Bobby or Jimmy that they could both wind up the same way. Jimmy or his protégé could easily turn on each other at the slightest provocation and never have any regrets. Being a homicidal, sociopathic, self-absorbed maniac is a truly lonely life.

Bobby faced another problem. He had nobody to share his accomplishments. He had no best friend or confidant to divulge his secrets. No one would believe him anyway. For a moment Bobby was not the exuberant, hard-ass, murdering bastard. He was a lonely sixteen-year-old with no one to talk to.

Vernon Price was in very good spirits. He felt invincible. Everyone who crossed him this day found out the hard way. "You don't fuck with Vernon. Man, oh man that little episode with that sweet little cunt Dumphreys was something else. Made that cunt squirm. Hell, made her like it. Yeah. It was a little touch and go for a little while but ol' sweet twat came across in the pinch. Man, oh man, good pussy too, wet, hot, tight and squirming like vermin. Got to have some more and soon. Ain't ever gonna wash her off me. Gonna let one 'a those little fresh meat cheerleaders lick the twat slime off my pole."

The only cloud in Vernon's skies was one Bobby Pierce. "Boy needs his ass whupped, again. I ought to go over there and kick his ass today."

Vernon felt it his duty to keep punks like Bobby on the straight and narrow, for their own good and the good of the country. "Might even get to fuck sweet little Ellen again. Can't figure that girl out. She give me and ol' Freddie Wilbanks the pussy twice in one afternoon and then acts like she don't know us. Good pussy, too. Can't figure it out. She sure sounded like she liked it. Fact is, don't know anybody who liked it more. Bitch is just weird. Entire family is strange."

Enough time in the wonderful world of Vernon.

No one had paid any special notice or attention to the absence of Mary Ann or Boyd Thomas. It wasn't strange for either to be gone for days with no forewarning or apologies upon return.

The bodies and the vehicle would not be found with any luck. Jimmy and Bobby were hoping people would assume the couple had run off together. By the time people got around to making inquiries, it would be hard to make any connection to the real killers.

The couple and their vehicle lay at the bottom of the strip pit approximately thirty to thirty-five feet below the surface. The last days of fall were here and not many people would be using the swimming hole until spring. It could be two or three years before anyone stumbled across the mangled forms and their steel coffin. The oily residue on top of the water would not be questioned because drums of various substances had been dropped in pits such as these for years. The limestone and frequent rains acted as cleansing agents and natural filters. By spring, the water would be so clear that people who wished could look real hard and see the bottom. This was not true but a lie told so often that no one questioned the accuracy of the statements. The pit would keep its dark treasure at least long enough that it didn't matter anymore.

Brandon was nervous and extremely self-conscious. He had had many girlfriends and was somewhat experienced but he knew this girl was different.

Some women are born with secrets that men can never know. This girl's eyes held a bemused cynicism that wasn't hard or forced. Passion was there. Passion she did not know she possessed. She had had lovers, but had never experienced love.

Brandon felt all this and for him it was the truth. Sixteen years olds feel everything so intensely that it is hard not to perish daily from the pure anguish and depth of feeling they have to carry around.

Brandon was pretty much full of shit. A hopeless romantic, he fell in love more often than he changed his underwear. This time he was right. Ellen Pierce possessed many, if not all, of these attributes.

She possessed other darker attributes as well.

Ellen Pierce at age seventeen possessed beauty, intelligence and womanly guile in great quantity. She came from the same environment and gene pool as her uncle and brother. They shared many same life experiences. It would be quite rare for her to come from such an environment unscathed. It is a credit to her strength of character that she functions at all.

Ellen knew by the age of six, not to be alone with any male member of her family. Most girls Ellen knew had had encounters with relations of "friends" of the family. Ellen's Uncle Jimmy had fondled her when she was four. He had attempted intercourse when she was six. Ellen's mother had walked in and for the first and only time in Ellen's life, that she could remember, someone had stood up for her.

Ellen's mother had raised so much hell that Maxi, Ellen's father, had beaten the hell out of Jimmy and had not let him back in the house for two years afterward.

Ellen recalls that at the time Jimmy was allowed back in, Bobby had started to change. Bobby had been outgoing and a happy child. He had become a sullen and withdrawn young man. Ellen suspected and rightly so, that Uncle Jimmy had been molesting Bobby for years.

She had lain awake at night and schemed and dreamed cruel, drawn-out tortures and slow, miserable deaths for her uncle. She now believed the cruelest punishment of all had been visited upon him. He had to be himself. The only problem was, the miserable bastard liked it. Ellen's mother had saved her before too much damage had been done.

Ellen felt Bobby had been sacrificed and had some measure of guilt. She went from one extreme to another in dealing with her brother. One minute, she was his strongest protector and friend. The next, she could become his vicious enemy and detractor. She loathed and loved her little brother but she flat out hated her uncle.

Ellen and Brandon met at the basketball goals. They sat under a tree and waited for Sarah Wheaton and Sarah's boyfriend, Chad.

Chad was nineteen and owned a '72 Nova. The car was not much to look at but it was one of the fastest in town. That made Chad one of the "cooler" guys around.

"Chad's gonna race Friday. Sarah says he's going to race Bobby Gantry in his little Maverick. The Maverick's supposed to be one of those little factory 302's that he had rebuilt and 'sposed to be faster 'n shit through a goose."

"You don't care much about cars and stuff, do ya?"

"Uh, no," Brandon replies uncomfortably. "None of my friends drove much. Some of their brothers had nice cars."

"Nobody raced much though?"

"We mostly just rode out to the mall or to the bowling alley or theater or something."

"Yeah. Well, cars are a big deal here. There's not much to do if you got a car and nothing if you don't. Chad's not the best looking guy around and probably couldn't buy pussy if he didn't own that Nova. You're blushing. Lord, would you look at that. Whats'a matter? Girls don't talk like that where you from? You have heard a girl say pussy before ain't you?"

"Yeah. It's just that, oh, oh forget it. I'm just not used to someone as pretty as you saying stuff like that is all."

"You think I'm pretty?"

"Yeah, sure. You're a knockout."

"You think I'm trash though, don't you?"

"No. I never said anything like that."

"Yeah, you do. I can tell. It don't matter though. I know I ain't like girls you're used to. Pretty little things is the latest little fashions, acting like ice cream wouldn't melt in their asses. Well just for your information, girls like that say and do the same things as any other girls. They just put on a big act and any boy that can't see through that kind a shit pretty quick deserves what he winds up with. I ain't one to put on airs for nobody but I ain't trash no more 'n anybody."

"I never said that. In fact, I never said anything. I just blushed for God's sake."

-91-

"Watch you mouth. Don't blaspheme."

"Huh?"

"Blaspheme. You know. Don't take the Lord's name in vain."

"What? You talk like a truck driver and you're gonna tell me to watch what I say?"

"That's right! There's a site more 'n a little difference 'tween saying pussy and shit and damn and things like that than there is in taking the Lord's name in vain. You city boys shore got some strange ways."

"Us! What about you?"

"You're judging me as something and accusing me of judging you."

"I may have been taken aback somewhat by the language you used but I am not used to people talking that way."

"Girls, you mean."

"No, anybody! I'm just not used to people being that graphic is all."

"Bullshit. City people ain't no better 'n we are. Shits, shit. Don't matter what kind a ribbon and paper you wrap it in."

"What does that mean?"

"It means that just cause I wear jeans and say what I think does not make me less than a city girl in her Calvin Kleins who tells you what you want to hear. Usually if a girl is telling you what you want to hear, she's playing you anyway and by the time you find out what you're really dealing with, it's too late."

"Why are you mad at me?"

"I thought you liked me."

"I do dummy. I like you a lot."

"I don't know why I'm saying these things. I guess I just want you to know how I really am. People say a lot of shit about me and mine. By that I mean people talk about my family and me. I just want you to know that whatever people say, one thing is, I don't lie and I don't kiss people's asses. I go where I want with who I want and I don't try to please nobody. I like you and if you like me, you better get ready for some bullshit. People around here think I'm strange and I don't care. I've never said these things to anybody and I don't know why I should tell you. I just got a feeling is all. I just don't want you thinking I'm trash."

"I don't. I think you're probably the prettiest girl I ever talked to. I just don't know why you're mad at me."

"Shit! I ain't mad. If I was mad you wouldn't be standing here talking to me. Shit, if I was mad you wouldn't be standing. Here comes Chad and Sarah."

"Cool. Let's resume this little talk later."

"Sure. You all right?"

"Fuckin' A. Hah, hah. You're blushing again."

Chad and Sarah approach. Chad looks a little pissed. Sarah motions for Ellen to talk to her alone.

"Ellen, Chad doesn't like this guy. He says this guy's dad is gonna make a lot of guys lose their jobs."

"Do what?"

"Yeah. Chad says if his dad finds out he's been chumming around with this guy and then his big shot father fires Chad's father that his dad will kick his ass.

"Ah shit. Can't he at least take us home?"

"Well, we'll take you, no problem, but he says he don't want that dude in his car. You better tell him. You're the one that got him out here.

"Okay, just give me a minute."

"All right, but hurry up. Chad's taking me to the movies tonight and I gotta get ready."

"To the movies, huh? Shit, that boy must really be horny."

"Oh fuck you. Just hurry, okay?"

"Yeah, sure."

"Brandon, come here a sec."

"Yeah, what's up?"

"Well, there seems to be a slight change of plans."

"Whadd'ya mean?"

"Well, I thought we was all gonna go over to the Tastee Freeze but Chad has suddenly got other ideas."

"That's cool, whatever."

"You don't understand. I don't have another way home."

"What are you saying?"

"I'm saying, I gotta get home and that's my ride."

"Oh, wait a minute. They don't want me to go. What'd I do?"

"Chad's dad works at the plant."

"Oh, I get it. That's cool. You don't have to say anything else."

Brandon turns and starts to walk away. This is not the first time his father's job has interfered with his plans.

"Wait a minute."

"What? Your friends are waiting."

"Listen, that's my ride home. I don't have another. I like you very much. Call me tonight. Chad's an asshole."

"An asshole with a car."

"Call me tonight! Don't let this be more than what it is."

"What is it?"

"Listen fucker. I like you. I don't know why but I do. Call me tonight. Right now I don't feel like walking eleven miles. Call me!"

"All right."

Ellen quickly stretches and gives Brandon a quick kiss on the cheek. "You better call."

She turns and quickly walks/run to the idling Nova. She gets in and Sarah scoots over. Chad guns the motor, takes off in a squeal of rubber. Ellen leans out the window and yells, "Call me!"

Chad flips him the bird. Sarah gives a little wave. Brandon is left standing at the curb. He feels like he just ran a mile

CHAPTER TWELVE

"Yo! Vernon! Watch out! Look out for that — POW! — mailbox."

"Hah, hah, hah. What's wrong Freddie?"

"Man, you is one crazy, sick, mother fucker. I'm glad this ain't my truck. Coach gonna kick yer ass."

"Bullshit! Ain't a scratch on it. This truck is made of steel, man. This ain't one a dem new Japanese pieces of shit. No sirree, Bob. This here's American metal."

"Yeah, if you say so. I just wished you'd slow the fuck down."

"Live a little, man, live a little. Hand me another one 'a them beers."

"Here you go. Where we going?"

"Well, Freddie, ol' son, I think we is going to pay a visit on my little buddy, Bobby."

"Oh shit! Here we go. Shit man, we ain't gonna find the little fucker nowheres. He gonna be hiding real good after today."

"Nah, he ain't smart enough. Besides, ol' man Pierce got animals and animals got to be fed. So ol' Bobby'll be at the barn or the pond."

"We just gonna drive right on up on him, huh?"

"Look out for that," — POW — "gate…"

"Hah, hah, hah. Man you need to relax. Eat a pill or something. You is tense and I mean tense."

"Fuck you! You'd be tense too if you had any sense."

"Bobby might be a punk, but his ol' man'll kick our asses good, he sees that gate down like that."

"Who's gonna tell him? You? Me?"

"Naw man, but ol' Bobby might."

"Shit, Maxi'd whup his ass worse 'n we going to cause he seen us and didn't do nuthin. He ain't gonna say shit."

Bobby was in the lower pasture. He was breaking up straw for the cattle. He had grain for the horses and salt blocks as well. He had to feed the livestock at least three times a week in mild weather. More in bad. Bobby liked feeding the animals. He considered the horses his friends and cared for them almost as much as the dogs he had killed.

He still had mixed emotions about the slaying of the dogs. He could still get excited at the memory. His blood would run faster and his fists would clench but he truly missed the animals. He had no trepidation about the rapes and subsequent murders of the two humans he and his uncle had butchered.

Bobby had loved the dogs and felt some degree of kinship with them. He had never felt close to other people. Most of his dealings with his own kind had caused him hurt, fear, pain or shame. Most of his dealings with animals had been positive. They fed him, gave him love, never complained and he didn't have to prove himself. Little wonder he preferred their company over his own kind.

The horses alerted Bobby to the approaching vehicle. He had been lost in his own thoughts. He spotted the truck and instantly recognized it as trouble.

Bobby got into his own truck and took off up an old logging road that curved through the pasture and up the mountain into some deep timber. Bobby was scared but for once he also had other ideas besides just escape. He had a vague stirring of an idea that if it worked, would give him a little revenge on his pursuers.

Bobby knew the terrain much better than Vernon. His truck was lighter and better suited for this type of driving. With a little luck, this could turn out to be not such a bad day after all.

Vernon spotted the truck going up the hillside and speeded up his own vehicle. Freddie began cursing and hung on tighter.

"We got him! We got him! We got him! That little fucker's heading up the old Robbins' logging road. That's a dead end. It peters out up along the next ridge line n' ain't nowhere's to go. We got that sumbitch."

"Well slow the fuck down. If he ain't got nowhere to run, let's least try 'n stay in one piece so as we can."

"Oh, you just leave the driving to me. This ol' Ford'll eat this mountain and we's gonna beat the pure dee fuck outta that rat faced little shit."

"Fine. That's great. Can't wait. Just don't get us killed doing it."

"Quit whining. You sound like your pussy hurts."

Bobby was at the top of the mountain and headed along the ridgeline. He knew the regular road came out into a dead end. He also knew something Vernon did not. Bobby and his family had been cutting firewood off this mountain for years. There was an old wagon truck where mule teams had been used to log off the mountain two or three decades earlier.

Bobby had snaked small trees out with his little ATV four wheeler. Bobby's truck could get over the hill without incident if he didn't get stuck. The ground was soft but if he was cautious he could thread his way through the trees and come around the top of the hill and down to the road on the other side. He would have to cut a fence at the end of the pasture but he was ready for such contingencies.

Vernon and the now terribly terrified Freddie Wilbanks were speeding up the logging road and closing the gap quickly. Bobby had passed the top of the hill and had threaded through the trees. At this point on the ridgeline the hill peaked and broke off all at once. The hill sloped at about a forty-five degree angle down the hill if you cut a sharp left. If you kept going straight, the hill appeared to be a gentle mount, but actually dropped straight down for about seven feet where the rock face had broken off in some past geologic upheaval.

Bobby knew the road and still almost forgot to make the sharp left. To facilitate matters further, he got out of the vehicle and dragged a good-sized piece of timber across the path behind his truck. This little trick, he hoped, would encourage anyone coming over the hill to continue in a straight line, which would take them over the drop-off and end the chase.

Bobby got back into his battered old truck and took off gingerly down the slope. He picked his way slowly for two reasons. He did not want his pursuers to hear his vehicle and he did not know what obstacle may be ahead that were not there the last time he had used the road.

"Vernon, slow down! You're going to get us killed."

"Don't sweat it. We got the little shit. There ain't nowhere for him to go."

"I don't see him, Vern, maybe we passed him already."

"Naw, he's on top of that rise. Shit, I didn't even know this road was here. The little fucker thinks he's slick."

Vernon, never having been known for following advice, did not slow down. He accelerated over the rise and immediately saw the error in doing so.

The vehicle never slowed. Vernon did not hit the brakes until the truck was airborne. Freddie screamed and Vernon cursed. The truck landed on the front bumper and slid about forty feet. Freddie was thrown through the windshield. He landed on his left arm and leg and rolled with the impact. His acrobatics notwithstanding, a small tree stopped the impetus of his fall. This same tree also shattered his pelvis.

Vernon's head collided with the steering column. He was dazed but not seriously injured. Vernon sat wondering what went wrong. He could not believe or understand what happened. It never occurred to Vernon or Freddie that Bobby, not dipshit Bobby, could have engineered or executed such a plan on purpose. The entire episode, in Vernon's mind, was a freak accident. The two friends were under the impression that Bobby had never realized he was being followed. They considered the entire incident the culmination of Vernon's over-zealous behavior.

Freddie lay wracked in pain. He yelled and screamed in agony. Vernon gathered his wits and stumbled to his aid.

Vernon had great prowess at inflicting pain. He had very little skill at easing it. Freddie lay in agony. The truck was wrecked and Vernon was at a loss. He didn't know what to do.

"Go get help, Vernon."

"We're a mile from anywhere. I don't want to leave you."

"Ain't nobody gonna come by, dude. I am in pain!"

"All right. All right. I'm going. I'll be back as soon as I can."

"Dude, give me your coat and something to drink."

"Sure man, anything. I'll be right back."

"Hey, see if dipshit's around, make him get help."

"Yeah, all right."

It didn't seem in the least ironic to Freddie or Vernon to seek help from Bobby. They would undoubtedly have beaten the shit out of him and left him lying in his own blood and pain wracked body. Bobby knew this and he also knew that everybody would have thought it was good, clean fun. Nobody in the entire community would have felt any empathy if Bobby were the person lying in pain instead of Freddie Wilbanks.

Freddie was a jock. Freddie was good looking. Freddie was popular. Freddie was a prized citizen in the community whereas Bobby Pierce was a nobody and if their positions were reversed, Freddie would laugh and walk away and brag about it later.

Bobby could not just walk away. It wouldn't be right to just leave Freddie lying there in pain. Hell, he might live.

Bobby disliked Freddie almost as much as he hated Vernon Price. Vernon and Freddie had been best of friends since Freddie's family had moved to town.

Vernon, like ninety percent of the people in the community, was a dyed-in-the-wool redneck. He hated everyone and everything that was different. He hated Jews, Polacks, the weak, the handicapped and niggers.

Everyone hated niggers. It was unspoken law. Somehow Pineville, like many towns its size, had adopted the Wilbanks family. No one ever called Freddie a nigger even though his mother was at least three-quarters black. Vernon and most of his friends would have hit anyone that said anything racist to Freddie or his family.

Freddie Wilbanks, himself, had long ago quit thinking of himself as anything but Freddie. Bobby was about to refresh his memory.

Bobby hated Freddie more than Freddie could ever know. To Freddie, Bobby was a joke. He didn't exist except as something to be harassed or laughed at. He was less than human. Freddie, like everybody else, treated Bobby quite niggardly.

Bobby waited until Vernon had disappeared from sight. He then walked up behind Freddie. He approached slowly and quietly. Bobby walked to within five feet of Freddie before he said anything.

"Hi, nigger," he whispered.

Freddie jerked at the sound. The quick movement engulfed his body with fresh pain. "What? Who's there? Oh! Oh, fuck! Shit, that hurts. Is that you Vernon?"

"No, nigger, it's not," still in a whisper.

"What'd you say? I know I didn't just hear you say what think you said."

Bobby stepped closer and knelt down beside the tortured, mangled body of Freddie Wilbanks."

"I said, nigger, nigger."

"Mother fucker, I'll beat your ass! You just wait. I'm gonna fuck you up."

"No, you're not. You are not going to do a damn thing. I owe you something and I'm going to repay you. In full."

Bobby was remembering everything that had been done to him by Freddie Wilbanks. Beatings, insults (real and imagined), mocking snickers. Everything.

"Hey, nigger. Do you remember when you and Vernon brought my sister home from that party? Do you remember carrying her unconscious form into the house? Do you remember Vernon waking her up by forcing himself up inside her? Huh, nigger? Do you? Do you remember taking turns raping my flesh and blood? Huh? Nigger? Do you?"

"Yeah, I remember. I remember shoving my dick in her face and her licking it like a sno-cone. I remember her moaning and coming like no tomorrow. I bet she does too, you little shit. Where were you? Puking, shaking in your panties while me and Vern poured the meat to her. Yeah, she was drunk. Yeah, she was passed out. Big fucking deal. She ain't nobody and neither are you, punk? You just get your little, white bread, punk ass in your little truck and go get some help, and maybe, just maybe I won't kick your ass for that nigger shit. And next time we fuck your sister, we might give you a turn. Hah. Hah. Oh shit, it hurts to laugh."

Bobby still whispering chuckled a little his own self. "No, nigger. I ain't going nowhere. You ain't going nowhere neither. You have taken advantage of me ever since I've known you. You have hit me. You have mocked me. You have laughed at me. You have taken advantage of my sister and disgraced my family name."

"Fuck you!"

"Shut up, nigger!" Bobby punctuates the statement with a backhand into Freddie's mouth.

"Oh, ah, ah, ah. That fucking hurts. Stop it, please. Stop." The blow knocked Freddie onto his side. His shattered pelvis erupted into explosions of pain.

Bobby grabbed a small stick and started poking Freddie in his legs and side. "Hah, hah, nigger. Crawl, crawl like the little piece of nigger shit you are. You ain't nothing. You ain't shit. You are a little piece of nigger shit that's about to die. You hear me, boy. You hear me, nigger. You are about to die. You ain't never gonna be nothing else except a piece of dead nigger shit crawling at my feet. Crawl, nigger! Crawl! Nigger! Crawl!"

Freddie was crying and blabbering in fright and pain. He did not know the person in front of him. He did not recognize the face of Bobby Pierce, but something deep inside of him recognized all too well the image he now faced.

Years of equality and being treated as a man fell away in seconds. The generations of oppression and four hundred years of servility and second citizenship reasserted their presence.

-104-

Freddie reverted to the frightened, animal-like, fear soaked wretch of a being that hides dark and small in all of us.

Bobby became a primal creature of hate and brutality that also dwells within each of us. His face held a maniacal grin of pleasure. Bobby had never been so happy in his life. Every time he poked and prodded Freddie, he laughed and chortled with glee.

"Crawl, nigger. Crawl, crawl like the snake you is, boy."

Bobby's seemingly mindless rage and attack, was in fact and act with direction. With each poke and prod he was making Freddie crawl back toward the truck. When Freddie reached the vehicle he reached up and tried to crawl into the cab of the vehicle.

Bobby quit hitting the young boy in front of him. He stepped back and watched the mighty Freddie Wilbanks cry and shake like a little baby.

Bobby was ecstatic. He had conquered an enemy all by himself. No, Uncle Jimmy to hog the glory. This was all his. He had set up the chase and the wreck. He had double backed and waited until his prey was all alone. He had bullied and tortured his victim until he was back into the vehicle. Now he would finish it.

"Hey, Freddie. You all right, man?" Bobby's tone was helpful, almost kind.

Freddie was confused. The beast that was torturing him was offering a hand and inquiring about his health.

"Let me help you buddy." Bobby gently rolled Freddie over and placed a jacket behind his head. He tried to make him as comfortable as possible. "Come on, Freddie. I'm sorry. Man, I just got carried away. You understand man, nothing personal. I just got a little out of control."

"What? Yeah, whatever, man. I'm hurting, man. Real bad. I think I tore something inside, man. Just get me some help, man. I won't say nothing. Just get me some help."

Freddie was in so much pain, he blacked out. Bobby used this opportunity to carry out the rest of his plan.

He got under the truck and found a gas leak. It was a small leak, but with a little help it became a rather substantial one. He then took his trusty stick and dug a trench directing the gas into a puddle that pooled about two feet from where Freddie was sitting.

Freddie awoke to Bobby standing about ten feet away. "What's up, man? You gonna get help or what?"

"Yeah, man. I'm on it. Here, I found some water in my truck." Bobby tossed a small plastic container to Freddie. It was full of water." "My sister puts them in the freezer and freezes them. They keep my cooler cold. It's melted now, but still kinda cool. Drink up, oh yeah, here's your cigarettes. They fell out of your shirt."

"Yeah, thanks man."

"Well, I'm gonna go get some help. Just keep still. I'll be right back."

"Oh sure. Just hurry, man."

"No hard feelings?

"Nah. Just get some help, man. I'll forget it all. Please, man. I'm hurting."

Freddie took a big drink as he watched Bobby walk up the hill. He was hurting bad, but he knew he wasn't gonna forget being made to crawl like a fucking dog and being called a nigger.

Bobby was sitting in his truck listening to an old Credence Clearwater Revival tape when he heard the explosion. He smiled to himself and started singing along, softly.

"Yep. I guess everybody's right about smoking. Damn things 'll kill you." He smiled to himself and slid the truck gently into gear and rolled off back down the old logging road. He hadn't had to cut any fence after all. This day just kept getting better and better.

CHAPTER THIRTEEN

"What's up, Uncle Jimmy?"

"Changing the plugs, Boy. Gettin' 'er ready to run that loudmouth Yardell Stuart's Chevy small block into the ground tonight."

"You running the Ranger, here?"

"Yep, he thinks I got a 351 in here, cause that's what we was talking about. But that there's a 400, boy and she's putting out about three hundred, fifty horses. Ol' Yardell will be shitting money right in ol' Uncle Billy's palm."

"Cool."

"Yeah, cool. I heard one of your little friends cooked hisself yestiddy. Little nigger musta thought he wasn't black enough."

"I guess. Where'd you hear about it?"

"Down at the Exxon. Lonnie told me about it. He said it was a damn shame. Said that boy had good hands, mighta took the team to State this year. He said that little fucker could catch anything ol' Vern could throw. I reckon ol' Vern's taking it pretty hard. You'd think he was sucking that boy's dick the way he's carrying on. Your Pa ain't none too happy they broke his steel gate and he says he's damn tired of everybody burning animals on his farm."

"Dad said that."

"Yeah. He gets off a good one every once in a while. You wouldn't know why those boys was out here, would you?"

-108-

"No. I don't know. They shore warn't invited by me."

"Yeah, I know…. You and them boys ain't exactly what one would call buddies, now were you?"

"No. I hate both those fuckers. I just wish Vern woulda stayed with the other one."

"You'll get him next time. You got a feel for it, boy. Hell! You're a natural."

"What? What're you talking about?"

"Boy, I ain't stupid and I been reading signs since a'fore I got long britches. They was two trucks on that hillside and neither of them boys was a wearing boots."

"I don't know what you're talking about."

"Good answer, Bobby. No need for it, though. Everybody bought the story just the way you laid it out. Only funny thing about it was Vern kept insisting that Freddie didn't smoke and that he couldn't have crawled anywhere because his legs were broke and twisted. People think Vern's just covering up because they's athletes 'n all. Of course, Vern ain't all that reliable anyways since he said Freddie was driving. We know that ain't true, don't we?"

"How? What do you mean?"

"Bobby, you know where you were yesterday, but you don't know where I was, now do you?"

"I guess."

"Well I was over on Randall's ridgeline looking for some of that girl's dope when I happened to notice a little commotion back here on the farm. I couldn't see everything after you all drove into the woods and started up the hill, but I somehow get the feeling that my favorite nephew, mighta helped ol' Freddie into picaninny heaven, where he's

sitting right now, eating watermelon and rubbing chicken grease into his balls."

"I didn't do anything."

"Well I shor hope you're lying cause I shor would be proud to know you killed that

little punk. I shorly would."

"Whatever. I was just feeding the horses. I never knew nothing about nothing."

"Stick to that, boy. You're gonna be a hell of a man."

"Thanks, I think."

"Yeah, you'll do to run the river with yet. You gonna come watch the race?"

"I'm gonna try. I think Pa's got some shit for me to do tonight."

"Well, we'll see. Catch you later."

"Yeah, later."

Racing in the country isn't your usual racing. There are no rules. The person

reaching the agreed upon finish line first is the winner.

The course for Jimmy's race consisted of about three and one-half miles of two-lane

blacktop, so narrow and curvy that the county had posted speed limits of 35 mph for over

two-thirds of the course. The route did have about four stretches in which drivers could

go all out for about a quarter mile at a time.

A lot of people had wrecked on the path chosen for this race, but Jimmy was fairly

confident he would win. He had driven the route since he was thirteen and was a pretty

good driver. He had also fixed the odds a little by doing a little work on Yardell's truck the night before. He hadn't done anything obvious because he knew a third party would check out both trucks if anything strange or funny happened during the race.

Jimmy had let air out of the passenger side, rear tire. Not enough to be obvious, but he figured it would be enough to effect the handling of the curves. He had also driven the course earlier in the day and scattered pea gravel in a couple of key points along the way. Neither item by itself would probably mean much, but both factors added together, he hoped, would at the very least, would make Yardell a little cautious and at best cause a slide, maybe even a wreck.

A big crowd was forming on both ends of the course. This could be a problem. The local police were wary whenever traffic increased in any one area of the county. The route chosen was known for being a popular racecourse and anytime traffic increased noticeably in any area, two or three old busy bodies along the way would call the Sheriff's Department. Plank Road cutoff was at least thirty minutes from town. If a cruiser happened to be in the area, it could end the whole event before it even happened but if everyone participating showed up on time, things should run pretty smooth.

The man Jimmy was racing lived nearby in Jacksboro Crossing. His name was Yardell Stuart. He hadn't lived in the county long and nobody knew much about him. Unlike most everyone around, he didn't have any kin in the area. Most people steered clear of outsiders and the only way to fit in was to be a relative to somebody or marry into local society such as it was.

Yardell was not married and had no kin to speak of. His story was, he relocated to the area when Toyota put a small plant in the area. He had worked for Toyota at the old plant and when it closed he had been given the option of relocating with the plant. A lot of people had moved into the area for the same reason. Yardell had been accepted into the community much quicker and with less skepticism than the norm.

Yardell Stuart's real name, Darrell Beasum, a police office with four years experience on the highway patrol. A routine traffic stop had turned into a major drug bust.

A young man named Albert Hall had been returning from a rock festival in Deerborn, Indiana. He had been a little high from the music and a lot high from the two gel caps of acid that he had acquired at the show. His girlfriend being a bitch at her best and a total cunt the rest of the time had been having one of her bad days. Another couple had ridden along to split the costs and keep the party going. Everything had been going pretty smoothly for the foursome until Albert and the other guy had gotten to talking about partying in general and places they had been in the past. Both guys had been in the military and had a lot of the same experiences. The girls had heard both of the young men's stories many times before and after an hour and a half they had lost patience. They were fed up and not hesitant to display their discontent in the least.

Albert's girlfriend was a large-boned girl of greater average height. She was not a fat girl but big in a mannish way. She had the unlikely moniker of Trixie Dawnell Connor. Trixie had started giving Albert shit about how all he ever talked about was his Army drugs and that she personally was beginning to wonder if he wasn't a little queer the way he obsessed about living with other men and everything. This statement brought forth a snicker from the other girl, aa small-boned and quite lovely girl named Bernice Johnson.

-112-

She stated that she often wondered the same thing about her companion, one Wendell Crawford.

The young men took offense at these statements and felt their very stature as men had been placed in a precarious position. To prove their heterosexuality, they felt nothing less than stopping at the next available wide spot in the road and engaging in ferocious carnality immediately would redeem them.

Unfortunately for the erstwhile lovers, but fortunately for Yardell Stuart, they chose a place called "Big Bone Lick" to consummate their redemption. Yardell had been off duty and noticed a vehicle parked in an area that looked out of place. He had also noticed a lot of movement from said vehicle. His first instinct had been kids making out and almost continued on home just having completed a very long, taxing ten-hour shift. The boy scout in him would not let him be derelict in his duty. Yardell had approached the vehicle after having called in the license place to his duty post. The dispatcher had run the numbers and had quipped, "Take a break and go home. Let somebody else play 'Dirty Harry' for a while." Yardell chuckled to himself because he had always felt he had a lot in common with the big screen cop that Clint Eastwood had brought to life with such hard edge realism.

He had approached the vehicle from the driver's side. He didn't expect to see anything but a couple of kids making out and sorta hoped he might get a shot of a nice looking ass or a shapely young breast or two. The vehicle, a large 1975 Suburban was a monster and sported so many bumper stickers from various alternative and thrash bands that you could not see into it from the rear and sides.

The couples were finished having sex and had decided to smoke a joint before continuing their journey. They were more than a little surprised to see a state trooper looking into the cab of the truck. Albert Hall suddenly felt very small and desperately wished he were somewhere else besides where he was.

Everything was fairly routine from that point. Inside the vehicle, investigators found three tanks of Nitrous Oxide or "Hippy Crack" as it is sometimes referred. Three thousand hits of very good LSD were also recovered, along with about an ounce of pot was spread among the individuals. All four suspects had some kind of illegal paraphernalia on or about their persons. All were arrested and the girls testified against the guys and Yardell's career was on its way.

If the boys did indeed have latent homosexual tendencies they would have ample time to purse them.

The bust got Darrell Beesum a promotion to Detective along with his first undercover assignment — a joint operation between the state and the ATF branch of federal government. Yardell was to infiltrate the local community and live there on a long-term basis. He would go to work at a regular job everyday and would become a regular at all the local booze mills. His mission was fairly open-ended and few limits were placed on what he could do in order to achieve results. If he could not buy illegal drugs, guns or alcohol, he would sell them, always keeping records of transactions both written and recorded. He had enough information on a lot of people to send more than a few to prison for a good length of time.

He had nothing on Jimmy Pierce — yet. Yardell had lured Jimmy into an argument about cars in hope of finding common ground to pursue a more intimate relationship. Jimmy's challenge to race played right into his hands. He planned on letting the redneck win and when he paid off he wanted to offer Jimmy the chance to make some easy money the same way. If everything went according to plan, Yardell would add another scalp to his already large trophy collection. Yardell felt pretty confident that he could beat Jimmy Pierce if he wished. He had done well at the academy and had been a good driver his entire life.

Jimmy Pierce did not know about Yardell's plans to let him win the race. All Jimmy knew was that he didn't have two hundred dollars to lose and that he'd run that summabitch off the road before he would lose.

The night was bright with a full moon and a clear sky. The roads were dry and conditions seemed perfect for a race. People raced at night for various reasons. Most worked during the day. Headlights and not as many people could see oncoming traffic on the roads. Unfortunately animals and debris could be in the way, but it wouldn't be fun if there weren't any risks involved.

The vehicles were lined up and getting ready for the signal. A pretty girl of about seventeen had been chosen to drop the flag. The flag was said girl's top, thus the reason she had been chose. The young girl's breasts were somewhat of a distraction but both drivers were focused on the task at hand. Counting to three, the pretty young thing waved the T-shirt straight towards the ground and the two roaring beasts of metal and rubber roared forth screeching and accelerating toward the first turn.

Yardell Stuart could tell something was amiss at the first turn. His truck was a bit sluggish in the turn and pulled a little to the right. He also knew he would be able to compensate easily if he wanted to. Jimmy Pierce was mad clean through to know his plan wouldn't work. His opponent could flat out drive and the low tire wasn't gonna slow him a bit. He knew he would have to do something drastic if he wanted to win and he did plan on winning. Yardell's truck got about three car lengths ahead in the first stretch he glided easily into the approaching curve with quick heel to toe action from brake, clutch, gas, all in one fluid-like motion. Downshifting smoothly, he slammed the accelerator coming neatly out on the other side. Jimmy's performance was not quite as smooth but he did get an idea watching the other driver take the curve in the manner that he had chosen. The drivers had completed more than hall the course when Jimmy decided to improve his changes. He knew the approaching curve was one in which he had placed the pea gravel. When the drivers approached the straight a way before the curve instead of trying to go around Yardell, Jimmy eased up on the gas slightly to let the other truck get squarely in front of his own. Yardell had planned on letting the other truck pass him at the very same time that Jimmy made his move. The sudden action momentarily threw him off. He hesitated and finally decided to hold off on his plan to let Jimmy get in the lead until the next stretch. He refocused his attention upon the oncoming curve. He started negotiating the turn much in the same way as he had the others until he felt the loose traction. Instead of accelerating through the middle of the turn as before he re-engaged the clutch and pulled the gear lever down into second with the intention of popping the clutch once and tapping the gas and then downshifting once again. A solid plan, except when he slowed the first time, Jimmy Pierce chose the same instant to floor his own vehicle and slam into the rear of the other truck from the side. Upon striking the other truck, Jimmy downshifted and floored it while turning into the other curve. This combined with the other vehicle slowing put him up along side the other truck and ultimately by the other vehicle. Jimmy passed Yardell and as he accelerated away he flipped him off. Yardell was pissed. Any thought of letting Jimmy win flew from his mind. He floored the little Chevy and it responded as if it were pissed at the humiliation that had been placed upon it. Jimmy being a man of questionable courage assumed Yardell to be likewise and figured the other guy would back off so as not to get injured.

Yardell had become a cop because he did not like bullies and never had. A dirty fighter or bad sportsman-like behavior left a bad taste in his mouth.

Jimmy Pierce was a braggart, a liar, and a thief and often acted like a coward. Deep down, Jimmy was a survivalist and much like a rat or a cockroach, his basic desire was to survive. If to survive he had to be tough or brave, he would come up with the goods.

Yardell Stuart had created a situation where Jimmy Pierce was gonna have to show some balls. Yardell floored his pick-up and quickly came within inches of Jimmy's pick-up. Jimmy seeing the pick-up so close, started to sweat. They were on a part of the road that had sudden curves one after another. To keep the other vehicle from passing, Jimmy had to swing into the curves on both sides no matter which lane he was in. Yardell forgot about the race and decided to run the other driver into the ground. He pulled out of a turn right behind Jimmy and tapped his bumper a little bit. He had hoped Jimmy would panic

a little bit and over-steer through the next turn.

Jimmy felt the other truck bump his own. He had been around enough not to freak

out. He was surprised that the loud mouth had enough squirt in him to do it though. A

straightaway lay ahead and Jimmy quickly came to a decision that would either get him

killed or win the race. He floored the little Ranger and made a gap of about four car

lengths. He widened the gap to about eight car lengths.

Yardell was confused. The Ranger was pulling away. He wondered if he had scared

the hillbilly into fucking up more than the wanted.

The road they were on was straight for about another quarter of a mile, but then it

quickly curved, a curve that Jimmy would not be able to complete at the speed he was

going. Yardell realized that Jimmy would probably wreck but doubted it would seriously

hurt the hardheaded bastard. Jimmy, meanwhile, had a plan. He kept pouring the gas

into his little truck. Yardell stared at the speeding vehicle ahead of him. He wondered if

the driver had lost his mind.

A house sat about two hundred yards from road. The driveway angled so as to meet

inside the curve. A mailbox was all you could see of it. Jimmy knew what he was doing

was risky, but he also knew the guy in the other truck didn't want to get killed either. He

took his foot off the accelerator and with the other foot he jammed the emergency brake

while hitting the regular brake. His truck slid sideways as he jerked the wheel, placing

him in a four-wheel drift in the middle of the road, directly in the path of Yardell Stuart.

Jimmy's truck was sliding and on the verge of rolling over. Jimmy had aimed his vehicle directly at the mailbox. He knew the driveway was gravel and hoped that when his vehicle slid off the asphalt and hit the gravel instead of catching and rolling as was likely on pavement, he hoped the gravel would allow his truck to continue its skid straight down the driveway, sideways.

Yardell being new to the area had driven the road before but was not aware of the driveway as his opponent. He saw the truck slide sideways in front of him and tried to avoid t-boning the other vehicle. There was nowhere to go or so it looked, so he decided to run off the road to keep from hitting the other vehicle.

Yardell's truck was going about seventy when it hit the ditch. It jumped over the obstacle and sailed straight into a large oak standing thirty feet from the roadway. He was killed instantly as was the tree.

Jimmy, meanwhile, had slid down the driveway broad-ways until he had hit a fence that stood along a gentle curve that arched around the property towards the house. His skid continued until he slid sideways up next to the front porch. He came to a full stop. Dogs were barking and lights were coming on inside the house. He shifted into first, released the emergency brake and spun out and away from the residence, trailing fence posts and front steps behind. He accelerated back down the driveway until he approached the roadway. When he got back on the highway, he could see the remains of the other vehicle and dust and debris that was still falling back down.

It never occurred to Jimmy to check and see if Yardell was still alive. His one comment summed up his feelings toward the entire incident. "Shit! There goes two hundred bucks." Jimmy didn't even bother to get out of the truck or even finish the racecourse. He quickly accelerated back the way he had come. No one saw him because everyone who had been at the starting point had gone back to town to await the news of who had won.

Jimmy Pierce, unaware that he had killed an undercover police officer and effectively saved ninety percent of his acquaintances from prison, drove away whistling. He felt surprisingly well considering he had just lost two hundred dollars.

The yard that Jimmy Pierce violated belonged to an elderly couple. The couple owned no phone and their nearest neighbors lived a half mile away. The gentleman suffered night-blindness and his wife could not drive. The accident was not reported until morning.

Yardell's real identity was not discovered until the following Monday morning.

CHAPTER FOURTEEN

Bobby Pierce had not gone to the race. He had intended to stay home but his father had come home in an unusually foul mood. Maxi started picking on him the minute he laid eyes on the boy.

"What the hell you doing home? You ain't never home when anything needs doing around here. Where whar you when that little picaninny got hisself cooked overn't the pasture? Huh? You better talk to me boy! I ain't in the habit of working my gums just to make a breeze and when I ask you something, you best be speaking up."

"Yes sir."

"Yeah, that's better. I'm going to Woodbine. Man over there says he got some blues I might wanna look at. You want to come along? I gotta admit you pretty good with hounds. Probably cause you act like a little bitch your ownself."

His statement startled Bobby from his father. It was the nicest thing he could remember the old man saying. If you left out the little bitch line, it was a compliment. Bobby would have leapt at the prospect except for the fact that he still felt pretty bad about killing the dogs and could not stand the thought of trying to look at another dog so soon.

"I got plans. I already promised Ellen I would take her to the burnt boy's layout."

"What the fuck for? He's burnt all the hell up. He's finally reached the state God intended for his sorry ass."

"She wants to go and I said I'd take her, if'n it's all right?"

"Shit yes. Take the little whore to look at the little burnt nigger. I don't care what you do. I just thought you might want to go see some dogs is all. You watch your sister close. That girl got some tramp in her like her mamma. I don't need any snot-nose little bastard spoiling my twilight years. Watch her close."

"I will. Don't worry."

"I ain't worried about nothing. I quit worrying about the whole lot of you when I caught your Mamma with that Kirby vacuum cleaner salesman. I probably shoulda put you three in the ground with them but, I always had a soft spot for young 'uns."

Maxi Pierce had become a hard man. He made these statements to his middle child and then turned and left. He didn't think anything more about the conversation.

Bobby sat stunned. He felt as though someone had kicked him in the stomach. He had always assumed his mother had run off and left his father. He had always felt betrayed by his mother. His father's confession made his hate come even more alive. He was confused and very disturbed. Bobby's state did not last long.

His sister Ellen came bouncing into the room. She had just got off the phone with Brandon. He had agreed to come to Freddie Wilbanks' layout. He had barely known Freddie and had agreed to come for the sole purpose of seeing Ellen. She managed to convey this to her brother in a very brief manner and then proceeded to inquire about Bobby's attitude.

"What's wrong with you? Why the long face? I thought you hated Freddie ever since him and Maxine been doing the deed."

"I do. I did. Whatever! Ellen, do you ever wonder about Mom?"

"Shit! Fuck Mom! Yeah, I wonder why she didn't come and get us away from Dad. I mean I can see why anybody would want out of these hollers but I can't forgive her for leaving us behind to live with that hateful old bastard, if she couldn't live with him."

"Okay. I can understand that. What if Mom didn't run off like Dad says? What if instead he had killed her?"

"What are you talking about? Mom's been gone for eight years. Why would you say something like that now?"

"Well, me and Dad was just talking and he said something about how he thought he woulda been better off if'n he would put me, you and Maxine in the ground at the same time as when he caught Mom and the Kirby vacuum salesman."

"Bullshit! Mom ran off. Everybody know that."

"Yeah, well who told everybody she run off? Who's heard or seen her since. She had people and ain't nobody heard nothing."

"Well, if he caught her with another man, he wouldn't have had to hide the killing. Ain't a jury around here would convicted anybody for nothin' if'n she got caught like that."

"I know, but I always felt Mom wouldn't have left like that. I always hoped she was coming back. That I'd see her again. When Dad said he had buried her, for the first time in my life, I knew. I fucking knew she wasn't coming back. The way he said it, like it was some distasteful chore, like wringing a chicken's neck. Nobody likes to do it, but it's gotta be done."

"I don't know Bobby. I don't know. If he did kill her, he deserves to die. If he didn't, she deserves to die. Either way, we're fucked."

The two sat in silence for about five minutes. Both children were remembering their mother and how good their lives had been when she had been with them. Their father hadn't been mean back then. Their mother had been the light of his life. She had made all of them laugh and their home had been a happy one.

Ellen had expressed what Bobby had been thinking. "If he had caught her with another man and killed her because of it, she had already destroyed our family and her death took the only good thing Daddy had. Living with the memory of her with another man probably hurts worse than anything else could."

To this Bobby replied, "I want to kill him."

Ellen came back with, "Don't do him any favors. Come on. You taking me to the layout or what? Brandon will be thinking I stood him up."

"You're the only person I know that goes on dates to funerals."

"Well, it's like they say, life goes on."

Vernon Price was loaded. He had drank two-thirds of a case of Budweiser tall boys and was working on the last eight. He had also raided his mother's medicine cabinet and swallowed three Xanax along with half a bottle of Tusselneck (codeine-based cough syrup, prescription strength). He was feeling numb.

People kept coming up to Vernon offering their condolences. He and Freddie had been the best of friends. Vernon's hopes for a winning season were also gone. No one in town could even come close to Freddie's ability on the football field. No matter how good a quarterback Vernon was, he still needed a receiver. He and Freddie had an almost uncanny ability to know right where to be in order to connect with each other on the field. Vernon would really miss Freddie.

A large crowd had gathered at the Baptist Church. Freddie's parents were members.

CHAPTER FIFTEEN

Ellen at first did not see Brandon. Bobby's revelation about their parents was preying upon her mind. Her father's transformation from lovable, outgoing, energetic husband/father into a hard talking, mean spirited, cold-hearted man had not been overnight. She had always assumed that their father was secretly hoping for his Katherine to come home and that everything would be like before. The confession by her father of their mother's infidelity and subsequent murder helped explain other actions their father had taken in their household. Maxi, for the most part, ignored his children. They did not exist. As time passed, Ellen began to favor her mother in both looks and mannerisms.

Maxi had loved his wife more than anything in the world. When he caught her red-handed betraying him with another man, he had lost all self-control. His act had been a true crime of passion and most likely they were deeds of the most heinous nature and were not all committed upon the same night.

Maxi had left for work that morning as usual. The children had caught the bus and Katherine Pierce had remained home alone. Katherine, for the most part, was a happy person. Her life with Maxi had run pretty smoothly. She was a good mother to her children and felt she had been good to her husband. Maxi Pierce was a man of good heart but little imagination. His wife had been fairly happy with their life except for the fact Maxi lacked passion. Their sex life was fair. They had straight sex in the missionary position about five times a week. Maxi did not approve of oral sex, at least not with a man's own wife. Good women didn't suck dick and real men didn't put their mouths where they put their cocks. A female cousin had introduced Katherine to the delights. She was a very enthusiastic supporter and missed giving as well as receiving lip service since her marriage.

The vacuum cleaner salesman had not been her first infidelity but she had always been very discreet and had never intended to hurt anyone with her actions. She just wanted a little something different from what she was getting at home. Every time she strayed, she told the person, in no uncertain terms, that the act would be a one-time thing and that she was happily married. She did still visit her cousin and felt that no one was hurt in the least by her actions.

Maxi had been raised in the "old school" manner and was of the opinion that men could have a little fun as long as it wasn't with other men's wives. Bar girls and whores were good fun and provided a valuable service. They did the things that no "good" woman should be asked to perform.

Anytime someone's wife strayed, it was a very serious matter. People laughed at cuckolds and a man could never look at one of his kids and be sure if it was his, if his woman strayed even once.

Maxi had taken off work early because he wanted to surprise his wife with a present. He had ordered a brand new washer and dryer along with a refrigerator that made its own ice cubes. They were to be delivered that afternoon and he wanted to get home in time to meet the delivery truck. He had also wanted to get a little pussy before the delivery guys got there.

Katherine hadn't planned her adultery that day. A friend of hers, one Madeline Albright had sampled the vacuum cleaner salesman's wares and called her friend to inquire if she would be interested. Katherine had awoke that morning in high spirits. It was her and Maxi's fifteenth wedding anniversary and she had half expected a little loving. Not only had Maxi not given her any loving, he had left without even mentioning the anniversary. She had told Madeline to send the man her way, half out of spite. She would not live to regret her resentment. The salesman had arrived at ten o'clock and had demonstrated two or three features of his magnificent machine. He had even showed her a vacuum cleaner or two, as well. They were heavy into a furious sixty-nine when Maxi walked in the door.

He didn't think anyone was home for a moment. He wondered whose car was outside but was not suspicious. His wife was an attractive woman but never acted less than a lady in public and he trusted her. He heard noises from their bedroom and his heart sank. The bottom dropped out of his soul and something in him froze. He almost turned and left his home without looking but he had to know. He would never have a moment's peace until he knew for sure. Opening his bedroom door had been the hardest task he had ever performed. He had been a combat Marine at the chosen reserve in Korea and that entire campaign had cost him as much torment as the turning of that doorknob. The first thing he saw was his beloved Katherine's eyes staring straight into his own. He watched as her mouth made the words, "Oh shit!" around the fat little penis of some toad who was busy flicking his tongue in and out of his little angel's asshole.

Maxi let out the sound of a wounded animal. He grabbed his wife by the hair on her head. He forced her face down onto the salesman's abdomen. He would not let her up. He put all his weight down on his beloved wife's head until she strangled on the adulterous organ in her face. She fought and struggled to dislodge the penis from her face.

She did truly love Maxi and felt that if he would let her up she could explain everything. Then she heard the words he was yelling. "You want his dick, you filthy cunt? Huh? You want it? Well you can have it. Take it! Take it all bitch. Choke on it! Get it all."

She couldn't breath. She struggled to remain calm hoping her husband would calm down.

"Is this my anniversary present, to catch you sucking a dwarf in the home I paid for, in the bed where we made our children? If they're even mine? Huh, cunt?"

Maxi got madder and madder. The pain inside him grew and grew. He pressed his wife's head down with his left hand and her ass with his right. The bodies writhed and wiggled in a sick parody of the act they were engaged in. He smothered the life out of the lovers with their own sex organs. He continued to grind his wife's body into her lover's for about thirty minutes. All the time berating her over and over. "Why? Why? Oh Lord, why?"

Maxi came to his senses at the sound of a horn in the driveway. His anniversary presents had arrived. He had greeted the deliverymen with a smile on his face and had them bring the gifts on into the house. After the deliverymen had left, Maxi gathered the bodies and put them in the boxes that the appliances had come in. He drove them to an abandoned strip quarry that the people had used for a dump for years. He took his big truck and towed his bobcat out to the dump. He worked until dark that night and the rest of the week after work filling in the quarry. He had to cover up the salesman's car as well as the two bodies.

Maxi had never looked at any of his children again without wondering whether they were his or not.

Ellen knew her father had problems. She knew that life couldn't have been easy for a man in this part of the world raising three children on his own. She had always thought her father had shown courage in keeping the family together. A lot of men placed in the same circumstances would have turned the children over to relatives or foster care. Remarrying would have eased her father's burden, as well. She had always secretly been glad that her father had not tried to replace her mother. She did not want another woman in her mother's house much less in her mother's bed. "Oh God! He's been sleeping in that bed forever. That's fucking sick."

"Hey! Hi! It's me. I'm here."

"Huh?" Brandon interrupted Ellen's thoughts.

The look on his face was a mixture of relief and confusion. The relief was because he had finally found her. The confusion was there because she didn't seem pleased.

"Did I do something wrong?"

"No, of course not. I just have something on my mind. Give me a minute to collect my thoughts and I'll be fine."

"Sure, whatever. Take as long as you like. You're the only person here I feel comfortable talking to. I sure don't want to screw that up."

"You mean that?"

"What?"

"What you said, that you feel comfortable talking to me. I don't think I ever met a boy that was comfortable talking to a girl. I mean, really talking with, not talking up."

"Yeah, I guess so. I mean I still get nervous when I look at you and remember how beautiful you are. I have trouble at those times. Otherwise, you are the closest I have come to making a real friend since I've been here."

"Damn! You're sweet. Ain't a boy or a man in this room that coulda said that in one breath and had me believe him. You're either the smoothest bullshitter I ever met or one real cool sumabitch. Either way, I'm about half scared of you."

"I didn't mean to scare you. I meant…"

"Shut up! Just hush. Don't spoil it. Take me somewhere away from here. Let's go somewhere and talk. I need someone to talk to real bad. Did you drive?"

"Yeah, sort of. I got a motorcycle. I understand if you don't want to ride."

"Oh shit, a bike! You got a bike? For real? You ain't playing with me are you? I'm gonna be pissed if you tell you got a motorcycle and you don't. I don't like somebody playing games."

"Yeah. I got a bike. It's outside. It ain't no hog or nothing. It's a little Honda but it does the job."

"I don't care if it's a mini-bike. I love motorcycles. Can I ride it? I mean by myself. My sister owns an old Triumph 650 and a Sportster. I've been riding both for years.

"Sure. I've never rode anything bigger than my dad's Goldwing and it practically does everything by itself. If you can ride a Harley, you'll probably laugh at my bike."

"I won't laugh. I promise. I love bikes. Let's go."

"Don't you have to tell somebody you're leaving?"

"I came with my brother. He'll know who I left with. I'd say half the room would just love to tell him I rode off on a motorcycle with the boy whose daddy is raping the county."

"What?"

"Oh, fuck it! Are we going or not?"

"Yeah, I guess so. What do you mean about my dad?"

"Hush. We got all night to argue and fight and hopefully make up. Right now, I just want to feel some wind."

Brandon led her to the parking lot. Ellen was correct about people noticing their encounter and subsequent exit. Small towns thrive on gossip and this would make fine talk around wood stoves and sewing parlors. Many an eyebrow would be raised and smirks make as neighbors shook their heads knowingly upon the couple. Brandon, being somewhat naïve, did not understand the extent of power a small town gossip mill produced. By morning, word of his liaison with Ellen Pierce would reach his father. His father would have some very strong thoughts on the subject. Brandon and Ellen exited to the parking lot.

Bobby saw them leave but had other matters to contend with. Bobby's life had thrown a lot of obstacles at him in the last few days but one thorn in his side remained consistent, Vernon Price. Vernon had spotted Bobby and was outraged.

"What the fuck is he doing here? It's his fault Freddie's dead. I'll kill him! Let me at him."

Vernon did not realize how true his statements were. He was relieving his grief in a manner that he understood, violence. Thus far, the night had not offered any outlet for him to vent his pain or anger. Bobby, who had been his whipping boy forever, had provided a target and Vernon was intent upon exorcising some of his personal anguish as quickly as he could lay his hands upon Bobby.

He lunged toward Bobby and nearly caught him. Bobby had not survived Vernon this long without becoming agile as a cat. He leapt to one side letting Vernon slide past just like he had done a thousand times before except this time Bobby did not sidestep and cower as per usual. He instead, punched Vernon in the ear, splitting it wide open.

The momentum of Vernon's own rush combined with Bobby's punch provided enough momentum to cause Vernon to slide into the charred remains of Freddie Wilbanks inside his coffin. The coffin, with said remains, toppled over and landed upon Vernon's right elbow, shattering it and along with his elbow shattered all the hopes for a winning football team. In a town where football ruled, Bobby had truly committed the greatest sacrilege.

The Sheriff just happened to be at the wake. Bobby was quickly taken into custody as much for his safety as anything. A lot of people had seen Vernon lunge at Bobby but just as many were willing to say Bobby had attacked Vernon unprovoked. A few were willing to lynch the boy either way. There were always a few like that in a crowd.

Freddie Wilbanks' layout had been meant to be a closed casket affair. The unlucky fall of Vernon Price had thrown the body out onto the parlor floor. People screamed at the charred remains. One lady vomited. A local man, Massey Ford, who considered himself quite funny, was later quoted "Anytime you get a bunch of coons in one place, ya' gotta have a little barbecue. Shucks, everybody knows that."

CHAPTER SIXTEEN

Ellen and Brandon knew nothing of Bobby's plight. Ellen would probably not believe it because she could not imagine her brother fighting back to Vernon Price.

If she had heard Massey Ford's remark she would have retorted, "Massey, would know, his daddy's mama was black." A true enough statement but Massey would not be bothered in the least. His theory was "Ain't where a man gets his start, it's where he's at that counts."

Brandon and Ellen had made their exit and were speeding through the night. The leaves had not fallen yet, but the first frost was not far away. Autumn was Ellen's favorite time of year. Spring ran a close second. Fall was the time of harvest and making sure everything was ready for winter.

Brandon had mostly lived where the seasons did not have the degree of change that the mountains offered. Brandon's little motorcycle sped along at a brisk pace. He was giddy with delight. This night had worked out better than he had planned. He had rehearsed long dialogues aimed at getting Ellen to leave and go somewhere private. All his scenarios were involved, drawn out affairs that sounded like one of those romance novels. The reality had been so much nicer. It seemed he didn't have time to mess it up.

The girl was as lonesome as he was. Ellen loved the wind in her face. The air was thick with a fog rolling up the hollow and valleys. People often made the mistake of thinking fog rolled down from the mountains, when it actually rolled up from the rivers. Warm air rose as fog and cooler air fell as mist or dew. The season had not progressed so far as to lose the sounds or smells of summer. Cicadas and frogs clicked and belched their calls across the stillness of the valley and a whippoorwill would blast its lonesome cry periodically through the night.

Brandon had parked the bike on a slight knoll overlooking a hollow of pine and spruce. The ticking of the bike's engine was the loudest noise of the night. They sat quiet for a little while. The couple felt comfortable together and felt no awkward need to fill the air with needless noise. Ellen broke the moment.

"What you thinking?"

"Nothing really, just sort of drifting along with the night. It's nice out here."

"Marshmallow weather."

"What? Marshmallow…?"

"Yeah, marshmallow weather. It's just right for toasting marshmallows. When I was a little girl, one of my favorite times all year long would be near the end of harvest before first frost flew. On nights like this, we would sit out and toast marshmallows and listen to crickets. It's a lot nicer than summer because the bugs are not near as bad and the thinner air feels better and lets the sound of the katydids carry further."

"Yeah, I know what you mean. It's like when everybody in the house lays down at the same time. It's a warm, good feeling of being where you belong after a full day."

The sound of the whippoorwill could be heard slicing through the tranquil night.

"That's a lonesome sound."

"Usually I think so too, but tonight that ol' whippoorwill can moan all he wants. I'm here with you and it seems so good and right that even his ol' lonesome cry don't matter none."

"I know Ellen. I just met you but I feel like I know you. It's like I've found something I needed real bad, something essential and I didn't even know I was missing anything. That didn't sound right."

"It sounded just right to me. I've been looking also but I done and gave up on everything in these hills ever filling the bill for what I was looking for. I want to tell you something and I don't want you to take this wrong and I want you to listen until I'm through. Okay?"

"Okay. I'll listen."

"You don't act like other guys. You act almost like a girl."

"Wait a minute!"

"Shhh, you promised you would listen. So listen. I don't mean you act like a queer or that you like guys and shit. I mean you don't act like you always have to be right. You don't strut around like no bantam rooster who thinks he's God's gift to the world. You don't talk all the time, sometimes you listen. I've been watching you since you got here. The thing I like most about you us that you are fair. You listen to people and not just their words. Mrs. Dumphreys calls what you have 'empathy.' She says it's the ability to put yourself in the other person's shoes and take into account someone else's feelings. I try to be like that, but with you its second nature. Just don't be so empathetic that you forget to take care of your own feelings. Remember the other guy might not give a shit about anyone but himself."

"You give me way too much credit. I have a healthy self-interest and for the most part I don't care about other's opinions. I spend a lot of time alone and I read a lot. My view of the world is naïve. I tend to credit people's actions to abstract moral codes and principals, much like characters in a book or play. Their true intent often passes me by. My dad says I'm a romantic and not in a good way at all."

"Dad says I'm a dreamer like my mom. She left us when I was four. She went off to find herself and her place in the world. When she left, my dad threw himself even more into his work. He became almost fanatical about his job. He threw all his energy into it. He doesn't want to do anything like we use to do. We used to go hiking, go to museums, camping, spend days at the lake, everything. We didn't always take mom with us. A lot of times it would be just him and me. She left. I didn't. He could at least look at me.

"Do you ever hear from your mom?"

"Yeah, she writes me sometimes or sends me a postcard. Last year I spent two weeks with her and her lover."

"Her lover? She got a man? Is that why she left?"

"Well, it's not that simple. She left with a dude about fifty years old, but her current lover is a big stripper named Wanda. She's about six-foot tall with enormous tits. Dad says she's vulgar."

"Your mom's a lesbian?"

"Not really a lesbian. She says she's just examining all her options."

-138-

"Wow, that must be weird as hell."

"Yeah, it is. When I was with them in Ontario, a lot of fucked up shit happened."

"Ontario? Canada?"

"Yeah."

"Your mom lives there?"

"No. They don't live there. They actually don't live any one place. Mom left with Stewart, the old man, in Vegas. Dad and her got in a big fight on vacation and she got mad and Stewart picked her up. He's an old fucker with shit loads of money and he owns a chain of strip bars. About six all together. Wanda is what you call a 'feature entertainer.' She travels from club to club all over the country and Canada and as far down as Rio de Janeiro sometimes."

"Wow, she must be hot."

"She's loud and trashy. I can't stand her. The first day I met her she offered to blow me."

"Does your mom know?"

"Yeah. She offered right in front of her."

"Far fucking out! What did your mom say?"

"She laughed. Here, I'll tell you what happened. Mom picks me up at the airport."

"In Ontario?"

"No, this was three years ago. She picks me up in Nashville."

"Nashville? How did you fly to Nashville?"

"I still lived in California. Mom and Wanda were staying in Nashville. Wanda was working at a place called 'The Perfect Pussy' or 'Classie Cat' or something like that. So anyway."

"I'm sorry. I didn't mean to laugh or interrupt, it's just fucked up is all. I mean there can't be places with names like that."

"Oh yeah. Fuck yeah. They got all kinds of fucked up names. Names like 'World o' Jugs,' 'Titty City,' 'Bouncies,' 'Bob's Big Butt Barn' and worse. But Wanda basically works at chain places. You know the ones that advertise on late night TV."

"Oh yeah, between those god-awful talk shows."

"Yeah, well anyway. Mom picks me up at the Nashville airport. I didn't even recognize her right away. It's twelve o'clock in the afternoon in July. She's got on some black mini-skirt with sequins, fishnet stockings with the tops showing. The skirt is so short you can see the garters holding them up. Big ol' platform heels and a platinum wig. At least I thought it was a wig. It turned out to be real."

"Wow, some get up."

"Yeah, I know. That's not even the half of it. She's got these big sunglasses on and you can't see her eyes. I first seen her walking past the ticket counter. I'm like, wow! That chick's ass is hanging out. You, know?"

"Your own mom?"

"I didn't know it was her. I'm standing there looking at this half-naked girl and not paying attention. She turns around and I still don't think it's her because my mom is a blonde and dresses casual and doesn't have a forty-inch chest"

"Wow! She bought tits?"

"Yeah, huge implants. I mean every guy in the place is just sort of staring at her. I can't blame them. Really, I mean it's hard not to look when it's all in your face like that, just hanging out. Well, she recognizes me and screams, 'My baybee, my precious, little boy,' and she comes jiggling right at me with her arms straight out in this little, hop run kind of jog because of the heels and all. She wraps her arms around me in a big ol' hug. All I could see is this big valley between those big, huge titties. She's got some kind of perfume on that takes two or three showers to get rid of. When she grabs me, half her ass is hanging out and she's got on a g-string. It was fucking awful. My mom had always been the epitome of class and elegance and here she was dressed and acting like some hooker straight off some bad movie. She takes me to the car and we are traveling to the hotel. I ask her 'Where's Stewart? Did he put you to work or something.'"

"Oooh! Good one."

"Yeah, she still had enough of the old mom in her to turn a little red at that one. She handled it well, though. She doesn't get mad or anything. She calmly tells me 'Honey, Stew and I are not together anymore. I have a new lover and I want you to be nice. Okay?' I just sat there. When she said lover instead of boyfriend, it should have told me something was wrong. We get to the hotel and the room is pitch dark, all the shades pulled and everything. They got a big suite at the Hilton. I hear the door open and this huge creature walks out in a towel. She's about six-foot tall barefoot and weighs about one hundred and forty with forty of that being nothing but breast. I know it sounds like I'm exaggerating, but Wanda is in magazines and everything. Her tits are 44DD. Each one is as big as my head. For the second time in less than an hour titties were devouring it felt like my head. My mom is standing there. She looks at me and says, 'Brandon, this is Wanda. Wanda is my new lover. I hope you two will be good friends.' That's when Wanda says, 'Camille honey, don't worry so much. Why I'm sure we'll get along just fine. Won't we honey?' and she actually grabbed my peter through my pants in front of my mom. Then she looks at my mom and says, 'Damn girl, he's a live one. It's moving. You do like Wanda, don't you, boy?' She drops the towel and puts my hands on her tits. 'You like? I'll let you touch all you want but we can't fuck. Me and your mom don't think it would be right but I'll blow you if you want. Anytime you want. Okay?'

"I'm standing there in shock. I mean here I am standing in a motel room being offered a blow job by a living triple X rated Barbie doll in front of my mom who I just found out is fucking the same Barbie doll."

"What'd you do?"

"I took a deep breath and said, 'I don't think so. I really need to use the bathroom.' Mom just laughed and tried to play it off but Wanda wouldn't let it rest. She looked me in the eye and she says, 'Don't give me no shit. I know a hard on when I feel one. Me and your mom got a good thing going. You be nice and act like you got some sense and I'll make you the happiest thirteen year old boy in the world. If you want it. I'll lick your asshole till you cry and suck you dry, but you try and cross me and you will regret it! Understand?' And then she squeezed my nuts hard, real hard. "I said, 'I understand' and went to the bathroom."

"Far out, then what?"

-142-

"Well, not much. I just sorta stayed out of her way."

"No. You know what I mean?"

"What?"

"Did you let her blow you?"

"I didn't let her but I woke up once and she had me in her mouth and she caught me looking at a video of her and some dude and another girl and she did me with her hand while I watched and wrapped those titties around me when I came."

"Damn, most guys would be in heaven."

"Yeah, I know, but there were other videos in there, some with my mom and her and other people. It was kinda fucked up."

"Did you fuck her?"

"No!"

"Did you want to?"

"Sort of. I mean she is built like a sexual prototype. What skin mags and media have promoted forever as a bombshell."

"Have you ever done it?"

"Yeah, lots of times."

"For real?"

"No, not really. Just with two girls."

"Oh yeah?"

"Uh huh, oh yeah. I had a girlfriend named Chrystal and we did it once and then she broke up with me."

"Why?"

"Why what?"

"Why did she break up with you?

"She met an older guy with a nice car."

"Sure you didn't do anything to her?"

"No, for real. She told my friend, Robert, that the reason she was breaking up with me was because she didn't want to have to be driven everywhere by her little boyfriend's father."

"You let your dad drive you on dates?"

"He dropped us off one time at the movies."

"That is so lame."

"I know. I was stupid."

"Did you love her?"

"I thought I did, but when she broke up with me I was more relieved than anything."

"Cool! Most people would never be able to admit that. Why were you relieved?"

"I realized I never felt at ease with Chrystal. I always felt like we were both acting the way people wanted us to. I guess I never let her see the real me because I never knew if she was real. She seemed phony."

"If you felt that way, why was you with her?"

"I don't know, so I wouldn't seem like a geek or queer. I felt like people would like me more if I fit in."

"I understand. Is that why you're with me?"

"What do you mean? Are we with each other? I mean, are you seeing someone?"

"No. If I was I wouldn't be here."

"Do you like me?"

"Yeah, I like you a lot more than I've liked anybody in a long time."

"You're the first person that's tried to be nice to me since I moved here."

"You aren't like anyone I've ever met. You don't fit in either. You could, but you choose not to on purpose. That's different."

"Fitting in around here would imply an IQ of a moron and a penchant for dating cousins."

"That sounds sort of snobby."

"My dad calls it 'acting uppity.' He says I've always felt like I was better than everybody else."

"Do you?"

"No. I don't feel that I'm better than anybody. I just don't think people have to submit and accept everything the world hands them."

"What do you mean?"

"Just because everybody around here thinks acting and living like little hillbillies and rednecks is the only way to live! They accept that as their lot in life. Doesn't mean I have to! I don't plan to spend the rest of my life accepting everyone else's ideas and plans for which I should be or how I should act. Parents and teachers preach all the time about how we should think and act for ourselves, but the first time a person shows original thought or does something different, the same people shake their head, click their tongues, point their fingers and nod at each other and say 'Yep, there goes that little Pierce girl with her snobby ways. Got her nose stuck so high in the air she'd drown if it rained.' If wearing shoes, reading books, taking baths and having enough sass to dream about something better in life makes a person uppity then I guess I'm uppity."

"It's the same way at my house except my dad thinks I'm a waste case. 'Boy, you got no ambition,' or 'What are you going to do with your life? I didn't get where I am at by being a slacker. You want something in this life you don't follow the herd, you tend it or at least get in on the shearing.' My personal favorite, 'I don't answer to people, they answer to me.'"

"He really says stuff like that? For real?"

"Oh yeah, he's a complete asshole. When I get in trouble, it's 'Explain yourself boy.' And the only answer he allows is, 'No excuse, Sir!'

"He sounds like a complete fascist."

"Yeah, but usually he just doesn't notice me at all."

"Yeah, my dad's like that. Most of my friends' parents are the same. They either got their own interests or younger, needier, little brothers and sisters to deal with and we just sorta fall through the cracks. The only good thing is we can do pretty much as we please as long s we don't get in trouble or do something embarrassing."

"You mean like staying out half the night with a new kid."

"The new kid whose father may fire half the town."

"I don't think so. The factory doesn't have any major problems. He may even recommend expansion. He may create jobs for the town. It won't be the first time."

"You admire your father?"

"In a perverse way my father is pretty cool. He is an individual and doesn't answer to or try to impress anyone. He makes a good living at a job many people don't even know exists. Most of the companies that hire him are either about to fold or some big corporation is trying to take them over. He, more often than not, is able to point out ways in which they can save themselves. People are so scared that he's gonna fire a lot of people. My father doesn't hire or fire anyone. He evaluates conditions and makes suggestions."

"Hah, hah, hah, hah. I believe you or I, at least, believe you think that's true."

"It's getting kinda late."

"All right, let's head back. My dad hardly ever checks on me, but if he did and I wasn't home, he'd have my ass."

"Mine would yell a lot and carry on. He would tell me not to leave the house but I would anyway. He doesn't really care. My little brother found out tonight he doesn't think we're his kids."

"Do you want to do something tomorrow?"

"Sure! We could ride out to the quarry. It's almost too cool to swim, but I love it out there. We'll probably have the place to ourselves. It'll be like our second date. Third, if you count meeting after school."

"You're a girl after my heart."

"That's not all I'm after. You can kiss me, you know?"

"Uh, sure all right…"

CHAPTER SEVENTEEN

"What the hell is your problem, boy? You try'n to destroy football in this town

single-handed? The quick little nigger fries in yer cow pasture and now you break the

first string quarterback's arm at the other'ns funeral. I oughter let chu out. Dem people

out front would dismember ye and spread yer innards alls over. Its times like this I feel

torn. My duty is to protect and serve. I guess I'll protect you, but what I'd really like to

do is serve yer ass up to those mother fuckers and see if we can't get that smile off'n your

little punk ass mug. What do you think about that, dipshit?"

"I think you need to brush your teeth and get out of my face."

"You think you're tough? Boy, I will show you tough! Just as soon as Sheriff

Boswell has left for the night, I'm gonna show you all sorts a thangs." Deputy Brewster

hissed this last statement through the slot in the metal door.

There being no juvenile facilities in town, Bobby found himself alone in a regular cell

that the county used whenever a juvenile was detained. The outer door being crashed

upon interrupted the brief interchange. The Sheriff entered the hallway and addressed the

Deputy and prisoner.

"We can't locate his pa nor any relative of legal age. Bonnie said she'd call the

Deuce and see if'n Jimmy's out thataway. If'n he is and if'n he's sober enough to drive

up here, we can sign Bobby over to him.

"That's a good 'un. Sign a thug over to a thug. I'm shor glad the system is working."

"Can I get a smoke?"

-148-

"What? What did you just ask me? You a punkass sixteen year old kid locked up for assault on a good kid and well liked member of society, you actually have the unmitigated gall to ask me, me, mind you, a servant of the law, you have the nerve to ask me for a cigarette."

The Sheriff, being familiar with his Deputy's diatribes, turned and walked away. His Deputy, non-plussed, continued to harangue his prisoner. "Why I'd rather suck the turds out'r a AIDS infected prostitute'n queer's ass than give you the sweat out'n underneath my nutsack."

"I didn't ask about your love life. I just wanted a cigarette. You ever notice how obsessed you are with faggots and shit? In general, I mean. You always got something on either subject."

"I'll kill you, you piece of shit! You are dead! Dead! Dead! Dead!

CHAPTER EIGHTEEN

Jimmy Pierce had indeed found his way to the Deuce. He was feeling in fine spirits. His race with the punk in the Chevy hadn't gone exactly as planned but he felt good anyhow. A good looking redhead was giving him the once over and he knew she was liking what she saw.

"Why hello. I do not believe I have had the pleasure of seeing you around there."

"No. I guess not. This is my first time here.

"Are you with someone?"

"Well, sort of. What I meant to say is, I'm here with my girlfriend, Carla is her name. I'm here with Carla but she done went out into the parking lot with some guy named Bud?"

"Well that ain't right. Ain't' right a-tall. Run off and leave a thang as pretty as yourself unattended why it ain't right at all. Let me by you a drink. What will you have?"

"Seven and Seven, please. I'm usually not much of a drinker and these Seven and Seven's are kicking my ass."

Jimmy chuckled to himself. He had seen this type of ol' gal before. She could probably out drink him. He would play the game if the old bitch needed three or four good stiff shots to get his peter munched than by all means, pour away. "My name's, Jimmy Pierce, and you are…"

"Shirley. Shirley Gidcombs. My friends call me Sugar. Some just say Shugg for short."

"Well all right. I think I'll call you Shugg cause I shore do plan on us a being friends. Wanna dance?"

"Yes, I do. I been waiting all night to dance and you are the first man to ask. I was beginning to think this whole town warn't nothing but faggots.

"You talk funny, you ain't from around here are you?"

"Shucks, no. I live down Hazard way. I'm just up visiting my daughter."

"You married?"

"Does it matter? Right now, I'm between husbands."

"Heh, heh, sorta like a Shirley sandwich?"

"Exactly! I got the new one to breed me but I still like the old one to feed me."

"Well, you look like a gal with a good appetite. Maybe I can help them fellers out a little."

"Oh my, yes! Please help me. I need some loving tonight! Let's hit the dance floor while the band's still hot."

Jimmy and his new found love attacked the dance floor. The woman had a butt that was at least five-foot wide. The rest of her was about average. Her breasts were 38 DD's and her waist about thirty inches. Jimmy was captivated. He adored a big ass.

Visions of those hips wrapped around his ears danced in his head. He figured if he stuck his finger up her asshole his hand would be buried up to the elbow in ass.

"Baby, you is a vision. I's got to git wit you and I do mean now."

"Why ain't you sweet. I do believe I's might be persuaded into some slight naughtiness if'n I had a couple more little ol' drinkee poos."

"Fucking-A! Set 'em up and keep 'em coming. Give the girl whatever she wants and don't scrimp on the likker, hoss. I's got a lot of woman to git likkered up."

"Oh yeah! Licker me up. Licker me up and down all night, all right?"

"All right. Fuck it! Give me a bottle and two glasses. Baby, we is goin to move this here little tete-a-tete' outside."

"You can move my tittie-ay-tittie-ay anywhere you wants, cowboy."

"Hell yes!!"

"Let's git."

Jimmy and his new love exited the building.

CHAPTER NINETEEN

The Sheriff's Department being unable to contact Maxi or Jimmy Pierce that evening had to keep Bobby over night.

Bobby was pissed at being locked up but he was also elated and delighted with the fact that he, Bobby Pierce, had broken Vernon's arm. He hadn't planned it and couldn't remember doing it, but he had truly inflicted pain upon his age-old nemesis. Whatever punishment or hardship he must endure would be worth it. He felt redeemed and for once Vernon Price was going home to nurse pain and humiliation that he had inflicted.

Revenge was indeed a sweet, heady drink. Bobby wanted more. He wanted everyone who had ever hurt him in any way to feel the pain back a hundred fold. Bobby didn't want to be a victim any longer. He liked his new feeling of strength and power. He would do whatever it takes to feel more.

The prey had become predatory. He had no regard for personal well-being. He wanted the town to feel. He wanted everyone to bleed as he had. He would do whatever it took.

Bobby laid down and tried to go to sleep. He felt strong and just. The world has a way of humbling everyone.

Bobby's buddy was back at his door.

"Sheriff's gone home and I shore would hate for you to leave here a thinking I had lied to you boy. You gonna pay for that smart-alecky mouth. You gonna pay hard."

The Deputy was more than your average brute. He was third generation in-bred, hog fed, homegrown mean. He didn't have a long memory except when he thought somebody had done him wrong or was laughing at him. He thought Bobby had done both. Bobby was not in an enviable position.

"Gonna git you boy. You gonna pay. You think you better 'n everybody else. Well I'm a goin show you a thang or two. Afore this night's thru, you gonna wish you'd never been born."

The big hillbilly opened the cage. He had in his hand a padded slapjack. The first blow hit Bobby in the side of his head. It spun him around and tripped on his own feet. He fell hard, his head bounding off the steel frame of his mattress-less bed. It came to rest on the piss-splattered surface of the stainless steel commode/fountain that stuck out of the wall.

"Ha, ha, ha. You ain't laughing at ol' Joey Dee now is ye. Us Mullins' got a good memory when we's been wronged. You 'bout to find out." The large Deputy continued his assault upon the hapless youth. The blows were all aimed at areas that would not readily show. Many to the abdomen, buttocks, sides, top and back of the head. The groin area became a favorite target.

"You been insinuating that I's a queer. Well I'm a goin show you who's a faggot, when I git this ten inches of man meat shoved up your little Mary ass! You'll know whose a queer."

The man's logic was impeccable and his commitment to justice a juggernaut. No one could hear Bobby's cries of anguish. No one there cared. Prisoners hooted and hollered

all through the night. Deputy Mullins, being a very virile man in his middle twenties
assaulted Bobby seven different times. He raped his anus four times and made Bobby,
suck him afterwards. Bobby could taste himself on the end of the hillbilly's dick. He
grinned in ironic bemusement.

He kept remembering how he and his Uncle Jimmy had done the couple at the quarry.
The Deputy, seeing him grin, expressed great joy.

"You like that, don't you? I knew it! I knew it! I knew it! You just said them thangs
to get me riled so's you wouldn't feel guilty about all this good lovin's. Shee-it, you ain't
got to pretend wit ol' Joey Dee. I'll give you what you need. You just come back.
Hear?"

The assault continued through the night. The sun came peeking through the bars
about five a.m.

Bobby's head lolled against the cell wall. A thin line of semen soaked drool slid
down his chin. The innate lifeless body of one, Joey Dee Mullins lay on the floor. His
head smashed beyond recognition by the very same slapjack that he had used to terrorize
and rape the youth.

Sheriff Arnett Boswell looked in disbelief. "Damn! I knew it was gonna happen
sooner or later. Boy, I'm shore sorry it had to be you. Joey's my wife's kid brother and
It's gonna take a hell of a lot of fast-talking to keep that bunch down. You keep your
mouth shut about what happened to you in here and we'll make this look like an accident.
You hear me, boy?"

"Yeah. I hear you. I've been trying to do that all night."

"What?"

"I've been trying all night."

"Trying what? What the fuck you talking about, boy?"

"I've been trying all night to keep my mouth shut."

Bobby puked on the corpse.

CHAPTER TWENTY

Jimmy had found him a live one. The big haired, big mouthed, big assed girl had turned out to be more than he had expected. The couple had danced a couple of dances and had decided to grab a bottle and have a more private party. Big Shirley, or Shugg, had Jimmy's dick out of his pants and in her face before he could get the truck started. Jimmy hadn't minded one bit. He blew his first nut and the ol' gall had just kept humming along.

He took her to a cabin down by the lake. A wealthy owner owned the cabin from Somerset. He only used it about five times a year. Jimmy didn't even have to break in. Kids from the surrounding community had already vandalized the residence and used it as a party house. Shirley hadn't minded.

"Just as long as they's a bed with no bugs."

Jimmy hadn't thought bugs would have stopped her. They had reached the cabin at a dead run. Both were laughing and out of breath. Jimmy stood in the doorway with the liquor bottle in one hand. He leaned into the wall and took a big sip and spoke to the woman.

"Damn girl, you shore is a horny ol' gal. Don't that man of you'n ever see to his bidness?"

"Shore baby. I gets me some. Most every night the ol' bugger likes to climb on with his ol' hot tobacco breath, a huffin and a puffin in my face. He'll get up there and waller aroun' like he's dying and all for a couple of minutes and squirt his little piddlin' mess all

-157-

over me. Most times as not, he go right to sleep after one little ol' time. He don't never give me oral and my 'Mademoiselle' magazine just swears that a girl gets her best by oral. You like oral, don't you Jimmy baby? I know you shore didn't mind a little oral when I blew you in the parking lot."

"Hell no, baby! I don't mind a-tall. Why a man oughta to be smacked for sticking a peter in something as fine as you. Anybody can see that's table grade. Yes sir. Howdy USDA prime. That ol' man of your'n must be a sixty-eight kind of a feller."

"Sixty-eight? I don't understand."

"You know, like sixty-nine except'n he wants you to do him and he'll owe you one."

"You shore is a funny mother fucker. Let's see if you can use that mouth for anything else besides bullshit."

"Well ma'am, I do believe I have been challenged. I do accept."

Big Shirley pushed Jimmy onto the bed. She rubbed her big titties in Jimmy's face.

"Bite 'em. I like it rough. Squeeze 'em and bite the shit out of 'em."

Jimmy sucked about three-quarters of one breast into his mouth. He clamped his teeth together and chewed furiously. The big girl screamed and started grinding her big ass into Jimmy's groin.

"Oh yes! Goddamn! Mother fucker! Fuck me! Goddamn yes! Suck my titty, you filthy mother fucker. Bite it! Chew it! Oh fuck yes!"

Jimmy continued to gobble her breast. He had never seen anyone get so tore up just by getting their titty chewed. He'd almost swear the woman was coming.

Big Shirley was indeed in the throes of orgasm. "Oh you got to fuck me. Come on, you dirty little bastard, stick some dick in me."

The couple tore at each other's clothes. Finally they were both naked. Jimmy was ready. His dick was as hard as he could ever remember it.

"Suck it! I want you to drown on my cunt juice."

Jimmy dove between the big girl's thighs. He found her clit almost immediately. He wrapped his tongue around the tip and bit down gently. He chewed lightly while swirling his tongue and slurping at the same time. He placed the tip of his index finger at the portal of her flesh. He kissed her twat like it was the sweetest mouth on the most beautiful model in the world. His tongue devoured the length of the woman's sex again and again. His finger moved faster and faster. It tried to keep pace with his lips and tongue. The woman bucked and shrieked as her passion rose. She cursed and screamed.

"Oh! Mother Fucker! You Goddamn mother fucker! Don't stop! Oh! Oh! Oh! Don't you ever stop. You pussy eating summabitch. Suck my pussyeee. Suck it! Suck my asshole."

Jimmy grabbed the woman's ankles, raised her legs high into the air. He placed his left arm under Big Shirley's abundant ass. He knelt down and further placed his right forearm across the back of her thighs. Her knees were almost by her ears. Her magnificent ass was directly in front of him. He licked his lips greedily. This was the biggest ass he had ever seen. It looked like it was breathing. The little asshole beckoned him closer. He attacked. He drove his tongue into her ass as deep as he could. He let it rest for a second and he drove it in at least two inches deeper. His teeth rested on the rim of her ass. He slurped and chewed the ass rim. He drove his tongue into her asshole again and again. He used his tongue like a little dick. No peter had ever fluttered and slurped and stayed so wet.

The woman was crying and blubbering. The sounds she made were like no creature ever born. Jimmy slurped and chewed the big ass for at least thirty minutes. Big Shirley grabbed his head and forced him to stop.

"Fuck me! You got to fuck me now! Fuck my pussy and then shove it up my ass."

Jimmy was more than happy to oblige. He drove his overexcited member into the hot folds of the big woman's love canal. It felt so good, too good. Shit! He was about to come. He couldn't believe it. He had just come in her mouth. No way in hell could he be ready to shoot again, already. Ready or not he came. A mind-blowing orgasm that had started at his toes. His whole body shivered and twitched. He squired what felt like a gallon into the horny woman.

"No! No! No! Honey, no. You can't come yet. Not yet, baby. It was so good. Don't stop. Come on baby. I'm dying. Fuck me. Come on. Fuck me."

"I'm trying. Just give me a minute. This ain't never happened afore."

"Bullshit! Come on. Don't do this. Let me have it. Fuck me you stupid hillbilly. If you can't fuck me, shove that tongue back up in there. I need something. Suck that come outta my pussy."

"Fuck that! I might eat some pussy. I might lick an asshole… but I ain't slurping no jism from nobody."

"Hah! Hah! Hah! You stupid, sad, punk ass, can't fuck, dick sucking faggot. I done and fucked three fat rednecks tonight. You already been sucking jism. Just not your'n. Hell, ol' Bub Forrester done and been up my ass. You probably done had some shit flavored spunk. Hah! Hah! Hah! Get on down there and suck me some more. Eat some more of that shit. Tell me how love tastes. You dumb piece of shit."

Jimmy and Bobby had many similarities, but one trait stood out. They both hated to be laughed at.

Big Shirley done and fucked up. She ran her mouth to the wrong mother fucker. Jimmy went apeshit. If the big whore had kept her mouth shut he would probably sucked her pussy sore.

He didn't mind sucking his own juices. He just didn't like her telling him about it. It was like she thought he was a punk. She really fucked up when she accused him of sucking other guys' dicks by proxy. The shit jism was the one that was gonna get her killed.

"I'll suck you alright, you fucking cunt. You want me to fuck you? Well bitch, you are fucked."

Jimmy grabbed a poker from the fireplace. He swung it at Wanda's head. Her shrieks of laughter quickly died and changed to howls of agony and fear. Jimmy pounded the big woman with the poker over and over. Blood flew all over the cabin.

"You still horny, bitch? Who's laughing now? Huh? I can't hear you! You still want me to suck your cum soaked crotch? Tell me some more about your piddled dicked husband. We're all real funny to you, ain't we bitch? You get a real kick outta sitting on

-161-

your big fat ass and sucking the life outta every man you meet. Probably on your third

husband and still got your claws in the first two. Women like you is what makes men like

me. Do you believe in the golden rule, bitch? I hear over in the east they call it karma.

Well, I don't know what it's called but tonight we gonna have what's called justice. I'm

about to serve up some justice on your big fat ass. Hear me, you whimpering cow. How

come I ain't funny now? You ain't amused? Shit bitch, this is the first time you been

real fun all night."

"You like this honey? You know what you is experiencing, baby? Emotion, that's

what! Honest, god blessed, heartfelt emotion. Fear! Bitch you has got the fear. But be

advised just cause you is skeered don't mean you be paranoid. No ma'am! You is not

paranoid because I am out to get you. You was liking that fucking. Yes ma'am, you is

one nympho-fucking maniac. Us maniacs got to stick together. That's right. I said us

maniacs. Now you see, I have in my life something you lack. A lot of people don't have

what I have. It's because they are not honest with themselves. What I possess is this. I

have clarity. You may be saying to yourself, 'Hunnh? What the fuck is he talking

about.'"

"Clarity of vision you fat tub of shit. I see things how they really are. I am a realist.

Before me I have one, big assed, lying, cum soaked, blood drenched, nyphomaniacal,

parasitic whore. A piece of the foulest vermin to ever plague mankind. I also have

myself. A man. A wronged man. A man who after giving his all on the altar of love has

been scorned. You have mocked me and defiled my manhood. I must redeem myself.

So, I say, we maniacs must serve each other. You a gaping hole of sexual need, a nymphomaniac needing something shoved in her twat. Me, a homicidal maniac, striving

to reassert his own manhood. How can we accomplish this task? I shall slake both of our

thirsts with one action.

Jimmy put the poker down and grabbed the curtains from the window. He rammed

the curtain rod into the now dry vagina of Shirley Gidcombs. He rammed and rammed

until he ripped the womb. He continued his assault long after Big Shirley's demise.

Jimmy noted that he had an erection while killing Big-Ass. He did not want to waste

it. "There's one hole I ain't popped yet." He rolled the corpse over and balanced it on the

curtain rod extending from her vagina. The knees came forward on each side of the

protruding staff. The corpse balanced precariously. Jimmy slid up behind Big Shirley

and positioned himself. "Man, I shore like a big ass."

He placed his penis at the opening of the woman's anus. It would not go in at first.

He grabbed a mixture in his hand of sex fluids and gore and smeared it upon his hardened

member. It slid in easily. He sodomized the corpse for almost an hour. Jimmy came and

started laughing. He felt like a king. The big whore had laughed at him and he had made

her pay. He stayed the night and repeated his actions at least three more times. Shirley

had turned out to be an all right date.

CHAPTER TWENTY-ONE

It had started out wrong but he had a back-up plan. Bobby's incarceration ended at noon on Sunday. Maxine came and got him. His father would not. When told of Bobby's arrest, Maxi had grunted and changed the television. When no answer was forthcoming his daughter had asked, "Well?"

"Well, what?"

"What are you going to do about it?

"Nary a damn thing. Let the little fucker rot. He got hisself in there, he can get hisself out."

Bobby didn't care. The assault by the Deputy had left him numb.

The Sheriff had been scared of what the boy would say upon his release. It was an election year and a scandal could jeopardize his bid for reelection. The death of his brother-in-law did not bother him. He had never liked the man and couldn't care less if his wife's entire family disappeared from the face of the earth.

The boy would have sworn he wouldn't say anything. The sheriff knew if he had the same experience he sure as hell wouldn't tell anybody. He didn't think anyone of today's generation was trustworthy. He would have died before he would let someone rape him.

This line of thought was dangerous. The direction it was headed did not look good for Bobby. The Sheriff was a strong believer that the best way to keep a secret was to leave nobody to tell it. The prisoners that may have heard something hadn't actually seen anything. He couldn't eliminate everyone that heard the commotion. The only person that was a real threat to his department was the punk. The more he thought about it, the more he knew what he had to do. Poor, punk kid. He didn't like it but he knew he had to do it. He quickly started planning how to go about eliminating his problem.

The problem in question had locked himself in his room and was trying to sleep. He wished he could sleep forever. The Deputy's death hadn't seemed real. The quick reversal of fortunes had thrown him for a loop. He had been feeling on top of the world and fate had thrown him back into a pit of despair. The fact that he had overcome his attacker and in fact he'd killed him didn't eliminate the helpless feeling the rape and attack had brought forth.

Bobby had spent his life as a victim. His recent role as victimizer had empowered him. His encounter at the jail had brought home to him, the people he had hurt, suffered and felt hopeless as he had. He did not want to be a victim. He would be more selective in his activities.

Bobby took pen and paper and made a list. This list contained the names of people that he felt deserved no pity. He wished his Uncle Jimmy would come home. He had a lot of things to tell him. He hoped Jimmy would be proud.

Bobby's, Uncle Jimmy hadn't thought about Bobby since the last time he talked to the boy. If someone were to inform him that his nephew placed such high regard upon him, he would probably snicker and call him a pussy, little, queer boy and begin immediately to figure some way to exploit and manipulate Bobby to his greater benefit. Jimmy for some reason had no feeling for Bobby. Bobby was a non-entity for Jimmy until a time arose wherein Bobby could be useful.

Bobby was about to become very useful to his uncle. Jimmy had put the incident at the abandoned strip mine out of his head. He and the boy had themselves a high ol' time and there just wasn't any reason for either of them to say anything to anyone.

Jimmy pulled his truck into the truck stop at the county line. A lot of people wound up there after the bars closed. It was the only place around that stayed open twenty-four hours. It served pretty fair food and damn good coffee. A man could get anything at the truckstop if he just sat and waited. The trick was to sit at the counter and say as little as possible. The waitresses and cooks knew something on everybody. If you tipped and were polite you could find out quite a few very interesting tidbits of gossip. Years of honky-tonks and barracks bullshit had given Jimmy a fairly reasonable ability to separate gossip from outright bullshit.

He was hearing some strange stories. Most of the talk centered around Freddie's funeral. People from the rural areas tend to place a lot of stock in being respectful toward the deceased. Bobby's actions had disappointed many and several were outright enraged. The Sheriff had been correct. The safest place for Bobby would have been locked away from the citizenry. It was just misfortune that his Deputy hadn't gotten along with the lad. Jimmy didn't like what he was hearing. The boy had never been in any kind of trouble. Jimmy had liked the idea that he had turned the town joke into a killer. It wasn't funny if the boy started trying to play Billy Bad Ass. People would notice and Jimmy didn't want anyone noticing. Jimmy, unlike the Sheriff, did not weigh any option. He knew what he had to do.

"Shit! I was just starting to get my hopes up that the boy might amount to something."

Jimmy finished his coffee and left a three-dollar tip. This made the waitress notice him. Jimmy wasn't perfect.

The remaining hours of Saturday night passed uneventfully. Sunday came down upon the valley with a perfect fall day. The morning started with a light frost. Jacket weather. By church time everyone had heard the events of the weekend. The dead state trooper was thought to be just another drunk hitting a tree. That would change on Monday. The talk was already going stale and people had put about every twist upon events that it had become almost indistinguishable from the facts. The more outrageous it became the more fun it was to tell. Some people were asking questions about the Deputy's death. The body of Big Shirley had not been found. Her absence had been noted and her family had tried to file a missing person's report. Monday would be the first official inquiry into her disappearance.

CHAPTER TWENTY-TWO

"Aw, shit! It's fucking huge. Not today. Please! Lord don't do this." The zit on the end of Brandon's nose was huge. He had squeezed it twice already. Both attempts had resulted in copious amounts of a yellow gooey substance the color and consistency of egg yolk. Brandon was very nervous. He couldn't understand his emotions. He had talked with and dated prettier girls than Ellen Pierce. He had never felt such trepidation at the prospect of meeting anyone. Upon close reflection he further surmised that the only time he felt somewhat comfortable was when he was actually in the girl's presence. The girl had some kind of hold on him. Whenever he thought about her he got nervous. His heart would pick up a beat. His palms would sweat. In her presence all his anxieties would melt away. He would forget to be nervous. He had finally found a person with whom he could connect (in more ways than one). He didn't know if he was in love but he definitely knew he did not want to approach his third date with a quarter-sized pimple on his beak.

Ellen had no trepidation about a forthcoming encounter. She was pretty certain how the day would go. If Brandon kept his cool he would probably find the promised land. She knew the moment she had seen him standing with Miss Dumphreys' panties in his hand that she wanted those panties to be hers that he was holding. Ellen was not a virgin but she was far from a slut. Her sexual adventures had been few and all on her terms. She had approached sex with a focused will. She had not fooled herself. She had felt stirrings but never any real passion. Brandon had lit a flame that threw real heat. She was finally beginning to understand why some girls acted so stupid whenever they met

boys. The clock read noon. Brandon was not due until one. That hour seemed an

eternity. Her mood kept flashing between irritation and expectation. She hadn't rode out

to the quarry in a long time. She loved motorcycles and was not bothered by the fact that

Brandon's bike was only a 250. She would let him teach her how to ride it. She had let

her second cousin Bill teach her how to ride his 350 when she was twelve on the days she

let him "teach" her about sex.

    Ellen had decided on her ninth birthday that Billy Elder would be her first. He had

opened the door for her and looked her in the eye when he had spoken to her. Most

people thought Billy a little slow because he didn't talk much. Ellen mentioned this to

Billy. He had chuckled wryly and stated, "Most people don't listen anyway and the ones

that do hear what they wants anyhow." Billy figured as long as people didn't expect

much and paid him little mind, he could come and go and do as he wished. He didn't

pretend to be something he wasn't. He just never revealed all that he was. Ellen admired

people that gave the world at large the part of themselves it expected and saved the rest

and best for those few who had enough sense to look. Diamonds aren't found laying in

plain view. You had to dig a little. Ellen felt Brandon had many hidden treasures. They

were not the ones that Brandon thought he was hiding. The young man emanated an aura

of "realness." Even when he acted "cool" it came off so awkward that he truly became

cool. A guy wouldn't thinks so but girls were the ones that truly decided these things.

    The air was crisp and clear. The temperature stood at about seventy-three degrees

with a slight breeze. It was a day that made her glad she lived in a small town. Everyone naturally assumed that Ellen was one of those people that grow up hating small town life. They get out as soon as the can and never look back.

Ellen wanted to get out. She wanted to see the world and she wanted to leave all the ignorance and shortsightedness of small town life in her past. She also wanted to save and cherish the good values and simple pleasures that her life had given her. She knew she was from a small town and that she would always be a small town girl. She knew something else. It was a small world and wherever you went, one thing would stay constant and that was yourself. If you know yourself and have decided who "yourself" consists of instead of letting others mold you to their expectations, you are always home.

She liked Brandon because by his own inability to fit in he had to shape himself into something original. Everybody paid lip service to the idea of individuality but let an individual show up and watch a crowd pick up rocks and stone the outsider.

Her father told her she was a snob. He suggested she "might oughter come down out'n dem clouds and find herself a good man afore one a dem town boys ruint her." She wondered what her dad was going to say about her riding up to the quarry with the son of the man who might close the mine and the plant. What would happen if she were to get pregnant and Brandon left town with his father before she could tell him? Ellen knew that no matter how much a boy liked a girl, no sixteen-year-old boy in the world was ready for that revelation. A rich town boy passing through shore weren't any way to be starting no family. Just to make sure, Ellen checked her birth control compact to make certain she was up to date and everything first rate. To be extra careful, she grabbed three condoms from the paper bag that the Health Department handed out for free.

If Brandon could have seen her placing three condoms in her pocket he would have jumped for joy. He had been nervous about taking one. He had felt he was being overly optimistic. At twelve, thirty-five Ellen could hear the sound of a high-pitched whine coming up the mountain.

"Somebody's in a hurry," her sister Maxine observed.

Ellen smiled to herself. "Yes, someone certainly was in a hurry."

Brandon had waited as long as he could. His patience had vanished. He had gotten on his bike and taken off at a reasonable rate of speed. When town appeared in his rear view mirror he gunned the engine and immediately felt the cool satisfying rush of air in his hair. He knew he would probably be early but he also knew if he tried to wait any longer he would be a nervous wreck and that the day would probably be ruined.

Ellen had every intention waiting coolly inside the house. The plan had been to keep Brandon waiting and to have her father speak with him. She wanted to make him squirm a little and see if he had any backbone. The appearance of the little, shiny red motorcycle at the end of the driveway had cancelled her plans. Her father had left the night before after talking with her brother about seeing some dogs. He had shown up at breakfast to announce he would be gone for at least two more days. His concern over Bobby's arrest had been less than heartwarming.

Ellen stood on the porch and waived away the dust from Brandon's entrance. Brandon was a bundle of emotion. He was jubilant, hesitant and expectant. Ellen looked stunning in a faded pair of jeans with rips in the pockets. She had on a half top T-shirt. To keep the wind away she had tied her hair into a ponytail. She had a jacket in case the day changed. Brandon stopped his bike at the bottom of the steps. Before he could

dismount Ellen rushed down the steps and jumped on behind him.

"I thought you wanted me to meet your father."

"He's not here. Let's just ride."

"Okay."

The couple raced away into the early afternoon sun.

CHAPTER TWENTY-THREE

The day had just begun. Bobby was down. No one knew where his Uncle Jimmy had gone and no one seemed to care. His father was out of town and would not be back for at least three days. His sister had a new boyfriend and he didn't have any close friends. Bobby packed some items into a duffel bag his uncle had given him. He loaded this bag and his 30.06 into his pick-up and took off down the driveway. He had no destination. He hoped destiny would take him to a better place. He would be back when he had decided just exactly which direction he should focus himself. He didn't care for the direction he was headed. He knew he could never go back to being the person he had been before the dogs.

Maxine Pierce watched her sister and subsequently her brother leave. No one said hello, good morning or goodbye to her. No one hardly noticed Maxine Pierce anymore.

Her Uncle Jimmy sometimes took notice. Her father would kill him and her if he had any idea of the nature of Jimmy's attention. Jimmy had first noticed Maxine about two weeks after arriving back home from the Gulf. He had come home drunk early in the afternoon. She had been alone in the house. She was singing along with the radio while she washed dishes. Jimmy had come up behind her unannounced and startled her. He had laughed at her small fright and had taken her into his arms and given her a friendly hug when she started getting angry. That gesture had elicited strange emotions within her and the comforting gesture of a friendly hug had turned into something more. She knew that they were not supposed to have feelings of a sexual nature because they were blood.

Jimmy never seemed to feel any remorse about anything. His lack of guilt or worry about getting caught had stirred her even deeper. She worried but Jimmy's attitude had been almost infectious. They had romped numerous times. Whenever Jimmy would catch her alone he would rub or kiss her. They seldom did "it" but the things they did do were Maxine's greatest joys and secretes.

Jimmy often borrowed money from Maxine as well as other women in the area. Maxine knew Jimmy was "no good" but he was also one of the very few people that she knew that would talk to her. He would sometimes call and flirt with her for no reason. She knew she didn't love him and that he didn't love her. She had several lovers but hardly anyone ever bothered to make her laugh.

Today being Sunday, she knew no one would call her. Her friends and acquaintances never called when Maxi might be home. Monday might bring a nice surprise.

Maxine decided to wash and tinker with her own motorcycle. Who knows she might even take a ride around sunset?

Jimmy Pierce had decided to leave town for a few days. He needed to clear his mind and figure out the best way to get rid of his little nephew. He wasn't for sure that Bobby had said anything that would connect Jimmy with any crimes. The boy was acting squirrelly and Jimmy just didn't like the feelings he was getting from the boy's unexplained actions. Jimmy didn't like leaving witnesses but he hadn't really felt his and Bobby's actions had been that big a deal. They had a little fun. If they kept their mouths shut they could have more fun later.

"Shit! Ain't nobody missed dem two assholes anyhow. Far as the world's concerned, the horny little bastards ran off and eloped. A child molesting coke fiend and an infant nymphomaniac and a future welfare mother." Jimmy figured everybody should thank himself and his nephew. The murder/rape of the lovebirds probably saved the country a million dollars. The prison system wouldn't have to support Romeo and Juliet could get her Section Eight housing in hell. That don't even count start-up and waste. Jimmy Pierce, social worker.

"Hah, hah, hah. Hell, should run for governor. Get elected on the anti-crime, anti-welfare ticket. Might even do a little "free drug" campaign.

Jimmy decided to avoid Lexington and Louisville and to go a little further north. He had a couple of friends that lived outside of Cincinnati on the Kentucky side of the river. His friends could always use a little weed. This friend kept a good stash of "throw away" weapons that had been stolen and could be used once and thrown away. A problem with using a weapon of this nature was that the gun may already have been used in a crime. It'd be hell to get pulled over on some bullshit traffic violation and wind up in jail on some other dumb fucker's felony beef.

Jimmy's buddy Lloyd also kept a lot of good chemicals. Jimmy had a talent for cooking crank. A lot of hillbillies could cook. Many "chefs" were sons and grandsons of moonshiners. Anyone who thinks making liquor is easy work has never been around anytime someone was cooking.

The new market was much the same. To cook good "crank" or meth, a person needed the right chemicals, a lot of heat, plenty of cold beer and balls. Some cooks would labor

-175-

day and night and only produce a lumpy brown residue that sometimes got referred to as

"peanut butter." Jimmy was more than a fair hand with substances. He was good at

using them. He was good at making them. Jimmy Pierce could take a couple of good salt

blocks and a few aluminum cans, two good propane burners, some acetone and inside of

about fifteen hours you wouldn't be able to stand within fifteen feet of him from the reek

emanating from his body. Jimmy didn't produce lumpy brown paste. On a good night,

Jimmy could produce pure crystal. Lay it out on a mirror and watch it glisten like glass in

the light. The stuff would be so pure that it had to be cut at a ratio of one to four to keep

mother fuckers from blowing their hearts clean outta their chest cavities.

Jimmy would be able to lay low for about three days, maybe four. He could do a little

cooking, sell some weed, possibly tag some new kitty and figure out how to solve his

nephew problem.

Lloyd Barnes had known Jimmy for years. They had gotten kicked out of high school

together. No one had been surprised at the end of their academic careers. Their

scholastic achievements had been less than exemplary. Attendance had been sketchy.

Neither had liked school or the people at school. Unlike Bobby, Jimmy and Lloyd had

both been bullies. Both had been left back at least twice. They were bigger, dumber and

meaner than the kids they were placed with. The only surprise at their expulsion had

been that it had taken so long.

Lloyd had been seventeen and in the ninth grade. He had his license and an old Nova.

He had been the only kid in the ninth grade to drive to school. The boys started skipping

school and rode around the back roads. They had stolen two 24-volt batteries out of combines and sold the batteries. They used the money to get drunk and then had driven

back to school. Once there, they had went on a spree of youthful exuberance. They cut

donuts on the football field and shot windows and underclassmen with a BB gun.

Lloyd had been driving so he had the responsibility for paying for the football field

repairs. Jimmy had to pay for the windows that had been shot out. Both students felt

they had done the right thing.

Lloyd now owned a little hillbilly bar and drove a new truck. His bills stayed paid.

He stayed laid. Everybody knew how he made it. Jimmy was not the success that Lloyd

was but he felt he had a good life. He never worked unless he felt like it. His belly

stayed full and he answered to no man.

Jimmy sometimes felt sorry for all the guys that had good jobs, nice homes and

families. Those guys had no idea what it felt like to be a free man. Never drawn a free

breath in their entire lives. Spent their childhood scared of teachers and parents. Spent

their youth scared of girls and pigs. Spent the rest of their lives scared of wives and

bankers. The whole damn bunch of 'em scared, too damned scared to live. Walk into a

room you can smell the fear on all of them. Stinking, pussy soured, soul eating stink.

Jimmy knew what it was to be scared. He was of low character and fairly a coward.

He knew he was not the only one. A man with nothing to lose has less to risk. Jimmy

was master at running a bluff. He had shot his mouth off in many a rough situation. Men

who could kick his ass sat and said nothing. It just wasn't worth the trouble of knocking

him out. Occasionally he would run his mouth at the wrong time and some ol' boy would pop him one. Jimmy didn't mind and never held a grudge. Many a coyote had fed on the

bones of wolves. Buzzards fed on lions. Wait and see. Wait and see.

Jimmy arrived at Lloyd's place around three a.m. Lloyd was awake. Many people

live their lives at odd hours. Bar owners and people in the "bar life" keep odd hours.

"Lloyd's Place" would be open again by nine o'clock. He opened at six a.m. during deer

season. Lloyd Barnes had an energy. He required very little sleep. Add in a little crank

and Lloyd could stay up for days on end. He worked until two-thirty every night and

would often open the bar the next day. Lloyd was not a troubled soul. He just didn't

want to miss anything. Activity blossomed around Lloyd. He was a rare individual who

never seemed bored. One of the few statements Lloyd remembered from school had

been, "Boredom is the sign of an unused mind." Lloyd agreed with this statement

wholeheartedly. "Lloyd's Place" was the name of his bar. Lloyd sat at the rear of the bar.

The building was very large. It sat on a two-acre plot. It was located about two miles

from urban activity. The highway passed in front and another road intersected to the side.

The place could have been called the prototype of the original roadhouse. The yard was

fenced in with a twelve-foot board fence. The fence had a gate that you had to be buzzed

through. Once in the compound, no one could see your vehicle. A lot of Lloyds'

houseguests preferred not to be found. The bar itself had plenty of parking out front, but

the fenced in area was for Lloyd's family and friends.

The bar did open onto the yard but only through one door. This door stayed locked.

Patrons that had been around long enough could get the bartender to let them out the

door. Once in the yard they could enjoy many activities that couldn't be offered inside.

Lloyd did a good business legally. He did a real good business illegally. His taxes stayed paid. He kept trouble to a minimum. The main thing was he always checked I.D. Personally he didn't give a shit how old someone was when they started drinking. He just didn't like to be surrounded by kids.

Lloyd's ol' lady encouraged Lloyd's dislike for underage patrons. She had been in the bars her entire life. Her parents had owned a small bar in Cincinnati and she knew people. Kids were trouble. They didn't have much money and they didn't control themselves.

Lloyd's catered to a rough trade. Letting underage girls into his establishment would be equivalent to throwing raw meat to sharks. A lot of people learned some hard lessons at "Lloyd's Place." Lloyd didn't mind. He himself had found the world a hard place. He didn't consider himself a hard man but he had planted a couple who were.

Lloyd and Jimmy went way back. They were not alike. Lloyd was tough and strong. He would face any man head on and let the chips fall where they may. He wasn't a coward in anyone's estimation. He followed his own rules of life. If you wanted to be his friend then you did the same. Lloyd treated people with respect and courtesy. He expected the same. You got what you paid for, whether it be a fifty-cent beer or a pound of cocaine. He stood by his word and had no time for people that did not.

Jimmy Pierce lacked many of these qualities. Somehow he and Lloyd were still close friends. Jimmy might fuck a lot of people over but Lloyd Barnes would not be one of them. Lloyd had a lot of friends; real friends that you could call and ask a favor and that wouldn't say anything but "Okay, I'm on it." You had to be that kind of friend to have one. Lloyd had put his property, his entire livelihood on the line to post bail for

characters that no one else, not even their families, would have trusted. These guys

would die for Lloyd. Lloyd expected no less.

Jimmy's appearance met with little fanfare. He simply pulled up to the gate, pushed

the buzzer, gave his name and drove through. A large man with cut-off bib overalls

without a shirt greeted him.

"Hey, pull up over thar." The beefy giant pointed toward a trio of old junk cars, two

of which were on blocks. Jimmy pulled his truck in behind them. He got out and walked

to the back of his vehicle. He took the plate off the bumper. The large man in the

hillbilly beachwear sauntered over to Jimmy's truck. "Air ye hiding her?"

"Yeah, I'm not sure I need to but I got a fucked up feeling."

"We'll it allus good to go wid dem feelings. Tell you what, you go on inside. I'll get

rid of er!"

"Thanks Grunt, I appreciate it"

"Hah, you might not be so appreciative when I'm done."

"I don't think so. The more I think about it, the more I think it's time this ol' truck

just disappeared."

"No shit! Well, looks like little Jimmy been up to a passel of hassle. Don't worry

bro' it's a done deal." Having said that, the big sunblasted, windblown behemoth turns

and barks orders at two lanky boys.

"Eustice, Gordon, get over here. We got a little job. Parnell open up that garage."

Jimmy reaches into his pocket, "You need the keys?"

"Nah! The bastards stole your truck. You still got your keys."

"Yeah, good idea. I'll just say the big, blond, greasy man cut him short."

"I don't care what you tell 'them.' I ain't see you or your truck. Furthermore, you won't see me again for about three days. That will be when we get introduced."

"Thanks Grunt."

"It's cool. You just make shore and return a favor. Save me some of that giddy-up dust bro."

"Cool. You know I will."

"Later."

"Later." Jimmy went on into the house. He didn't bother knocking. No one would have heard him anyway. Inside the back door was an anteroom much like a screened in porch. Two guys in denim vests and leather pants were smoking a joint with a very large woman. The woman looked very stoned. She had a very pretty face but she probably weighed three hundred and forty pounds. She wore a T-shirt with a slogan 'Bikers Keep It Greasy' emblazoned on the front and nothing else. One of her pudgy hands held the joint and the other was fisted around the cock of the shorter of the two gentlemen.

"Hey dude, want a drink?" The taller of the two asked. As he spoke he offered a bottle of Wild Turkey in Jimmy's direction. Jimmy accepted the bottle.

"Don't mind if I do. Name's Jimmy. I'm a friend of Lloyd's."

"Thought so. I'm Clutch. This is Robert Earl Simms and the young lady is his wife, Purdy."

"Glad to meet cha," Jimmy spoke.

"Hey," said Robert Earl with a nod. Purdy just smiled and took a hit off the joint, handed it to Jimmy, bowed her head and took her husband's member into her mouth.

Jimmy accepted the joint and tried not to think too much about where he had just gotten it and took a big toke. It smelled faintly of sex. He figured it wouldn't be too healthy to act overly finicky with these people. He released the smoke and offered the cigarette to the tall biker named Clutch. Clutch took the joint and nodded toward the couple.

"They just got married. Robert Earl's letting Purdy show a little class. Wants everybody to know what a good ol' lady he's got. Get you some if you want. After tonight that's private stock.

Jimmy glanced at the fat bleached blond who at the moment had her new groom's balls on her chin.

"Yeah! I'll take some. Can I get the pussy or she just feeding her face."

"Hah, hah, hah! You're all right dude. Nah, if you want some butt or pussy you ain't even got to wait."

Right on cue Purdy bent forward and turned her back toward Jimmy. Without hesitation, Jimmy handed the bottle back to Robert Earl and unzipped his pants. He pulled the girl's T-shirt up to display a large, round, cum splattered ass. There was blood and semen on her thighs. She was still seeping.

"I ain't a member," Jimmy spoke.

"It's cool, just do the right thing."

Jimmy, not a new man to a biker wedding knew he was receiving a very high honor. A biker letting you fuck his woman on her wedding day was almost the same as letting you ride his Harley. Jimmy's not being a brother (member) to the biker club was an even greater gesture. Jimmy felt in order to show that he realized the enormity of the good fellowship being offered he should make a gesture in return. Jimmy placed a palm on each buttock and lowered himself to his knees. The girl expecting another assault with a male member was more than a little surprised when he grabbed her tight and shoved his entire face deep into her snatch.

The man called Clutch let out a yelp. "Hot damn! Go man, go! Show some class!"

Robert Earl let out a rebel yell. "Fucking-A, right. I'll ride that river any day with a brother got balls like that."

Jimmy pulled it off. It took a lot to impress men like this. He lapped at the overflowing gash and slurped the love juices like it was ambrosia. He thought to himself, "This is a good place to hang low for a few days."

CHAPTER TWENTY-FOUR

The temperature had reached a mild seventy-seven degrees, unseasonably warm. Ellen felt wonderful. It was like everything had been special ordered. Her mood was contagious. Brandon had stopped for gas and to get sodas. The couple had laughed continuously while in the gas station. The store clerk, a toothless, old biddy of about sixty laughed also. She said, "Does my heart good to see young lovers." Each had looked at the other and blushed. This caused them both to laugh harder.

Ellen couldn't stop thinking, "Is it that obvious?"

Brandon was the only one who couldn't see it. Brandon was not clueless. He wanted Ellen very much. He had some concerns. He wondered if she always acted this way or if he were somehow special. He wanted to tell her she was special but knew he wouldn't be able to handle it if she didn't feel the same. What if she laughed in his face? What if she did this all the time? What if she were willing to do this all the time with him?

The twosome had been at ease at the store. The ease had disappeared by the time they arrived at the quarry road.

A cool tension had replaced the easy energy of youth, part sexual tension and part youthful mistrust of new relationships. The gifts of emotion traded cautiously but placed upon the block. Both parties wanting to rush forward — a sea of churning eddies of feeling.

Brandon eased to a stop. He turned the engine off. He had always likened the act to a small murder. He felt a tiny guilt every time he shot the engine down. It seemed to him

-184-

that the little engine had given him its all and he for its effort always killed it. "I guess that's why it's known as killing an engine. I guess that would also make for a lot of cowboys. I guess that I better not talk like this when she starts talking to me."

Ellen would have smiled and would have been delighted at these thoughts. She, herself, often had thoughts of such a nature. The fact that Brandon had similar thoughts would have seemed like fate – kismet.

"It's a beautiful day. Can you believe it's this nice?"

"Well in a way I guess I can. We lived in California for four years. It hardly ever got colder than this."

"Wow, that must have been fucking fantastic."

"It was nice. You just sorta' took it for granted. The days that stand out were always super hot or super wet or just shitty. Good weather never seems like a big deal until you move somewhere that doesn't have it all the time."

"I know. It's like running out of panties."

"Well, I wouldn't know about that."

"You know what I mean. When I was little, I never even thought about it. Whenever I needed panties I just went to my drawer and pulled out a pair. I never thought about how they got there. The first time I realized my Mom wasn't coming home was the day I reached into my panty drawer and there were no panties in the drawer."

"Gee, I'm sorry. I didn't mean to make you sad."

"You didn't make me sad. I just feel I can share that with you. I mean your mother isn't dead but you don't see her every day."

"I know. I understand in some ways you have it better and in some you have it worse."

"How could I have it better?"

"Well, if your Mom is dead, at least she didn't leave you for another woman. I know that's weak but you have anger of one sort that I relate to and you have it at your father."

"I understand, but my father told me my mother left me and up until a few days ago I felt betrayed like you do. Now I feel even more so. Now I feel my father stole my mother from me. I'm also not sure I blame him. I remember my father the way he used to be. He was full of laughter. His eyes would sparkle. They would shine their brightest when he looked at my mother. My father may have killed my mother and her lover but my father died that day as well. Her lying with that vacuum salesman was a dark, treacherous thing. It brought out something in my father I don't think he even knew was in him."

"Reverend Parker says there is good and evil in every man. God's gift to mankind was 'free will' and we each and everyone must decide which way to go — evil or good.

"I don't think it's that simple. Your mother's actions were wrong. I agree. I feel your father overreacted."

"I'm not sure you do. My mother presented herself to my father in a certain way. He fell in love and created a life with that person. He devoted his future to that person. Her betrayal proved to him that she was not that person and perhaps she had never been. He killed her but she killed the woman he loved. I think if I loved someone and they were murdered I would want to kill the person that had murdered my love."

"Wait a minute. That's fucked up! What if she had just fallen out of love? People do change and grow. It has been known to happen."

"I agree, but I feel my father realized when he caught my mother that she had never been in love with him."

"I don't know. It just doesn't sound right — killing somebody because you love them. What do you do to people you hate?"

"Hah, hah! I don't know but I'll think about it."

"This is gloomy talk for such a perfect day. Let's walk down to the water."

Hand in hand, they strolled down to the quarry.

"The water is real clear this time of year. People don't come here much when it gets too cold to swim. There aren't any fish in the pit. I guess it could be stocked and they would probably breed but if it did any good somebody would try to make you pay to fish.

"Yeah. It's pretty neat you can almost se the bottom."

"Yeah, they say that when the coal ran out the company didn't even take out all their equipment. They left two or three earthmovers and one of them real big cranes over on the other side near the big cliff, you can see way down. People say if the sun is just right you can see all the shit.

"Where? I want to see."

"Well, I'm not sure, up by the road a little further out."

"Show me!" Realizing the implications of the statement, "I mean I really want to see, not that I want to make out."

"Oh, shut up!" Ellen says laughing. "I know what you mean. I'm not sure if I should be pissed or not but I know what you mean. Last one there is a lily, livered Yankee who gets no lovin' a'tall"

Saying this she sprints toward a little knoll on the side of the road. Foreseeing her destination, Brandon sprints past her. She is quicker than he thought she would be and he quickly realized he is in a race. He pours it on and barely reaches the hill before her.

"Oh shit! I haven't ran like that in a long time."

"Us hill girls gotta learn how to run. Especially if they's men folk at home." Ellen Scarlett O'Hara in a parody of a Dixie accent, "It's amazing how good Southerners can mimic themselves."

"Damn! That's good. Is it true about hillbillies and incest and all?"

"Well, it do get cold in de winter and houses are fer apart. No. It's not like that. Some people marry cousins n' all. Some families are so distrustful of outsiders that the only people they let their kids talk to or go around are family. People considered it a lowly thing and people that do it are considered disgraceful. You can't blame the children but they become the biggest victims. Everybody knows why they are they way they are. Animals kill their babies when they are first born if they are the result of incest."

"What? You're kidding."

"It's true. We had a pair of chows that were brother and sister. The female went in heat. We pinned her up but her brother got to her. She had her puppies and he would not let her near or let anyone near her. She finally had to eat her puppies or else starve."

"That's awful."

"All animals answer nature's demands. Man is the only animal that tries to bend nature to his will. My dad says 'Man is an arrogant beast.'"

"Yeah, I guess. Let's check out the pit."

The couple laid down on the cool grass. The air was warm for November but the ground still held a chill from the morning frost. They moved closer together without knowing they were doing so. Brandon was the first to notice the pressure of the young girl's body against his own. He instantly tensed. Ellen noticed and started to pull away. Each looked at the other and with a self-conscious laugh. They had their first kiss. Their lips met with a tenderness, a hesitant pressure, then more. Brandon brought his head back a couple of inches. He looked into Ellen's eyes. He pressed his lips onto hers this time with a firmness and growing passion. She gave a taste of tongue and wrapped her arms around Brandon's shoulders. Brandon rolled her onto her back and cupped her hip with his right hand. Her head rested in the crook of his left arm. He opened his eyes to stare into hers.

When Brandon's eyes opened and focused on Ellen's he screamed and threw her from him. Ellen, totally confused, lay in the dirt.

"What the fuck?" Recognizing the panic on Brandon's face for pure fear. What's wrong? What is it?

Brandon pointed past her head down toward the water. Ellen could not, at first see anything. Something bobbed up and down in the water. She thought it was a doll's head except it was larger and had pieces missing. She recognized the face and started

screaming.

"Oh my God! It's Mary Ann! Mary Ann! Somebody's killed her! Oh no! Oh God!

Oh shit, fuck damn. You fucking bastards. They killed her. She wasn't even fourteen-

years-old. Let's get out of here. We've got to tell somebody."

"Are you sure it's real?"

"Yeah, mother fucker. It's real. You know it's real just like I do. That's why you

screamed."

"You think the people who did it are still around?" Brandon asked with a touch of

fear.

Ellen stopped screaming for a second. "I don't think so. They been missing for a

week or so."

"They?"

"Her and her boyfriend, Boyd Thomas. That son of a bitch probably killed her and

skipped town. He probably thought she would never be found."

"If she's been dead that long, how come her head is just now floating up?

"I don't know. What do I look like, fucking Quincy? It's probably gas or something.

Let's just get out of here. Now!"

"Okay."

"Okay."

"Let's just be careful. I'll take you to your house and then we can call the police."

"Bullshit! You stop at the first place with a phone and when the cops come we are going be right there. Boyd's uncle is the deputy and I want to make sure nobody does any tampering to cover up for that fucker."

"How do you know it was him?"

"I don't. Who else would have a reason? He ain't been around. Everybody just assumed they ran off together. His daddy probably been sending money to hide out on. Poor Mary Ann. I hope they fry that mother fucker!"

"You don't know he did anything. You don't even know that's your friend. Calm down."

"Oh shut up! You would stick up for him. You're a man and men stick together. She probably never seen it coming. Sneaky bastard!"

"Let's go. We aren't helping the situation by standing here shouting at one another."

"Okay! Okay. You're right. Let's just go report this and get her out of there. This is gonna kill her daddy. Man this is bad, really bad."

"Yeah, and it was turning into a really nice day."

Brandon took Ellen in his arms. "Today will always be special. We certainly won't have any problem remembering our first kiss. Let's just make sure it's not the last."

To seal the statement, Ellen places her hands on each side of Brandon's head and plants one square on.

CHAPTER TWENTY-FIVE

Events over the weekend had provided for a hectic Monday morning. The little police

station had been swamped with reporters, parents, supporters, scared people and

onlookers in general. The Sheriff was most concerned about the death of the State

Trooper on Friday night. He hadn't know an undercover operation was being conducted

in his jurisdiction.

This "oversight," if that's what it was, made him very nervous. He couldn't help but

wonder if his department was under investigation. If so, he had plenty to worry about.

His small town hadn't had a murder in three years. Every year someone got

"accidentally" shot while hunting or cleaning a gun. Not one unsolved death in his entire

nine years as Sheriff. Every time someone had killed someone else in Pineville they had

turned themselves in.

The town had a lot of good people. Right now it had a lot of scared people. These

people wanted answers. Rumors abounded in the small town and the outlying

communities. The fact that all the deaths had in some way, involved the Pierce family

hadn't gone unnoticed. Not one had gone as far as to say it outright but people were

speculating that the Pierce family may be involved. The most vocal of the speculators

had been the Sheriff's own wife.

Divers had gone down into the pit after Brandon and Ellen had called and reported

their find. The Sheriff had interviewed the couple before the divers had located the car

with the bodies inside. Ellen's insistence that Mary Ann's boyfriend be arrested had convinced him she had nothing to do with the girl's murder. The look of shock on her face after finding out Boyd had been killed had erased any doubts. The head had appeared out of nowhere. The throat had been cut almost to the bone. Fish and turtles or some critters had probably chewed the rest of the way through the neck. The girl's head was in fairly good shape. The young man had not faired as well. The body had been ripped and chewed and savaged by the brutal attack and the wildlife in the pit.

The Captain of the State Trooper barracks had come to town to investigate the death of their agent. The FBI would soon be there. Preliminary investigation had declared the event a one-vehicle accident. Everyone knew that assessment had been absurd. The investigating officer at the scene had written his report the night of the accident. The officer had no idea that the dead man had been an undercover police officer. He had assumed the corpse had belonged to another good ol' boy that had a few and gotten into a little road race and hadn't been able to cut the muster. The officer had thought he was being generous. He had written the report as a straightforward accident to ensure the widow no problem of collecting insurance. He had also felt a degree of sympathy for whoever the guy had been racing. Both parties had known the risks and the guy that had won could have just as easily been the dead guy.

Daylight had revealed facts that laid the single vehicle accident theory null and void. The skid marks clearly revealed excessive speed and more than one vehicle. A lot of people had known about the race. It had been no trouble for the Sheriff or the visiting officers to get the name of the second racer. The question on everyone's mind was, "Where is Jimmy Pierce?" No one had any idea.

The Sheriff was having second thoughts about his decision to let Bobby Pierce go. He had little doubt that the boy had killed his Deputy in self-defense. The fact the he himself had signed the official report that he'd labeled the death an accident, was worrying on his mind. He wished he had killed the boy and had labeled the deaths an escape attempt turned bad. Too many people asking too many questions. The Sheriff knew his department was in for a big shakedown. Yesterday his biggest worry had been getting reelected, now he knew he would be lucky if he could just stay out of jail himself.

The Coroner had four bodies to investigate. The Sheriff had not one suspect in custody. There were at least two falsified reports on two of these deaths. Outside police agencies were investigating his town and its people. His department was in deep shit.

Monday afternoon, the body of Big Shirley was discovered by a couple of twelve-year-olds out riding their bicycles. This body was an obvious murder. Combined with the murdered couple in the abandoned strip pit it made for three. Three blatant homicides and no suspect. Preliminary inspections of the bodies showed similarities. All three were raped and beaten. The forensics specialist from the FBI believed from the first appraisal probably all three had been killed by the same person or persons. Further examination would be done, but the Sheriff already knew he had a fucking serial killer in Pineville. Some fucking hillbilly was out there raping and killing and his chances for reelection were gone. He would be lucky if he didn't get arrested. No one had linked the murdered trio with the other two deaths.

The Sheriff was looking for Bobby and Jimmy Pierce. He wanted to talk with them and make sure they got their stories straight. He wanted to cover up his own fuck-ups along with his officers (the one that had reported the dead State Trooper as an accident).

Tuesday morning found Sheriff Boswell pulling up in front of Maxi Pierce's home. The only people home were Maxi and Maxine.

"Morning, Maxi."

"Hello Arnett. What brings you out here to God's country?"

"Well, I need to do a little follow-up with your boy, Bobby. I would also like to bend your brother Jimmy's ear a little bit. I dropped down to the schoolhouse and was told Bobby won't be allowed back until Friday."

"Yep, that boy, he's a fuck-up. Sometimes I wonder if'n he's even mine."

"Hell Maxi, the boy favors you plenty."

"Well, whatever. What's he done?"

"No. It ain't like that. As far as I know, he ain't done nary a thing. I just want to do a little follow-up questioning about my brother-in-law's unfortunate accident."

"Well, if that ol' faggot's dead, the world's a better off. You don't think my boy had anything to do with it do ya?

"Maxi, I just need to talk to that boy to make sure his story ain't gonna change none if'n the federal boys get a hold of him."

"Shit, Arnett, my boy ain't gonna punk on nobody. I'd kill him myself. We don't hold much favor with no rats or snitches in these parts. You know that."

"I know. I would just feel a lot better if'n I could speak with the boy in person, that's all."

"Well I ain't seed hide nor hair of him since Friday night afor all this a taken place."

"Maxine. Hey Maxine."

"Yeah, Daddy."

"You seen you brother anytime the last couple a days?"

"Just when you was yelling at him on Saturday."

"Oh yeah, that's right. I seen him right after he got outta jail. Why didn't you talk with him then?"

"I did talk with him. Things have changed some since then. Your girl, Ellen and that town boy found them bodies out at Peavy's pit. It has brought a bunch of federal and state boys around. I don't want them boys talking to Bobby or Jimmy afore I do."

"I bet you don't. Who you think 's gonna be Sheriff come election?"

"Fuck you, Maxi."

"Hah, hah, hah! Lord, would you lookie dere? That shore is a purdy shade of red Arnett. I ain't seen that boy or his uncle, but you can bet yer ass when I do, I'll shore tell 'em you want to talk to 'em."

"Did Jimmy say where he was heading?"

"Hell no and ain't nobody around here would give a fuck if he had told. I'm about tired of this bullshit and I'd just as soon you get the hell off'n my property."

"All right. I'm going. Thanks for all your help. It's good citizens such as yourself that make this job such a joy."

"Glad to hear it. You probably won't have worry about it after election."

Sheriff Boswell was not angry about Maxi's gruff talk. Most landowners in the

county didn't have much use for the law. If anything happened out in the county, people

tended to handle it themselves. By the time the law arrived, the situation would be under

control. Old timers had a saying, "No matter what happens, all the law does is figure out

who owes the law money." This was feuding country and people knew how to nurse a

grudge. People had been shot over cows wandering through fences. You could live next

to a man for twenty years and never have a problem. That man sees you on his land while

you're supposed to be working. He might kill you because he thinks you're there to fuck

his women or to steal. He's probably right.

The Sheriff decided to interview Ellen Pierce. Not only had she found the bodies, she

might know where her brother might have gone.

Ellen thought this day would never end. Everyone was avoiding her like the plague.

She could hear snippets of conversation and everything she had heard had been bad. The

police may not have suspects but the citizens of Knott County had suspects.

Ever since the wreck and subsequent death of Freddie Wilbanks, Vernon Price had

been telling anyone that would listen that Bobby was a murderer. At first, people had

laughed. No one was laughing anymore. Everybody that had been found was in

someway connected to the Pierce family. The connection between Big Shirley and

Jimmy hadn't been made yet, but people already had suspicions.

No one had accused Ellen of anything. Some boys had made comments about

retribution.

"If'n we find out your family killed Boyd and Mary Ann, there'll be a few more bodies floating in the strip pits."

Ellen knew people were scared. She also knew scared people were dangerous. She had been almost relieved when her name rang out over the intercom asking for her presence in the Principal's office. Her relief was short lived. Her relief had faded as soon as she had seen the Sheriff's cruiser outside of the school's entrance.

"Oh fuck! Here we go."

"Come in. Come right in. Mr. Boswell, this is Ellen Pierce. She has been an exceptional student during her stay here. I'm sure she will be happy to answer any questions you may have."

"Thank you, Mr. Coats. Could I possibly speak to the young lady in private?"

"Oh! Excuse me. I thought this was a matter concerning a student."

"It is. I would prefer to speak to Miss Pierce in private."

"Well, by all means." The little man huffed out of his own office.

"What an ass! Is he always like that?"

"Pretty much."

"I hope he doesn't cause you any problems over this."

"He won't have to, the kids will give me enough grief."

"I know. I know. I hate to have to take you out of class, but I need to ask you some questions."

"I told you everything I knew yesterday."

"Yes, you did. You told me everything about the discovery of those bodies. What I need from you today is to see if you can help me locate your brother and your uncle."

"Why? Do you think they have something to do with the killing of Mary Ann?"

"No, nothing like that. At least I hope not. No. I need to speak with them about a couple of incidents that occurred over the weekend."

"You mean the race and what happened at the layout for Freddie?"

"Do you know anything about those incidents?"

"Not really. I was outside when the coffin got knocked over and I haven't spoken to my Uncle Jimmy in over a week."

"Doesn't he live with your family?"

"Yeah. He lives there but I don't have much to do with him."

"Why is that?"

"That's none of your business. I just don't care for my uncle. I don't start anything with him. To keep the peace in the house we avoid each other."

"Has he done something to you? We have laws you know...."

"No. It's nothing like that. He doesn't bother me personally. I don't like the way my little brother follows him around. He puts ideas in Bobby's head. I think a lot of the problems Bobby's been going through can be laid at Jimmy's feet."

"Does he put the boy up to no good? I'm not sure I understand."

"Jimmy is a braggart and Bobby is a teenage boy. Bobby believes crap Jimmy tells him. To Bobby, Jimmy can do no wrong."

"Well that's not so strange. A lot of young men look up to their uncles."

"I know that. It's just Uncle Jimmy is probably less mature than Bobby. It's like the blind leading the blind."

"Okay. I think I gather your meaning. I still need to talk with both of them."

"You said that, but you never said why you want to talk with them."

"Well, they were both involved in some pretty serious incidents over the weekend. There is no indication that they were involved with the three murders but people are getting antsy. They're looking for people to blame. A lot of state boys and federal agents are in town. If those boys talk to your kin folk afore I get a chance to, things could get sticky."

"If they haven't done anything, then surely they have nothing to worry about."

"Normally I would agree. The fact that they are both missing at this time, when things are all stirred up and all, makes them look like they got something to hide. Do you think they could be together?"

"No. Jimmy hasn't been seen or heard from all weekend. Bobby disappeared sometime yesterday morning. He was gone afore Brandon and me found those bodies. He probably doesn't even know about them, much less have had anything to do with them.

"I never meant to imply any different. I need to speak to Bobby about an incident that happened at the jail."

"He should have never been in jail. If anything happened while he was there, it's your fault. Bobby did nothing wrong. You should be in jail for locking him up and if you are the one who beat him I hope you burn in hell. If'n my daddy gave a shit and was worth the salt it took to keep him breathing, he'd whup your ass."

"Now listen here, young lady."

"No! I'm not gonna listen to anything you got to say. It seems to me instead of looking for answers, you are just trying to find someone to heap your miseries on. I wouldn't tell you spit. You and your kind have never done one decent thing for people like my family and I seriously doubt you plan on starting now. You just go and do your own dirty work."

"Goddamnit! I'm trying to save these boys a lot of hassle. If you know where they are at you best be telling me. I've got a good mind to haul you in for withholding information."

"Bullshit! I don't know where they are and you sure as hell don't have a good mind. Good day, Sheriff. I got a class."

CHAPTER TWENTY-SIX

Bobby had spent a sleepless night held up in an abandoned doublewide at the top of the holler. The road was washed out but he had driven up behind the domicile through pastureland. No one had used the property for months. There was little chance for discovery.

The owner of the trailer used it to house Mexican farm workers in the summer. These workers would travel across the South helping to get the tobacco crop in. A group of about fifteen Mexicans would descend on a farm and chop and house an entire crop in one day, two at the most. It was cheaper and quicker than using local help. Besides, there just wasn't enough local people to meet the need. The people that lived around the county looked down on the Mexicans. Some people that never lifted their hands to any kind of work thought they were better than the migrant laborers.

Bobby could not figure out this type of thinking. A person could not control the circumstances surrounding their birth. America was supposed to be a land of opportunity. His Social Studies teacher called it fear — by labeling a group of people inferior for reasons they could never change — their heritage. People allowed themselves the luxury of earned superiority. In a true capitalist society, the only limitations a man should encounter would be those encountered by supply and demand. The person who worked the hardest and the most toward a goal should eventually succeed. The person who does nothing, in a true capitalist society, would starve.

Bobby could not get the incident at the jail out of his mind. He still had a black eye and a lot of bruises. His asshole burned like fire and he could still taste the foul stench of the Deputy's sperm. Bobby had never had normal sex. The only sex he had encountered had been the rape of Mary Ann. The fear and helplessness of his own rape brought home the enormity of the crimes he had perpetuated against the innocent couple.

Boyd had been decent to Bobby and he wished he could bring him back. Mary Ann had been a little tease and he was glad he fucked her. He wished he had kept her and could do it again right now. He could still remember how she had started to respond while he was tonguing her. Under different circumstances, maybe they could have been lovers?

Who was he kidding? Girls like Mary Ann Smith did not date sixteen-year-old boys with junked up pickups. They dated pretty boys who drove Trans Ams and never had to work for spending money.

Bobby felt humiliation and profound sadness for the acts he and his uncle had committed upon Boyd and Mary Ann. His biggest regret was not killing the couple. His biggest regret was he hadn't killed someone that he felt deserved it.

He had brought his list with him. He got out his pen and added a couple of names. His list was getting quite extensive. It still had Vernon Price's name at the top. He had definite intentions of paying back that mother fucker in spades. He wished he could have burnt Vernon along with his little buddy, Freddie. He wished there was some way to kill all his enemies at the same time. If only he could get them all in one place.

A bell went off in his head. Ninety percent of the people on his list went to his school. All he would have to do would be to blow up the school. He started making plans for blowing up the school. The more he thought about it the less of a good idea it became. It would take a ton of dynamite spread all over the building to detonate all at the same time. Another problem was a lot of people he wished retribution upon did not go to school. He needed an event, a gathering where everyone would be at the same time — Friday night's football game would be perfect. Small towns were notorious for being football fanatics.

Bobby had very easy access to dynamite and detonators. The mines in the areas all had their own blasting equipment. The mines were guarded at night but usually it was a joke. The guards, at most places, checked in, stuck around for a couple of hours then split to go party or fuck off. A lot of night watchmen would have visitors — women or buddies. They would get fucked up at the site.

As long as Bobby was discreet and didn't take everything in the shed at any one site, the explosives he stole might go unreported. Even if someone noticed stuff missing, they might just assume one of their friends took it. No one liked to start any shit. Order more and change the lock on the door. Most people that got stuck watching coal tipples and strip mines were the never-do-wells in the families that owned the businesses. No, Bobby would have no problem finding his explosives.

He wished he could talk with his uncle. Jimmy would know what to do.

CHAPTER TWENTY-SEVEN

"Damn! Son! You are the one. Look at that boys. I ain't never seen nobody cook

any finer than this ol' boy here, shit. Ain't no purdier snow this side of Alaska. Jimmy,

son, you the best ol' boy ever cooked."

The man singing Jimmy's praise held in his hand a softball sized rock of pure crystal.

Jimmy had been cooking for thirty hours. He had distilled about twelve kilos of a

crumbly substance that was pure jet fuel. This "first run" was often sold as is on the

street (more like gravel road).

The good ol' boys called it peanut butter. He had taken the first run and cooked it

with more acetone and aluminum cans. He had re-cooked and re-cooked. The final

product had turned into a gleaming block about seven pounds. This was pure crystal. It

sparkled like a diamond. It could not be inhaled in this form. Good crank sold for about

a hundred dollars a gram. This crystal that Jimmy had produced would be cut and re-cut

until it's worth would be in the quarter million dollar range. Everybody was celebrating.

Crystal was a rarity. Many a hillbilly could cook up some crank. Very few held the

magic required to cook crystal.

Jimmy had the knack. He knew when to lay on the heat and the very exact, on-the-dot

moment of truth of when to snatch the prize from the fire. One moment too long or one

drop of sweat too many in an already precarious mixture and everything could explode or

evaporate. It was a testimony to friendship that Lloyd let Jimmy make the attempt to

cook crystal. Very few people got the chance to "re-cook."

A first batch run by a new guy was enough to be considered part of the family. A man would usually be asked to cook a couple more batches before being trusted to burn off a batch. That way, everybody would at least be able to recover any loss if a batch did pop or cook off. A lot of people who had been cooks had been sent to prison and once released had discovered they had lost the touch.

Jimmy's skill was such that he had fired a batch of crude peanut butter before it had even cooled. Instead of venting the room and letting the dope set-up, he had ordered another heater to raise the room temperature and started spooning ingredients with a ladle and firing with a propane torch in the other hand. He only set down either item long enough to kill another Budweiser, empty cans going directly into the mix. The room in which he worked was little more that a closet with the temperature approaching one hundred, thirty-nine degrees. Many volatile chemicals sat in the room. Some of these chemicals had firing points of just over one hundred, seventy degrees. Jimmy was literally playing with fire. Lloyd had no hesitation in allowing Jimmy a chance to run crystal. The first time he had ever seen Jimmy work a torch he had likened the intensity and focus upon his friend's face to that of a surgeon or a painter. Jimmy was no crankster-gangster pumping out low-grade giddy-up powder. He was a fucking artist. He took a handful of raw materials and he made art. Jimmy's crystal could take a seven to one cut and still make you fly like good coke. If you cut it less than three to one and sold it, people would die. Smokers be warned. Hardened dealers would sound like the Surgeon General when dispensing dope this good. It put a good feeling in a man's heart to know he could turn a fair profit and still take care of the consumer.

Everyone was riding high and the new batch was ready to be christened. A pretty young blonde, who probably should have been home doing algebraic equations for third period math class, stood poised over a small carnival mirror with a cut-off McDonald's straw in hand. The door suddenly burst open and two young guys who looked like younger versions of Lloyd came into the room, breaking the spell.

"Uncle Lloyd! Uncle Lloyd! We got trouble."

Everyone started talking at once.

"What! What's the fucking problem! What have you two little shits done now?"

"No, it ain't like that. This ain't even concerning us."

One boy aims his finger toward Jimmy. "It's about him. Lorna Garrett said her Mom ran this guy's plates through the computer and said he's got every cop in the state looking for his ass. He done killed some trooper."

"What the fuck you talking about? I ain't killed no damned body. Who the fuck is Lorna Garrett and how the hell does she know what the fuck I do?"

"Lorna's a good ol' gal whose mom just happens to work as a dispatcher down toward Hazard."

"We gonna have to find out what the fuck is going down! You didn't come here with no posse on your ass, did you?"

"Not far as I know."

"I believe you."

Once more the loyalty of a childhood friend stood the test. Lloyd's word again held inquiries from curious souls at bay. These bikers and rednecks came from the same school of thought as Jimmy Pierce. Jimmy wanted to kill Bobby just to be careful. The bikers wanted to kill Jimmy for the same reason.

Good for Jimmy not many cooks were magicians.

CHAPTER TWENTY-EIGHT

Maxine was ecstatic. Everybody in the whole country was looking for her Uncle Jimmy and she was the only one who knew where he was. She hadn't even been questioned by the police or her father. All her life, people had always assumed she knew nothing of any value. This time, she didn't mind. Her Uncle Jimmy had called her and no one else. He had called that morning at five a.m. and had given her a number. He had said to call him when she talked to her brother. He had said he needed to speak with Bobby as soon as possible. She was not to tell anyone, not even Bobby, how to get a hold of him.

She hadn't seen Bobby since Sunday. Here it was Wednesday and nobody had seen hide nor hair of him. She had no idea where her bother was, but upon his appearance she would call the number Jimmy had given her.

Everybody asking everybody else. Nobody asking her anything. Serves them right. She had something to tell her Uncle Jimmy when she did see him.

Oh, she was happy. She couldn't remember being this happy.

Maxi Pierce was not a happy man. Far from it in fact. Not only had he lost his dogs, he was gonna have to give money back to people that had paid for pups in advance. It was gonna take years and every penny he had to rebuild. He just wanted to kill somebody. He wasn't quite sure that his neighbor, Randall Smith, had killed all his dogs by accident. Maxi was a suspicious man in his later years. His poor departed wife had taken his faith in people and crushed it.

It just seemed funny to Maxi that ol' Randall "accidentally" killed Maxi's dogs and

not two weeks later, Randall's little girl finds herself feeding turtles down at Simm's pit.

Guess that was an accident too.

The more Maxi thought, the thirstier he would get. Thinking being dry work and all.

Maxi decided to moisten up things and work with a little lightening. He had some of the

best moonshine in three counties put away for such occasions. The half-gallon of mash

he was drinking on had been distilled through a charred oak barrel that had been burnt

inside another barrel. The liquor sat in an abandoned mine for twelve years. To Maxi

Pierce, there existed no finer whiskey on earth. He got a gallon every year when his

buddy would make a new batch. Ol' boy down Pinetop way, if he didn't know you or

like you, you couldn't buy this liquor at any price. The big towns and stores might get the

best of the hill younguns but a lot of the old ways had been lost. They'd never get all the

good liquor. It was a dying trade, though. No money in it like there use to be.

Everybody was growing dope. Got all the kids hooked on the shit. Hell, his own brother

was on the pot. Probably a lot of other stuff as well, stupid shithead.

Maxi sat and drank. The more he drank the madder he got. Sometime around dark,

he decided he had enough thinking. He needed to do something. He thought he might

take a walk and visit an old neighbor. Hell, he might oughter offer his condolences.

Better take his Remington just to be careful. A lot of accidents around these parts lately.

He stepped off the porch whistling. The tune was a cheery one.

Maxine began humming it herself. It seemed to her the whole world had become

infected with happiness. She knew somehow her Uncle Jimmy was responsible.

Jimmy Pierce had certainly brought a little joy into the heart of one Sheriff Arnett Boswell. Preliminary test on the corpse of the fat girl from the boonies had matched sperm samples from the bodies dragged out of the strip pit. Further investigation had placed the big ol' gal at the Deuce on Saturday and a couple of other night spots. Unfortunately the old girl had been busy. He now had a list of suspects. It was just a matter of time now. Election day might not be so bad after all.

He figured he might want to check these guys out himself. It was obvious all his Deputies were worthless.

"Gawd," he could remember being a man. It seemed so long ago. He wasn't sure he would even recognize one. The Sheriff had narrowed his field. He knew at least one person had been involved in at least three homicides. His task now was to find that person. He would have to rely on old-fashioned police work. He would start by finding out as much as he could about where the people had been and who they had talked to. Once he backtracked the days of the victims he would have some idea of who killed three people.

The State Police had sent a team of detectives to investigate the death of their agent. Yardell Stuart had been actively investigating twenty to thirty people in a three county area. Primarily a narcotics agent, he had made buys from a lot of people. He had also dabbled with the trafficking of guns and stolen goods. Criminals were not limited in their range of activities. A man that could provide you with an ounce of cocaine would probably be able to find an M-16 on fairly short notice. In a six-month period, Yardell had enough information to send at least fifty people away for five or more years. These people may get arrested and may even become indicted but out of fifty arrests, no more than five or ten would do any "real time." A few would rat out the rest. Many of these would be dismissed because of witness unreliability or lack of evidence. The main problem with convictions in small communities is no matter how hard you look; it's almost impossible to find an impartial jury. Everyone is only a cousin or in-law or two away from a hung jury and/or mistrial. Out of twenty or thirty cases Yardell was actively working, two or three hundred people are going to be involved as fringe elements upon those arrests. When you get two or three hundred people scared in a region of about thirty thousand, you have got a fair percentage of the population paranoid. Scared people take drastic measures.

The State Police was making little headway in its case. The local law and political machines were not cooperating because they had not known of the presence of an undercover agent. They were scared of what that agent may have uncovered and they had to watch whose toes they stepped on. They had determined that Yardell had been scheduled to race Jimmy Pierce. They had not been able to find Jimmy or his pick-up. They had no reason to suspect Jimmy at this time. Jimmy had not been under investigation by Yardell.

Most people in the local community had very little dealings with Jimmy. He was bad for business. He could make big scores two or three times a year but he was not dependable enough for regular trade. A lot of criminals operate on a trust basis. A man's word was only as good as his last deal. Most people think drugs are cash and carry. Usually dope is "fronted out" for a certain price with the understanding that more could be had when you made good on what you already had been given. Failure to pay for dope you had fronted would get you cut off. Word would spread quickly that for some reason you had become a bad risk. From that point on, you would have to pay cash. The worst thing you could be if you were a small time dealer was to be cut off. Cutting someone off basically put them back to customer status. Dope made money, lots of money if your habit was such that you could no longer sell enough to pay for what you used, you were pitiful.

Jimmy had never outright burned anyone and he was a known moneymaker as far as cooking dope. Jimmy was no good at dealing. He was constantly short on pay for what he had been fronted. One man holding up the works for everyone. In a business where everyone depended on being paid by the guy below him, a guy like Jimmy could hold up production. Jimmy wasn't actually out of the game. He just wasn't a steady player. Jimmy made a better customer than he did a dealer.

In this particular instance, his instability had worked in his favor. The cops wanted to talk with him but they did not yet believe he had been involved with the death of their officer. The police did believe Jimmy had information about who had run the trooper into the tree. They felt like he had left town to avoid questioning. A statewide search had been launched to find Jimmy. Known associates were being rousted and resentment was building.

Jimmy's friends were getting nervous. It was time for him to relocate. Jimmy had a cunning nature when it came to personal survival. He knew the last thing anyone would expect was for him to go home. He felt the risk was small and he needed to know what his nephew had said. Jimmy still believed that Bobby had given him to the cops. He

planned on killing his nephew before the police could get him in front of a jury. No

witness, no case. Jimmy did not know the body of Big Shirley had been found. He did

not know the bodies had been taken from the pit. He supposed that if Bobby told his

story enough, somebody would look and ask if indeed someone had dumped a car with

bodies in the strip-mine. Jimmy was under the impression that all the cops had on him

was the truck wreck. He was not worried overly much about that. No one had any proof

that he had been involved directly with the crash. The truck itself had ceased to exist.

Jimmy himself would not be able to find that vehicle. It had been chopped up and parted

out.

The fact that the redneck loudmouth had turned out to be a cop didn't bother Jimmy

in the least. He had never dealt with the guy and he knew a lot of guys were going to be

grateful. If he went to trial over the cop's death he would probably be at the most

convicted of reckless endangerment or some driving bullshit. There was no proof of any

premeditation and all he had to do was stick to his story. He had plenty of people willing

to testify he was somewhere else when the event occurred.

Jimmy knew he had obtained a lot of status with the undercover's death. For the

moment, everyone was wary of dealing with Jimmy. He knew that after the bullshit died

down he would be a legend. The underworld would roll out the red carpet for him he

pulled this off. If he went to jail, the population would not fuck with him. He had killed

a cop. He was a hero.

Jimmy knew all these things and he also knew that leaving now would take the pressure off his friends. Jimmy's friends would not say anything but they would understand and appreciate the gesture. Jimmy had always been a minor player, a bullshitter with a little talent for cooking dope. A moneymaker; yes, but not a major bad ass. The class he was displaying by going away and taking the heat off his friends would definitely elevate his status. After this, anything Jimmy asked for would be given without hesitation, as long as he didn't punk out at a late time.

Jimmy had called his niece Maxine. She was a big ol' gal and not too much to look at but Jimmy knew she would die for him if he were to ask. She had good pussy if you could stand to look at her. He kept her happy. She was useful. Most people overlooked other people like Maxine. Jimmy had seen her and people like her as untapped resources, much like Randall Smith's daughters or daughter now.

Hah, hah! Jimmy could give a little smile and slip them some peter every now and again and could get about anything he needed from them. From money to head to fucking a friend. A good ol' fat gal was worth her weight in favors and blowjobs. More loyal than a coondog and easier to train.

Jimmy had called Maxine two days before and had told her to call him when Bobby had come home. She had either lost the number or the boy was hiding. He dialed her number. The phone rang twice and was quickly picked up.

"Hello, who is it?"

"Whoa, hold on a minute."

"Who is this? This is Maxine."

"Well hi baby, what's wrong?"

"Uncle Jimmy, come home please. Daddy's been hurt bad."

"Maxi hurt? Who'd hurt that old fart?"

"I don't know. Ellie came home crying and said that he'd been shot and that she had to go to the hospital. I'm so scared, please come."

"Okay, okay baby. I'm on my way. You ain't told nobody where I'm at have you?"

"No. I ain't told nobody nothin'. Bobby ain't come home. I don't even think nobody's seen him."

"All right darling. Calm down. I'm on my way. You just keep on doing like you doing. Stay quiet as a church mouse and ol' Uncle Jimmy will be home as soon as can be. Can you do that sugar pie?"

"Yes I can do that. Jimmy, I got a secret. You are gonna be so proud. I can hardly wait to show you."

"All right, just hang on you can show me when I get there. I'm sure whatever it is you done good. Okay sugar buns? You gonna be a big girl, right?"

"Yes, Jimmy I'll be as good as gold."

"That's good. You know you're my best girl. I'll be there soon as I can. Love you, mean it."

Jimmy quickly hung up leaving a stunned Maxine sitting staring at the receiver. He had said he loved her. She couldn't remember the last time anyone had said that. She knew he had probably been kidding but he had said it. "Oh! Oh! Oh!" She had never felt so flustered.

Her brother was missing (no big loss), her father was in the hospital (hope he dies) and her uncle had said he loved her. The best part was he didn't even know her secret. He would be so happy. Everybody would be happy.

CHAPTER TWENTY-NINE

Maxi Pierce had been drunk and in a foul temper when he paid his neighbor, Randall Smith, a visit. The entire episode had been a royal fuck up. Maxi had walked up into the yard amidst the clamor of dogs barking. This pissed him off even more because he didn't have any dogs and the asshole responsible still had dogs. "Fuck this," Maxi thought to himself. "I'm gonna shoot something." He leveled his Remington 1100 at the nearest dog. Just as he applied pressure to the trigger, a porch light came on.

"Whose out there?" A voice yelled from the darkness. The Smith family was a bit on edge. They had no idea who had murdered Mary Ann. Randall Smith, himself had not sobered up since he had gotten the news. To make matters worse, the police seemed to think he was the main suspect. He had even been asked for a DNA sample.

"Goddamned bunch of dipshit, asshole, punkass, motherfucking, dickless, cunt slurping, yuppie bastards! Wish I could shoot the whole damned bunch."

Now, here in the middle of the night, someone had disturbed his dogs. "Whose out there? You better answer me or I'll blow yer damned head off."

"Fuck you!" Maxi roared. "You little piece of shit. I wish you would pull a gun."

"Is that you Maxi? If'n that's you, you know this ain't no time for fucking around. My family's a grieving. I ain't a having no more damn pain shoved down our throats."

"You don't know what pain is. You goddamned little piss ant. You done and went and killed the only thing that meant a damn to me and I'm here to settle up."

Randall Smith stood as if slapped. The raw nerve of this yellow cad of a man. "You son of a bitch," he whispered. "You low down, sorry miserable, son of a bitch. You going to stand in my yard, pointing a damn shotgun at me and talk about loss. A few mangy, flea-infested rag tag hounds are blowed up accidentally and I done and paid you cash money for the whole damn lot. There you stand a waving a gun and talking about loss. My sweet thirteen-year-old daughter is laying down there on a slab. Raped, murdered, defiled and discarded like a goddamned wrapper off a cheeseburger and you gonna talk to me about some filthy dogs. Maxi Pierce, you got one damn second to turn around, get out of my yard and don't ever come around me or mine again."

"Fuck you! You damned dog-killing bastard. I'm here to get satisfaction." Having said this he leveled his Remington.

Randall Smith raised his 30-06. He fired one shot that went through Maxi's chest putting him on his ass. "I hope yer satisfied."

Bobby Pierce had no idea that his father had been shot and lay in critical condition. If he had known, he probably would not have cared. Maxi Pierce had been shot Tuesday night. Bobby had been busy stealing more dynamite and detonation cord.

Bobby had decided upon a plan. He would wire the bleacher at the football field by the high school with explosives. His plan would call for him to set said explosives off during the game. He hoped to kill a lot of people with his "bombs." Bobby had also decided to watch the entire thing from the roof of the gymnasium, which overlooked the field. He had three rifles, a 30-06, a 30-30 and an M-16. He had access to other weapons but figured these would be enough for his purpose. From atop the gym he would have full three hundred, sixty-degree field of fire and more than fair cover. Bobby had listened

to his Uncle Jimmy many times talk about setting up fire positions. There were two

access ladders to the gym roof. Bobby would not be able to watch both. He hadn't

worked out all the details but he would. First things first. He needed to place his

explosives, rig an ignition device, set up his fire points and do so without being noticed.

The game would be on Friday. He had two nights to make everything ready. He had not

figured on an escape plan. He wasn't concerned with escape.

Bobby wished he could find his Uncle Jimmy. Things would go so much smoother

with his help.

Jimmy Pierce wished he could locate his nephew. Jimmy was a fool of sorts but

possessed and ingenious talent for self-preservation. He knew, given enough time, the

State Police would link him indirectly with at least two bodies. The dead cop wold be

tricky but no one had seen him run the man off the road. People had seen him with Big

Shirley, but she had been with several men that night. He figured he could get out of that

one.

The only direct evidence against Jimmy was Bobby. The bodies in the strip pit had

been found and Jimmy was scared. He had re-entered the county in an old potato chip

truck. The truck had a mattress, cooler, and several fuck books. Jimmy had driven to the

ridgeline where Bobby had murdered the nigger. He had a clear view of the Pierce

homestead. He would wait for his favorite nephew to appear. He would then eliminate a

problem.

Jimmy had a cell phone with him. He had given Maxine the number so she could call him if she heard from her brother.

CHAPTER THIRTY

Thursday morning found Brandon tired and worried. He could not concentrate. Mrs. Lola Dumphreys had reprimanded him twice for not paying attention. Mrs. Dumphreys' long legs and big breasts usually ensured that at least half her students were listening to her — the male half.

"Brandon, what is your problem?"

"Nothing, Mrs. Dumphreys. I just can't seem to concentrate."

A nerdy voice spoke up from the back of the room. "He misses his little girlfriend."

A deeper voice came back with "He's probably planning on how to help his father kill the town."

Wednesday afternoon had heralded the official announcement of the plant closing. Brandon's father had said it would be okay for him to skip school and that it might even be better if he went and stayed with his mother for a while. People could get pretty ugly when faced with joblessness. You take away a person's livelihood; they sometimes felt they had nothing to lose.

Two men had arrived that morning to "assist" his father with his "evaluation." Their real purpose was to be bodyguards. It would take another week to finish al the details for his father's report and subsequent plant closing. His father had tried to get Brandon to stay home. Brandon had refused because he hadn't been able to get a hold of Ellen. He felt he would be able to reach her at school. Upon arrival, he had quickly determined that she was absent because her father had been shot. Brandon had spent the first two periods trying to come up with some excuse to leave school. The loudmouth had given him an idea.

"Fuck you, Mullins!"

Noise in the classroom came to a stop. The very air in the room seemed to still. Terry Mullins was no loudmouth. His family had lived in town for four generations. The closing of the plant would hurt his family immensely. His father and uncle were both line foreman. He had about twelve aunts and cousins that worked on the lines or on the loading dock. Terry Mullins had a big stake in the plant closing. He was a Junior and a first-string fullback. He did not wish to move.

"What did you say mother fucker?"

Brandon stood and spoke very slowly, accentuating each word. "I... said... 'Fuck... you... Mullins.'"

Terry Mullins jumped over two desks and nailed Brandon in the mouth with a right and followed with a left. The fight lasted less than a minute. No one tried to pull the larger boy from the smaller one.

Lola Dumphreys waited a full thirty seconds before buzzing the Vice Principal's office. This was indeed a factory town and no northerner or his punk boy was going to get any free rides here. Closing the auto parts factory was tantamount to placing the entire county on welfare.

Brandon had expected no less. He had mouthed off to the larger boy with a fight in mind. It was the quickest way he knew to get out of school and to the hospital where Ellen would be with her father. Brandon had not planned on getting three teeth knocked out or a broken nose. Terry Mullins would not be sent home The entire incident seemed to be forgotten. Brandon did get to the hospital and was able to locate lovely Ellen. Ellen sat by his little mechanical bed in one of the garish orange chairs that seemed to grow in hospitals everywhere.

"Nice! You sure ain't no de la Hoya are you?"

"No. I'm more of a lover than a fighter."

"I hope you are cause if you love like you fight, I'm definitely going to need some batteries."

"What?"

"Shh. I'm just kidding. I think it's sweet you getting your ass whipped so you can see me."

"Yeah. How's your dad?"

"He's hurt bad, but Dr. Copeland says he's going to live. He'll be eating through a tube in his belly for awhile but he said he could make a full recovery."

"When will he be able to go home?"

"No way, before Monday. Why?"

"I just wondered. I mean are you going to stay with relatives or something?"

"You horny, naughty boy. I just adore your concern. My poor ol' daddy lying near death and all you can think about is taking advantage of little ol' distressed me."

"No, no, no. I didn't mean anything. I was just hoping you wouldn't have to stay with relatives. I mean, I wouldn't be able to see you."

"Calm down. I'm just playing with you. I'm fine. I'm not going anywhere. I'm going to stay at home with my retarded sister and idiot brother."

"Where is Bobby? I haven't seen him at school in a long time."

"He got in a fight with Vernon. Remember? He got suspended. He goes back on Friday."

"Cool. I guess he's raring to go back."

"Oh yeah. No doubt. I bet he can hardly wait. Everybody will throw a party. Yahoo! Bobby's back. The goober has returned. Maybe they'll throw a party. Yeah, I'm sure. It'll be a real blast."

CHAPTER THIRTY-ONE

Jimmy Pierce awoke from a very pleasant sleep Friday morning. He had been

dreaming of a sumptuous blonde nymph lying naked on a beach of pure cocaine. Little

black girls with platinum nipples that dripped Budweiser stood on either side of Jimmy's

head while an endless line of beautiful teenage girls stood single-file anxiously awaiting

their turn to kneel and engulf his rigid manhood in their tender little vaginal orifices.

From his paradise, he was torn by the incessant buzzing of the cell phone he had

brought with him. The caller was Maxine. Bobby had come home at daylight. He had

been filthy but happy. After a long shower and a quick breakfast he had rushed out to

catch the school bus. Jimmy was ecstatic. His island of sex and dope completely

forgotten. He had been prepared to wait out the day and possibly one more but he knew

his luck was running thin. If he could eliminate Bobby from the picture, he would not

worry about the other murders.

Jimmy, like most egomaniacs, assumed everybody but himself was an incompetent.

He felt with his cunning and smarts no cop in the world would be able to put anything on

him. No witness. No crime. Sorry nephew of mine, but today you must die. Jimmy

stepped out of the truck. It was a beautiful fall morning, just a hint of frost. As he stood

pissing, he started whistling a tune. He could not believe how fine a day it was going to

be. It was a great day to be alive. "Yes sir, a glorious day, a fine day for a murder."

Bobby had finished late on Thursday night. He had expanded his original plan. After

checking his "wish list" of names of people he believed needed to be taught a lesson, he had realized several would not be at the ballgame. He had sat and mulled over his options

and had decided to restructure his original vendetta to include these individuals. His

original plan had called for one big explosion during halftime activities. Bobby knew that

in all likelihood not all of his bombs would explode. That was the reason he had planned

on sitting atop the school with rifles. He would snipe at the stragglers and survivors.

Aside from the original three rifles, Bobby had rounded up materials to barricade himself

on the roof. He had cement blocks and sandbags a plenty. The roof was a flat tar roof

with gravel lain on top. When he had seen this, he instantly decided upon the sandbag

idea.

Bobby knew that all survivors would be rushed to the local hospital so he had taken

additional precautions. The hospital had a large propane tank right outside the In-

patient/Out-patient receiving pharmacy. Bobby had placed a timed charge to go off at

midnight. He seriously doubted he would be alive to see it, but the thought of all those

"survivors" getting blown up did his heart good.

The biggest problem with his plan had been figuring a way to fire the charges. A line

of detonation cord and an electric detonator going to all charges would increase the

chance of discovery. He needed some way to blow up the entire bleachers at one time.

His plan had culminated into two placed chargers that he had set the night before along

with the one at the hospital. The chargers were hooked to electric timers and shaped C-4

charges Jimmy had shown him how to use. These were placed on each end of the

bleachers. If they were found, in all likelihood, they would be ignored. They were

wrapped wet soggy bags from the local Burger King. The timers were only good for twenty minutes after being activated. Bobby would have to attend the game to activate

his "babies."

The snack shop at the football stadium also used propane. Bobby had placed twenty-

four sticks of dynamite under the propane tanks. Detonation cord had been run under the

bleachers along the speaker cable wires on each end of the field. A detonator lay beneath

a tackling shed covered with old mats. Bobby hoped the dynamite would go off from the

first two charges. If it did not he would have to detonate it manually.

The bomb at the hospital was a work of art. His Uncle Jimmy had made several like

it with mini-charges and had blown up various things around the farm. Everyone knew

Jimmy was nuts and liked to play with bombs. Bobby hoped Jimmy didn't get blamed

for any of his doings. He was not overly concerned because his Uncle Jimmy was a killer

and had deserted him.

The only bomb Bobby had complete confidence in was a gasoline bomb he had

placed on the roof of the gymnasium. This bomb was to be lit by a wick consisting of an

M-80 firecracker taped to a gallon can of Coleman Lantern Fuel. Atop the can he had

placed two cement blocks. This device was to cut off one access point to the roof.

Bobby wasn't sure he could go through with any of this madness. He figured if the

first two blasts went off he would follow through with the rest. Bobby had decided all

this on Thursday. Friday morning he went home, got cleaned up, ate and went to catch

the bus. As he approached the bus stop he could see his old friend, Vernon.

Bobby let the day unfold as a normal day. With each insult, imagined or real, his

resolve strengthened. He knew Vernon would be sitting down on the bench because his injury would not allow him to play. He had placed one charge directly behind the team bleacher.

"Good luck, Vernon. Have a nice day. Burn in hell fuckface."

Ellen had decided to ride the bus to school but not to attend class. She had needed a ride to town in order to meet Brandon. They had decided to spend the day together after he got released. The hospital had insisted he stay over night but his father had agreed to pick them up at noon. He did not want Brandon walking around alone. He had tried to press charges but the local police were not too supportive. It seemed that four or five bodies were floating around and they needed to give them their highest priority.

Bobby hadn't realized the police were anxious to see him. People at school assumed that they had seen him and the police had decided they were never going to see him. Somehow he went the entire day without being questioned.

Jimmy Pierce had come down from the mountain. His day was getting better. Not only had he found his nephew, he was pretty sure the boy hadn't told anyone, anything. Maxine had been tickled to death to see him. She kept telling him she loved him and giving him big hugs and little kisses. She had cooked him a huge breakfast of pancakes, sausage, biscuits and gravy, coffee, milk and a spot of good corn liquor to spice the coffee with. She kept giving him sidelong glances like she was the fox in the hen house. He felt so good he didn't even get aggravated. He kept sipping until about one o'clock and decided to take a little nap. He let Maxine "nap" with him. Throwing the dog a bone if you will. "Hah, hah. Yes sir. A glorious day."

Brandon and Ellen were finally alone. His father had returned to work after making Brandon promise not to leave the house. An "assistant"/bodyguard stood outside the deck playing with a Gameboy when not playing with himself.

"You got a nice house."

"It's just rented."

"I know that. I also know one or ones your dad owns are probably a lot nicer. I like you Brandon. I like you a lot. Most boys would be trying to build themselves up right now. You play down your money and your material things. It doesn't matter either way. I like your smile. I like your eyes. I have since the first time I noticed you with those crusty panties in your hands.

Brandon blushes but smiles.

"We are alone Brandon. If you want me, I'm yours. I know you'll be leaving soon and that I will probably end up married to some numb nuts because I forgot a pill one Friday night. It doesn't matter. I want you to be the guy I tell my daughter about when she gets older. I want you to be my sad, misty could've been, should've been. Make love to me. Give me a strong, honest, sweet and pure memory to carry me through. You're a good guy and you'll probably wind up with some sneaky little showpiece of a wife that you won't be able to stand. You'll probably fuck her friends while she fucks yours and you'll own all kinds of things but you'll always have a what if? Let me be your what if. Let today be about two people who just care about each other because they do. Let's make no plans or promises. Hold me, love me and keep a little place for me in your heart. Cool?"

"Cool? Cool."

"Don't fuck it up. Just kiss me."

So he kissed her and the afternoon flew by for the young lovers.

Bobby's afternoon was not near as sweet. Every time he would begin to doubt his course of action, some asshole would provide the motivating element needed for him to proceed with his "wish list" of death. He had planned to warn his friends to stay away from the game. He discovered there was no need. He had few friends and none of them ever attended football games. This should have been a good thing but it just brought home how pitiful his life had become. He did feel the need to warn his sister, Ellen. She sometimes went to ballgames. She was no fan or organized athletics and showed no interest in jocks. There just wasn't anything else to do. Since Steven Eurkel had left "TGIF," Fridays were a bummer.

"What time does that bus run, Maxine my queen?" Jimmy asked his chunky, not un-pretty niece at about two, forty-five.

"They usually get home about three –fifteen. Why?

"Oh, nothing much…. Just need to speak with that nephew of mine is all."

"Oh. Okay Jimmy." Maxine spoke tentatively.

"Yeah girl, what's on your mind?"

"I got a secret."

"Well, good for you. What about that? Maxine, my queen has got herself a little ol' secret. What is it? No wait let me guess. Ed McMahon done and brought you ten million dollars for buying *Mad* magazine?"

"No. It's better'n that," she blushed. The girl practically shined with joy.

Jimmy almost felt a slight attachment to the girl, real feelings for his evil ass.

"Better'n ten mil? Damn girl, what you got a gold pussy that squirts champagne?"

"No. I ain't even never heard of such."

"You ain't? Shit now, stop teasin' and tell ol' Uncle Jimmy what you gots that's so special."

"I'm gonna have a baby."

"Damn! No shit! Well lord a mercy. Whose the buck done and been sporting my best gal?"

"Nobody's been sporting me 'cept 'n you. I'm having your baby.

On any other day this news would have gotten Maxine smacked in the mouth and probably kicked down some steps. Jimmy's attitude about kids was not what you'd call Christian.

"Well girl, that's fine. I ain't gonna say it ain't. Just let me tell you something. You better never let nobody, and I mean no damn body know that it's mine." Jimmy twisted the girl's wrist as he spat the words between his teeth.

The girl, a fountain of love and joy a moment before, leaked tears and whispered as she looked into her lover/uncle's eyes. "I won't say nothing. Don't you love me no more Jimmy?"

A brief flash of mercy or pity, ignited inside the sick, infected heart of Jimmy. His tone softened and his grip loosened. "Yeah, queenie, Maxinie. I love you fine. You just remember you don't know who the daddy is. Okay?"

"Sure. I knows I can't say nothing about love. Plus my friend, Henrietta gots a baby and she tolt she didn't know the father and she gets a check every month."

"Damn girl! Whoever said you was dumb? You a damn site smarter'n I ever thought. What you plan on doin with a check every month?"

"Whatever you wants me to, I guess."

Jimmy's heart softened. "Damn girl, this day just gets better and better.

The school bus ran and nobody got off. Jimmy started to get surly. "Where the fuck is that boy?" he growled.

"I don't know. He's always on the bus. Daddy gets mad if he don't get right home and water the dogs."

"What dogs, you stupid cow?" Jimmy raises his hand as if to strike.

Maxine stiffens. "I'm sorry. Don't be mad."

At that moment the phone rings. Jimmy grabs her by her shoulders. "Answer it. If it's anybody but Bobby tell them you're by yourself. If it's Bobby, let me talk with him."

"Okay." Maxine picks up the phone. "Hello, who is it?" she chimes.

Bobby answers on the other end. "It's me, Sissy. Is Ellie home? I need to talk with her."

"No. She's probably visiting Daddy. Bobby there's somebody here wants to talk at you."

"Who?" Jimmy takes the phone. "Hello," he says in a deep smooth announcer-like voice. "How's my boy?"

"Jimmy!" Bobby exclaims.

"Shh. Shhh."

"Where you callin' from?"

"Oh, sorry. It's okay, ain't nobody around. I'm using an extension in the Counselors'
office. I got two weeks of homework assignments she's gonna give me. She says I will
have to make it up or fail a half year."

"Huh, well you get that homework boy. I need you to get on home, now. Me 'n you
got some talking to do."

"I can't Jimmy. I don't have a way. Can you come and get me?"

"Listen up, boy. I'm a little hot right now but I can meet you. Walk down to Beaties
old store off River Road. If I ain't already there, wait for me."

"Sure. It's great to hear your voice, Jimmy. I got something great cooking, Jimmy."

"That's good boy. I'm damn happy for you. You just make damn shore you're there.
Don't tell nobody nothing. Okay?"

"Sure, Uncle Jimmy I know when to keep my lip zipped." That was an expression
Jimmy used.

It softened Jimmy a little. "Damn I'm gonna miss that kid," He thought to himself.

Jimmy felt a hand on his crotch. Maxine fell to her knees and was unzipping him.
Jimmy looked down. He unbuttoned his trousers with his right hand. He hung up the
phone with his left. He cupped the back of his niece's head with both hands. He closed
his eyes and leaned his head back as she engulfed him. "What a day! A fine day!"

Bobby arrived behind Beaties store at four-fifteen. He did not see Jimmy at first. He
had expected to see the little Ford Ranger but instead he was confronted with an old

Lance potato chip truck. Jimmy's buddies at the crank farm had come up with the

vehicle. It was ideal because it stood out so bad that no one noticed the driver. The

plates were still good and the sides had been white washed but the old insignia shown

through,

"Nice truck," Bobby said and meant it. The boy had an affinity for old vehicles.

"Yeah, I like it. Hell, she's an automatic."

"Bullshit!"

"Yeah, you're right, but she ain't hard to drive."

Bobby stepped up into the vehicle. He noticed the mattress.

"Damn man, this has everything."

"Yep, friend of mine used this truck to follow The Dead," Jimmy lied easily,

thoughtlessly.

Bobby could tell Jimmy was lying a red flag went up on his head. Anytime Jimmy

went to the trouble to lie to Bobby, he knew his uncle wanted something.

Bobby asked the older Pierce, "What? What's on your mind?"

"Well, boy it seems to me you been pretty busy while I been out of town. You ain't

been talking out of turn have ye?"

"Jimmy, I ain't said shit about shit. I got as much to lose as anybody."

Jimmy believed the boy but that changed nothing. His nephew had always been a

rock. He never changed, predictable and simple. Jimmy didn't trust Bobby anymore

because he couldn't tell what the boy might do. He couldn't just kill him either. He

needed some way to make it look like an accident or somebody else did it. Jimmy's head jerked up. He had been lost in his thoughts about how to kill his nephew and something the boy had said had penetrated.

"What was that boy? I missed something."

"I said, you won't have to worry about nobody asking nobody anything after tonight."

"Oh yeah? Why is that?"

"Because I'm gonna blow all the bastards to hell and probably wind up dead myself."

"Uh huh." Jimmy replied doubtfully. "How do you propose to do that?

Bobby outlined his plan. The more he spoke the more admiration shown on Jimmy's face. Bobby had told him everything except how he had wired the hospital to blow up. He didn't think Jimmy would let him blow up the hospital with his father inside. Bobby certainly had no idea about his Uncle Jimmy and his father's relationship. Jimmy would have been tickled pink to blow Maxi Pierce to hell. He had daydreamed about killing Maxi many times.

Jimmy listened to Bobby's plan and the more he listened to his nephew's vision of vengeance, the more certain he became in believing that Bobby's actions were tailor made for his own needs as well. He formed a plan. He would convince Bobby to let him go along with him on his night of terror. Hell, he would even help shoot people while the boy detonated the dynamite under the propane grill inside the snack bar. They would never be able to tell who or how many people were involved. He would do all these things and at the right moment he would kill his nephew in front of witnesses, of course and stop the carnage. Not only would Jimmy shut his nephew up and cover his own sins, he would be a hero for stopping a psychopath during a mass murder spree.

"Hot damn, this day just keeps getting better."

CHAPTER THIRTY-TWO

Brandon and Ellen had lain in each other's arms until four-thirty. Brandon had broken the spell. His father would be home at five and they had better, at least, be dressed. Ellen had felt the afternoon had been everything she had wanted. She felt to try and draw it out would only taint the beauty of the moment. As she dressed, Brandon started to speak of the future.

"Shh! Don't. I know you ain't leaving right away and that this is probably not the last time we will hold one another. This is the afternoon I wish to carry in my heart. When I'm a wicked old lady with a mischievous glint in my eye. I want this afternoon to be the one that put it there."

"Okay. Do you need a ride anywhere?"

"As a matter of fact, I do. Could you drop me off at the hospital? I want to visit with my father and then I may even go to the football game. I don't want this day to end. Are you coming to the game?" she asked.

"Probably not," the young man replied. "I don't think my father is going to let me go by myself. Plus, I don't cherish the thought of having to have a bodyguard."

"I understand and it's okay. Today was great. If you change your mind, kickoff is at seven o'clock."

"I know. I've been to a couple of games before."

After dropping Ellen off Brandon returned home. His father met him at the door.

"What in the hell do you think you are doing? Didn't I tell you to go no where without Patrick?"

Patrick and Brian were the "assistants" assigned to guard Brandon and his father.

"I just dropped Ellen off at the high school"

"I don't give a shit what you were doing. I told you, not, I said absolutely do not for any reason leave this house."

But Dad... I..."

Brandon never got to finish his sentence. A backhand from his father across the mouth finished it for him. Brandon's parents were not the type to hit. They were talkers, whiners, word manipulators. Brandon could not believe his father had hit him. Without any conscious thought of his own he hit his father back — a quick right to the mouth. His father stumbled back about three steps. The punch stunned him less than the shock. Brandon's words further amazed and befuddled his father.

"I did nothing wrong. I refuse to hide from the world because of your job. I was in no danger. I provoked the fight in school so I could leave and see Ellen. There is a world outside of you and your work. I am sixteen-years-old. When do you want me to make decisions for my own life?

"You just did. You ungrateful little shit. You think you can hit me in my own house. You pack your shit and get the fuck out of my house."

"Where do you want me to go?" Brandon yelled at his father.

"Well, Mr. Big Shot, high and mighty, sixteen year old mother fucker, you decide."

Brandon for the moment stood motionless. He didn't know what to say. His father sneered at him and turned his back toward his only child. Brandon startled by the entire exchange yelled at his father. "Don't forget your babysitters, you old fuck! It's a hell of a life when a grown man has to have other men keep him safe just because he makes his living destroying the lives of people he's never met just for money."

His father turned and looked his son in the eye and said, "You've lived a damn good life off that job. You've never wanted for anything. Remember when you pack the clothes I paid for with that job and ride the little motorcycle that you paid for with a job that I got you because of the contacts I made with that job."

"If you will remember I sometimes save people's jobs. I've kept as many places open as I've closed. My job isn't easy and I take damn little pleasure in closing factories or mills or whatever. The simple nature of the fact is, places like this are being closed because they are mismanaged, poorly run or unnecessary. This town has become complacent. Its citizenry hold me in contempt. I am not biting the hand that feeds me. I do my job and I do it well. If the people in this town had done their jobs with any pride or vigor, they would still have them. You get out of life what you put into it. You get your shit and get. You raised your hand to me so you must feel you are a man. You ever raise your hand to me again and we will fight as equals. No quarter given. From this point on I have no son."

"Fine! I don't need anything."

"I realize that. You will just go live with your mother. Oh! Oh! What a great, big, independent, young man. He beat his father and now he's on his own. Mommy, can I have gas money? Mommy, will you take me to school? Mommy, did the money come from Daddy? You are pitiful, boy, pitiful. Get out of my sight."

Brandon ran from the room. He gathered some jeans and t-shirts and put them into a bag. He took six hundred dollars that he had hidden from underneath the carpet. Grabbing his helmet and keys he left his father's house. He was not mad and there were no tears. He was numb. He felt nothing. He would get Ellen and see if she wished to go with him. If not, he would still go. He and his father had never been close. He could not believe the contempt in his father's voice. He must have been disappointed in Brandon for years. He had always known his father was a hard man, but he had no idea of the depths that his father's dissatisfaction with his son had reached. His father thought him weak and dependent. Brandon had worked, but all his jobs were jobs that his father had found for him. He had never thought about refusing to do these jobs. He realized now that his father would have respected him more if he had just outright refused to work.

Brandon headed for the high school. He could hear the band playing the pre-game warm-up. The players were being ushered onto the gridiron. The announcer's voice rang through the clear autumn air. Town was pretty dead. The only traffic on the roads was a few stragglers headed toward the field. Brandon didn't care for sports. Much like Ellen and others, he attended because that was the only entertainment offered in their small town lives. It didn't really matter who won. People still went to almost all the home games. A winning season would have half the town following to away games as well. The season so far had been a winning one.

CHAPTER THIRTY-THREE

Some concern was being shown because of the loss of their starting quarterback and receiver. Vernon and Freddie had been known as something as a dynamic duo. Freddie would easily have made All State and probably All American. Vernon Price was a good player when playing with Freddie. Without Freddie, he was at best fair. Vernon had ridden Freddie's coattails since Junior High. He had always known it wouldn't last.

He wasn't worried. He could milk the cast on his arm until the end of school. He graduated in May and would go to work in Lexington with his uncle. Vern was riding pretty high. He was slamming ass with Lola Dumphreys and any little cutie that would give it up. Everybody was being extra nice to him because he had lost his best friend. Best of all, everybody was mad at that little, shit, Bobby Pierce. He hadn't believed it when the little shit had shown up at school. He had hoped he had enough balls to come to the game.

One of the greatest joys of Vernon's life had always been beating on Bobby. The entire town had finally seen the light and decided also that they too would have the little shit. Vernon had spotted twerp face's sister earlier. For once she was by herself. He nailed shithead's oldest sister, Maxine, but Miss Priss Ellen thought she was too good for him. It wasn't just him she disliked. It seemed she didn't like anybody.

A few of the dingy tramps that hung out down at the Dairy Queen had said she was seeing the new, nerdy punk Brandon. Little, city fucker. His father comes in and closes Preston down and his little peckerwood, pimple-dicked, faggot of a son tries and scores all the best ass. Normally, Ellen would not rate this high on Vernon's scale. He was half

drunk on 'Boone's Farm Apple Wine' and he hadn't blown a nut all day. He hadn't even

jerked off. Vernon had planned on shoving his pecker up Miss Dumphreys hot little box.

She said her husband would be arriving home tonight and that the would be at the game.

Vernon had laughed. "I ain't never hurt it before. Hell, seems to me the ol' mother

fucker likes licking the mayonnaise jar."

The first time Lola had heard Vernon use the term she had gasped and giggled,

"Licking the mayonnaise jar?"

"Yeah, you know, sloppy seconds. Don't sit there and try and tell me that you don't

run home as soon as I dump a load and straddle his ol' bald head and make him swaller

every drop."

Lola gasped again. This was indeed what she had done on several occasions. The

thought of how nasty she was being had turned her on so much that she had all but

smothered her husband. She had came so hard on these occasion that her husband had

forgotten to ask about the slimy slickness of her cunt.

"Don't be vulgar. It's not that. Our fifteenth anniversary is coming up and I intend

on being extra special nice to my man."

"Oh! Oh! Oh! Excuse the fuck up on out of me. I didn't know Miss Lola was

working toward a new shiny doodad from ol' sad sack."

"Whatever Vernon, however you want to put it. The fact is I'm not giving you any

tonight, maybe never again if you don't stop being so crude."

This little conversation had taken place after lunch in Mrs. Dumphreys' classroom. She had a free period after lunch. Thirty minutes of time was set aside for each teacher everyday in order for them to do lesson plans and grade papers or take care of personal business.

Lately, Miss Dumphreys had been having a lot of personal business, Vernon's. The boy had gotten too cocky and arrogant. She had decided to reel him in a notch or two.

Vernon hadn't liked her remark or its tone. Instead of backing off as she had intended, he had grabbed her by the neck. Fingers entwined in her hair, his face inches from her own, he had snarled, "Listen bitch, I'll take some of this ass if I want." To emphasize his statement, he squeezed her left buttock hard enough to bruise her. "Everybody knows we're getting it on. You try and stop. I'll just have everything exposed. I can see the headline now, 'Jilted Teen Lover Reaps Revenge on Slutty Teacher/Lover.' Shit, we might get on Springer. You might think that you got me pussy whipped, but I get the feeling that after a day or two you'll be calling me. You just give ol' sad sack his little piece of my pussy. Let him buy you whatever it is you got in mind for him to buy. Then you come and get me and be ready to take it up the ass. I'm talking up the ass, dry."

This interchange had the desired effect. Lola was hot and loved being treated crudely. Vernon may only be seventeen years old, but he already knew a whore when he spotted one. He also knew how to treat a whore.

"Damn you nasty little shit. Come on, I've changed my mind. Fuck me, punk."

-244-

"Naw, I want Daddy to get his baby and maybe it's time the teacher got taught a lesson."

Vernon had gotten a kick out of his little power trip at the time. He was now starting to have some regrets. "Shit! Need some pussy. I mean, I need some pussy now!"

While Vernon had been having this deep insight about the unnatural act of turning down pussy, Ellen had been getting a Coke. After getting her beverage, Ellen had decided to walk down to the area cul-de-sac with a slight rise behind the arena and grand stands.

People sometimes snuck into the games by coming over the rise by using the adjoining lot. A graveyard lay above the ball field and it was fairly simple to cut through and over. The games were cheap but that wasn't the point. Sneaking into the game was an event unto itself. Mostly younger kids from junior high or freshman snuck into the games.

The stoners were another group that often took the indirect route into the games. These people being constantly in need of their money for other endeavors. A lot of Ellen's friends were in this group. She figured to sneak up and have a little fun. The kids were always a little paranoid. It was a rare Friday night when somebody didn't get caught by the Assistant Vice Principal and asked to leave. Some of the finest entertainment occurred when people who were asked to leave refused. The law had to be called on more than one occasion. The local toughs didn't seem to mind at all when they were rousted. Very seldom did anyone actually get arrested and the entire episode gave them something to talk about all weekend.

Ellen stopped behind the bleachers. She stumbled and almost fell having tripped over some cable on the ground. "Shit! What the fuck is that?" She looked down at the obstacle. "That's plumb dangerous. Somebody should move that before someone gets hurt."

Vernon had turned at the sound and smiled to himself. An answer to his needs had arrived. Vernon had never been a person to miss an opportunity when it came a knocking. Ellen began her stroll down behind the bleachers. Vernon quickly fell in step behind the young girl, his intentions not completely clear even to himself. He had seen Ellen trip and had chuckled.

"Stupid bitch," he muttered to himself. He glanced at the cable running behind the bleachers.

"What the fuck?" Vernon had helped put the light into the bleachers and knew no cables were on the ground. Coach Fredericks had pitched a bitch when someone had suggested it. "Goddamn insurance liability, son. Them cables got to be run overhead and to code." The school had finally hired an off-duty electrician to do the job. If Vernon hadn't been so intent on his mission, he might have pursued the matter further.

Ellen had heard Vernon behind her. Turning she spoke hesitantly into the darkness. "Who's there? Whose back there?"

The figure continued to bridge the gap between them. Ellen starting to sense something is amiss starts backing away from the approaching figure. Meanwhile the figure picks up speed. Ellen gets ready to turn and run screaming all the way. Before she does, the approaching figure speaks. "Wait up. Hey, Ellen. Wait for me."

Not recognizing the voice immediately because of the friendly tone, Ellen stopped her

retreat. Recognizing Vernon, she relaxed. "What do you want, Vermin?" Ellen had been

calling Vernon, Vermin for years.

Vernon hated it. It was something he really hated. He definitely resented the snotty

little bitch's choice of words and the shitty little tone of dismissal was going to cost her as

well. Vernon may have been undecided in his actions when he started following Ellen,

but with every step and wicked thought he was becoming more decided.

"Where's your pisshead, little brother?"

"Bobby? Why? What have you done to him?" Fear for her brother was overriding

her better sense. Ellen started walking toward Vernon. "If you have harmed one hair on

his head I will rip your fucking guts out. You overbearing fuckhead."

"I ain't even seen the little shit. When I do, I'm most definitely gonna harm him and

it won't be his hair."

"Why are you always picking on him, Vermin? You're twice his size and he has

never done anything to you."

Vernon hearing the hated nickname again, lost it. He backhanded the young girl

across the mouth. She didn't fall but she came awfully close.

"Don't you call me that! You sleazy, little piece of shit. I'll tell you what I got

against your little, punkass brother – the same thing I got against you. You're trash. It's

just like Mama says, trashy little whores like you are worthless. Your whole damn family

ain't nothing but shit heel, hillbilly, redneck trash. You got nerve, whore, calling me

Vermin."

He hits her again. Ellen is laying on the ground. Vernon stands over her, belt in hand. She kicks out and hits the boy's knee. Vernon stumbles and almost falls. His arm being in a sling has him off balance.

"Lie still bitch! Take your fucking medicine." Vernon brings down the belt across her face. It lays her left cheek open and slices her ear. He pulls back to flog her again.

From the darkness, an arm grabs his wrist. "Hold up, dude. That's a chick you're whaling. Ease up man or the cops are gonna be here."

One of the local potheads had heard the noise and had come to check out the disturbance. Seeing a man beating a young girl, the youth had stepped in

The chivalrous gesture was not lost on Vernon. He was not impressed. He was mad. "Who the fuck are you?" Before the boy could answer Vernon spits directly into the young man's face. The boy makes a serious error in judgment. He released the wrist to wipe at his face.

Vernon, never being one to miss an opportunity, swings the heavy belt. He connects with the back of the man's head. Blood flies. Ellen screams and runs. Vernon continues the assault alternating between kicking the boy and lashing him with the belt. The boy is barely conscious. Blood is streaming from the boy's face, hands and arms. Vernon is cussing and spittle is flying from his lips. Two of the boy's friends finally decided to help their friend. One guy grabs Vernon from behind and the other tries to pull Vernon's victim out of his reach.

"Get off me, you fucking potheads."

Vernon and many like him do not see the hypocrisy involved in calling people derogatory names when they themselves do the same things.

He slams his good elbow into the would-be rescuer's head. The punch is fortunate for Vernon. He connects with the guy's nose. Splat! The boy falls to the ground screaming, his nose obviously broken.

Other people from the crowded bandstand start to appear. The scene is confused. A group of Vernon's friends arrive.

"What's up, Vern?

"Yeah! What's going on?"

Again, Vernon displays his knack for seizing the moment. "Nothing I can't handle. Just some pot smoking, white trash, pieces of shit trying to rough me up some. I guess they figured it would be a good time to try me, seein how's I got only one arm to work with."

"Damn, Vern! They jumped you? Bunch of dirty cocksuckers. Three on one. Man, that's low."

The startled dopers were a little late recognizing what was going on around them. A tall, skinny, redheaded boy called Squiggy was the first to take action. He kicked the boy with the broken nose, hard. His steel-toed shitkickers connecting solid into the bleeding boy's ribcage.

"You fucks like fighting three on one? Well, we can play that way. Can't we boys?"

"Damn right."

"Fucking-A."

"You better damn bet ya!"

For the next three minutes the three youths were subjected to a horrible beating. The group of young men and women forming a circle of humiliating pain around them. They were beat, punched and choked by the boys. Most of the girls were content to scream obscenities and throw coke containers and bottles at the hapless youths. The commotion was finally so great that several adults were sent to stop the incident. No one had paid any attention before, figuring it was some ordinary adolescent dispute — two boys fighting over a girl — more bluff and bluster than anything. Unfortunate for the Galahads on this night.

The Vice Principal, upon seeing the condition of the three youths quickly called for an ambulance. The ambulance drivers at first thought the call was a joke. The game had barely started and as far as they could tell no one looked hurt.

"Behind the snack concession. Hurry! We got some people hurt bad."

"How many?"

"At least three. Get somebody back here."

The paramedic crew that sat at the games called for back up. The two young men on duty quickly worked their way through the crowd.

"What the fuck happened to these guys?"

Everybody got quiet.

"I said, what happened?" the ambulance driver yelled.

"What the fuck does it look like? Some punks beat each other up." This from a beefy, greasy-haired kid with scraped knuckles and bloody boots.

A couple of other joined in. "Yeah they were just whalin' on each other. Man we even tried to break them up man. They were wild. Yeah. They must've smoked something really toxic this time."

"What do you mean? Are you saying these young men are on drugs?"

"Fucking-A, man. Those fucking burnouts are always high."

"Is this true, Mr. Albie?" an off duty Deputy asks the Vice Principal.

"I'm not sure. You know how it is. I don't know anything for sure, but I certainly wouldn't want to accuse anyone's children of any wrong doing without all the facts."

"Well maybe I'll just ride with these boys and make sure they aren't up to anything."

The crowd loved it.

Vernon was in ecstasy. He beats up some spindly stoners and not only does the crowd get on his side, they beat the boys. Then the local cops want to arrest the guys he beat up. You got to love it. Life is so fucking good. Nothing could fuck this up. Nothing.

Just as Vernon is concluding this sick and joyous thought a girl screams and falls within inches of his head. He hears the unmistakable sound of a high-powered rifle. The girl is laying at his feet. Blood is gushing out of her abdomen. Shooting continues, more bodies fall. There is mass confusion.

Vernon dives for cover beneath the bleachers. More shots ring out. More bodies fall. Vernon makes himself as small as possible. He burrows deeper under the bleachers. His foot gets tangled in some wire. He yanks hard to get free. His bad shoulder makes it difficult to move. He looked down to see wrapped around his shoes some thin wire. This wire had fallen from atop the speaker poles. The speaker wire was still where it belonged. Vernon briefly remembered Ellen Pierce tripping on something. He also recognized the wire. Vernon's dad and uncles had worked the mines. The cable was detonation cord and he was smart enough to know what that meant.

"There's a fucking bomb here! Oh shit!" Vernon's thoughts were a blur. For once in his life his thoughts included someone other than himself. Lola, he had to get to his precious Lola. He could still hear the sporadic melody of rifle blasts. The firing seemed to be centered upon the entrance gate. A crowd of people were trying to push through. Something was blocking the way. People were clawing over each other to get away from the stinging deadly spray. Many had run in the other direction. A blind panic had taken over the crowd. Mothers and fathers were screaming for their children. Injured children were yelling for their parents. Amidst the confusion, Vernon could see his Lola. She lay slumped next to the snack bar. He started to rise and bridge the short gap between them. He crouched in a sprinter's pose, his good hand on the ground, his bad shoulder and arm tucked tight to his chest. Vernon had a plan. He would get Lola and take her up the hill behind the arena. Others had the same idea. A few had died at the top of the hill. Some had not. Vernon figured he would risk it.

A lot of people were lying very still under cover hoping to wait out the gunman or men as the case may be. They did not know about the detonation cord. Vernon wasn't sure himself but something told him he was right. Just as he started to spring a voice whispered to him, "Hey Vernon, stick around. The fun's just beginning."

Vernon knew that voice. He just couldn't place it. "What the fuck are you talking about?" Turning his head toward the sound Vernon recognized his neighbor and punching bag, Bobby Pierce.

"Get down shit head. Can't you see somebody's shooting people? Besides that I think some sick fuck has a bomb."

Bobby was touched that Vernon was worried about him. If it had come a little sooner, it might have made a difference.

"Really? I don't think you need to worry too much."

"Oh yeah? Well what the fuck do you know?"

"I know this." Bobby places a Colt .357 Python against the back of Vernon's neck. The gun is his father's. He figures he won't be needing it. "Bye, bye fuckhead." Bobby squeezes the trigger and smiles triumphantly as Vernon's head is torn almost completely from his body.

Nothing in Bobby's life has ever felt so right. He hadn't been sure if he was going to activate the timers. Now with the rush of adrenaline that Vernon's murder had provided, he knew he wanted more. Oh yeah. This was so right. His entire life had shaped him for this day.

He quickly located his two bombs beneath the bleachers. He activated them both. He knew his Uncle Jimmy would continue to fire into the crowd at its thickest point. He made his way toward the gymnasium. A few people had also wandered that way, seeking shelter. Occasionally Bobby would shoot somebody if they came into his path. These killings were not out of any malice. He needed to get in position for when the bombs went off.

Bobby had detailed his plan to his uncle that afternoon. His uncle had made a few changes. He did not want Bobby to have a chance to chicken out. Bobby had planned on attending as a spectator. He would wait for an opportunity and then would sneak under the bleachers and activate the timers. He would then sneak over to the gym, climb into position, wait for the bombs to do their work and shoot the stragglers. Jimmy had convinced him that it wouldn't be safe for him to be that visible. Just because he slipped through school unnoticed that day did not mean he would be able to do the same that night. Bobby had agreed. He hadn't liked the idea of trying to go in unnoticed in the first place. He hadn't had a choice. But now he had his Uncle Jimmy and everything was gonna be fucking-a-okay.

The sound of the gunfire had changed. Jimmy had switched to the M-16. The 30-06 must need reloading or maybe it just didn't shoot fast enough. People were still trying to drag friends and relatives to safety. A lot were being dragged toward the equipment room. Jimmy was purposely avoiding shooting in that direction. He was herding spectators like cattle into the slaughter pens. He needed to get into position and give Jimmy the signal. They had a big surprise for the gathered masses of Pineville.

Jimmy was having the time of his life. This was more fun than the Gulf War. He hadn't known any of the people that he had helped kill in the Gulf. There had been greater risk of personal injury. This was easier and more personal. He hadn't realized exactly how much contempt and hate he had for this town and it's inhabitants. Bobby's plan had been perfect for Jimmy's needs. His nephew had been on a suicide mission. Bobby's idea had been to kill as many people as possible after the bombs had exploded. Jimmy had liked this idea but figured it would be easier to set the bombs to explode during the confusion after the shooting had started.

Jimmy had an ulterior motive for having Bobby to go down and set the bombs. He wanted Bobby to be seen. His goal was to blame Bobby for the murders. He hadn't figured out all the pertinent details as yet, but he had always been good at improvisation. His plan involved him, Jimmy, helping to capture the boy, dead of course, along with any accomplices little Bobby used. Jimmy was tinkering with dragging a victim over near the ladder at the exit route. Firing a few rounds using the victim's hands to pull the trigger to insure a positive paraffin test and creating a story. The story would have to include Jimmy trying to stop the murders and hell, he'd probably be a hero.

Everything was working out perfect. Bobby was blasting people left and right. Highly, fucking visible that's what that boy was, highly, fucking visible. Jimmy figured he had killed at least twelve to fifteen people. Thirty or forty more were wounded. The crowd over on the visitor's bleachers were huddled together. Neither gunman had fired toward them. Those stupid fucks probably thought they were safe. Little did they know they were in a world of shit.

Bobby's third bomb placement lay underneath some abandoned tackling sleds and workout equipment. Bobby had said there was C-4 wrapped around twenty-four sticks of dynamite. Jimmy figured with the way the building curved around the 'bomb site' the blast would be projected out toward those bleachers. This would probably have been enough to injure and/or kill fifty to sixty percent of the visiting fans. Seventy to eighty people were currently huddled in the little cul-de-sac right on top of the explosion. Jimmy's only fear was someone might find the device and disconnect it before it could be blown.

Bobby had gained the rooftop. It was time to blow the exit ladder. After picking Bobby up and hearing his plan, the two of them had gone back to the farm and gathered some more equipment. They had gathered more ammunition for all the weapons Bobby had 'borrowed' plus they had picked up Jimmy's pride and joy. Jimmy's M-60 machine gun complete with tripod and three boxes of ammo sat on the roof. They had placed sandbags all around it. It would take a howitzer to blow them all out of position. Jimmy had decided he better not fire the 60. It would leave a distinctive blast residue on anyone's clothes. The ammo for the M-60 was all mercury tipped. Those and others would leave different blast particles. He had told Bobby that he was letting him do the 60 because it was his plan and he deserved the honor. The boy had been elated. Jimmy almost hated having to kill the little maggot. He had such potential. He wished he had discovered Bobby's gift for murder earlier. It wouldn't matter between the two of them they would probably be able to kill two hundred people tonight. They'd be fucking famous if everything worked out like Jimmy hoped. Bobby would be dead and he would be a hero for having stopped the little savage.

If Jimmy somehow got caught he'd be an old man before he got executed. This was the greatest day of his life. It just got better and better.

Gravel flew into Jimmy's face and then he heard a muffled report. Fuck! Somebody

was shooting back. The fucking nerve of that guy. Another shot came even closer than

the first. Jimmy raised his head to see where the bullets were coming from. He located

the gunman just as the man was preparing to fire again. Jimmy's asshole puckered.

"Oh fuck, I'm dead."

The man had been waiting for Jimmy to raise his head. He had him dead to rights.

Jimmy heard a shot and the man's face exploded. Bobby shouted with glee. "I got the

fucker. Pow! Right twixt the eyes. Did'ja see that Jimmy. I plugged him center."

Jimmy was shaken. He hadn't even noticed Bobby's use of his name. He had

dropped the uncle. Unconsciously the boy had become an equal with his uncle. Jimmy

turned and Bobby was holding the 30-30.

"Man the 60, it's almost show time."

Jimmy had the firing mechanism for the dynamite. He had gotten Bobby to sneak

down and splice the det cord. He had run an additional fifty yards and attached a

claymore firing mechanism. Three clicks on the clicker and BOOM, the bomb would

explode.

He hoped the resulting panic would send everyone racing back toward the other

bleachers. The timers would be ready to fire the explosives planted underneath. Bobby

brought the sixty-caliber machine gun to life. He fired a long burst of about twenty

rounds into a huddled mass of schoolmates. "There goes the band," he shouted in joy.

"Watch out, you little shit. You're going to blow that weapon."

"Sorry," Bobby grinned sheepishly. He knew better. A 60 could fire all night if you maintained low, steady fire. Six to nine round bursts. Long bursts would melt the barrel and render the weapon useless. He began choosing his targets more wisely. People were falling all over the place.

"Get ready," Jimmy yelled to Bobby. "I'm going to let her blow."

Both killers ducked for cover behind the sandbag bunkers they had built for that purpose. Jimmy clicked the charger once, twice, thrice. At first nothing happened. "Shit, you little fu…"

BOOM, BA BOOMS. The blast was magnificent. A fireball exploded outward into the night. Jimmy's hope that the school walls would funnel the blast toward the visitor section worked perfect. Bodies flew apart. Limbs and bits and pieces rained down upon the roof. Shrapnel from the blast had acted like a shotgun blast. A gigantic wave of death and terror engulfed the visiting end of the school. The electronic scoreboard had blown over and landed on a fat lady's chest. She lay crushed beneath it, splayed like shish-ka-bob.

The air was thick with the acrid stench of smoky death and gunpowder. Jimmy sat staring at the confusion. Bobby had maintained enough presence of mind to start blasting again with the M-60. He let fly with two long bursts and then a short. The boy was a killing machine. Jimmy smiled. There had had to be at least a hundred people dead from the single blast. At this rate, he wouldn't have to kill Bobby. There wouldn't be anybody left to say who had done the damage.

"Where were the cops?' Jimmy could hear the sirens — fire engines. He knew the
National Guard wouldn't be here right away. He had expected more trouble than this.
Jimmy regained his focus and started firing into the crowd again. He chose his targets by
the degree of terror he witnessed upon their faces. The more scared a victim seemed was
more reason to shoot that person. Jimmy's thinking went along the lines that he was
doing them a favor. He didn't want them to have to sit and be terrified. A sort of
kindness was how Jimmy would have put it, if asked.

Bobby stopped firing the M-60. He yelled at Jimmy, "Get ready, the bleachers are
gonna blow any second!"

By this time the crowd was in blind panic. A lot of people had escaped and were
trying to get assistance to those hurt or hiding. Everyone was assuming the bomb to be a
singular event. Ambulances were arriving with paramedics and life squads already
attending to the injured. Jimmy had taken to shooting anyone he had seen giving aid to a
fallen victim.

The bleachers were swaying back and forth from people falling and bumping into
them. The bombs erupted within seconds of one another. To people standing out of the
blasting area, the bleachers appeared to be bubbling in a cauldron and suddenly they just
erupted. The earlier blast had caused blind panic. The second blast had people too terror
stricken to move.

Bobby's knack for carnage once again outdid itself. The misery and bloodshed would
take days to dig through. The bombs had been placed in such a way that caused the ends
of the structure to lap over each other. The blast spread toward each other meeting in the

middle. Some people were blown to bits. Metal cross braces had been blown clean

through bodies and limbs. A girl of about thirteen stood in a delicate pirouette. Frozen in

a study of grace and elegant anguish. Dust rose in a torrent. People ran blindly, tripping,

falling. The screams of the injured and dying carried through the night, echoing madness

and pain.

Bobby and Jimmy sat atop the gymnasium firing into crowd. They couldn't pick their

targets clearly. They fired at flashes of limbs or torsos. The scene looked like something

out of Dante's ninth circle.

Bobby swept the scene with the M-60. He had gotten into a semi-trance. He was

drunk with power. He felt invincible. Nothing could stop him. This night was the night

that the meek sought their inheritance. The world might not be his, but he sure as hell

ruled Pineville High's Friday night Double A football game.

"Lord, yes," Jimmy was thinking it was time to make his move. He wanted to make

sure his nephew got blamed for everything and that he (Jimmy) hadn't done anything but

try and stop the boy.

"Let's go down and see who we're shooting."

Bobby agreed. He cherished the idea. "We can walk around and put them out of their

misery." Visions of putting people down like animals at the slaughterhouse danced

through his head. He was positively giddy with delight. The hurt, frustrated adolescent

had completed a sick metamorphosis. He was now a raving, homicidal maniac. Little

chance of salvation remained. Bobby had given himself to the darkness completely.

Jimmy had retained enough of his own meager supply of humanity to want to escape the situation without consequences.

Before either Jimmy or Bobby could make a move to resign their position atop the gymnasium, shots rang out inside. Bullets ripped through the ceiling. Someone was firing through the roof. They were trying to hit them blindly. The duo seemed shocked. Somehow they had come to the conclusion that they were the only people in town allowed to shoot at people. Destiny had somehow given them free reign over terror and somehow they had a monopoly.

No one had told Arnett Boswell. The Sheriff had been on the outskirts of the county trying to track down the whereabouts of one, Jimmy Pierce. He had somehow pieced together information he had with information the FBI had given him. His conclusion had been as much drawn on instinct as research. One man's name kept coming up in all the investigations. Jimmy Pierce was connected to the fat bitch found in the cabin. He had been earmarked to race the state trooper. A Pierce had found bodies in the strip pits. Jimmy had been out of town all week. Conveniently out of town, if you asked Sheriff Boswell.

The radio had broadcast an emergency alert for all units. Something about an explosion and gunfire at the football game. He was about to ignore it thinking it was probably some kids firing M-80's and shooting squirrel guns in the parking lot. Responses started coming across the frequency. Emergency vehicles were requested from three counties. Boswell knew something bad was wrong. Those units would be paid out of the county budget and that meant people were hurt. This was no prank or teenage hijinx. Something was bad wrong. Something told him in his gut that punk Pierce was involved. "I'd bet my last dollar."

Arnett reached the school just as dust was starting to settle. He could hear machine gunfire as well as a high-powered rifle. People were running around without any purpose. Everyone had a dazed look. They looked like people in photos from war torn countries, refugees from some conflict in some third world coup. Boswell got out of his vehicle. He spotted one of his deputies standing amidst a crowd of confused onlookers. They were looking toward the roof of the gymnasium.

"Hawkins! What the fuck are you doing?" Boswell's voice cut through the night.

As the decisive tone rang in his ears, the deputy's eyes came into focus. He shook confusion off his shoulders like an old shawl. "They're on the roof. The shooters are on the roof."

"Well, why in the fuck are you standing here looking at them? Get these people out of here! Do some damn crowd control. Don't they teach you dip shits anything, anymore?"

"There's people dead out there!"

"Yeah? I kinda figured that. Get those people moving. Set up a perimeter. Surround that building! Make sure those bastards up there don't come off that roof and try to blend in with all this confusion."

The deputy looking sheepish replies, "Yes, Sir!" His face coming alive, shock dissipated, as he gained purpose.

Boswell thought to himself, "Is this the kind of men we have in this world today? Lordy, help us."

He went to the trunk of his car. He retrieved a twelve-gauge pump assault shotgun, some ammo and his own personal 30-30 deer rifle. He kept the rifle in the car for killing injured deer or any other varmint that found itself crippled on the highway.

Arnett Boswell had given up most of his self respect while in office as Sheriff. He seldom looked in the mirror anymore. His job was an elected position. Being a politician had not sat well with him for a long time. The people in the community had lost respect for him as a man. This night, Arnett knew, would make him or break him. He knew his days as Sheriff were done. His goal now was to regain some sense of self worth.

Upon entering the gymnasium, Boswell has been able to locate the gunmen easily. He could hear the thud of the M-60 as it shattered into the night. The gunman or gunman, he wasn't for sure, were not trying to hide their whereabouts. He got underneath the sound, aimed the 30-30 at the spot where he felt he could do the most damage. Arnett fired three rounds going from left to right. He stepped back three steps and turned half-right and fired three more. He took shells from the boxes he had bought, reloaded and moved about sixty feet further down. He could hear movement from the roof. He got on his radio.

"Turn off all the damn sirens. I got the sumbitch trapped."

"How the hell you do that?" A voice came over the radio.

"Because I'm in the fucking gym underneath the fucking roof. Get some people to cover the ways off that fucking roof. Secure the area. Get everybody out of the area.

Whoever is up there has got to come off sometime. When that happens all we got to do is be waiting on the ground."

Jimmy had to smack Bobby to get him to calm down. The second trio of shots from Sheriff Boswell's deer rifle had been close. One round had burned across Bobby's ankle. Luckily for him, he had on a pair of his uncle's combat boots. A finger wide groove had been dug neatly from the smooth surface of the boot. Jimmy had jumped clear as soon as the first three rounds had stopped. He had seen the next three come through the roof. He had calculated the angle and fired back. His 30-06 was a bolt action, so his return fire was slower but more paced. He spaced the shots evenly, walking the width of the building.

Bobby had freaked out. The mighty killer had doubled up into a fetal position and started screaming. Jimmy had grabbed the boy and smacked him across the cheek and then with a backhand.

"Stop it! Chill out. You ain't hurt, you little shit. We got to get off this rooftop. Somebody down there has pulled their head out of their ass and we gots to git a'fore it becomes something catching. Hell, ain't hardly nobody left to shoot at anyway. They's all hid or dead. The good 'uns done runned off. I'm going over to the other side of the roof. I'm gonna make some noise. When that bastard shoots at me, you watch where the bullets come out of the roof. You walk that 60 back and forth till I tells you to stop."

"I... I... uh d-don't know, Jimmy. What if, what if he shoots me again?"

Bam! Jimmy knocked Bobby on his ass. "Listen up, you little shit! You said when you come up here you was planning on dying. We gonna kill this mother fucker. If you don't do exactly like I say, I'll shoot your chicken shit, little ass."

The sirens suddenly stopped. In the distance some still wailed. Units were still responding. The only sounds were from the wounded and the concerned.

Arnett Boswell waited patiently. He hoped his dumbass deputies had done as he asked. If the building was secure on the ground, he knew it was just a matter of time. Boswell had one concern. "What if there was more bombs?" He needed to catch this fucker or fuckers. The more he considered it; the more certain he became. There was more than one person on that roof. He had heard at least two different weapons firing when he arrived. Shit! There could be a whole slew of people involved.

The Sheriff got back on the radio. "Did anyone see anything on the ground? Do we have any idea who we got on that roof?"

A multitude of people tried to respond. Boswell tried to clear the confusion. "Will someone from my office please get their ass in here with me?"

Jimmy made his move. He stepped as quickly as he could across the roof. Taking a sandbag in his left hand, he lobbed it toward the position Bobby had vacated. Holding the rifle in his other hand, he ran across the roof.

A shot rang through the night. A bullet cut through the ceiling right in front of him. He dove right and barely evaded being killed by his nephew. Bobby had done exactly as he had been told. He had waited until Jimmy had drawn fire, then he had answered it. It was Jimmy's turn to be scared and shaken. Bobby kept firing and firing.

Jimmy shouted at the boy. "Move! Move! You dumbass. Don't stand in one spot."

Arnett Boswell was hurt. The first shot that Jimmy had fired had ricocheted off a

steel support girder in the ceiling of the auditorium. The bullet had lodged in his thigh.

He had returned fire and had even retained enough sense to walk the bullets in a pattern.

He quickly emptied the 30-30 and grabbed the shotgun. The weapon was loaded with a

combination of buckshot and flechette rounds. Every third round was flechette. These

were little dart shaped projectiles. There were nine in each round. They were very

deadly. Whoever was on the roof had certainly gotten lucky with that first shot. All they

had to do was wait and pinpoint his location. He couldn't move.

Bobby didn't know his opponent was unable to move. He continued to work the

automatic weapon back and forth across the rooftop, just as he had been told.

Boswell quickly noted that whoever was firing was not moving their position. He felt

that it must be some kind of trap. No one could be that stupid. But just maybe, in the

heat of the moment, somebody lost their good survival sense. He hated to reveal his

position but he had to take a chance. He emptied the shotgun at the area he guessed the

killer to be located.

The first two rounds blasted into the ceiling, making fist-sized holes. The third round

took out a larger chunk and suddenly the gun from above went silent. Boswell emptied

the remaining six rounds in a spiral pattern working counter-clockwise outward from the

third round he had fired.

The third round had hit Bobby's calf. It was the same leg that had been shot before.

He had thrown the M-60 down and grabbed his injury. The flechette dart had pierced deep, but the wound was far from fatal. The seventh round from Arnett Boswell's shotgun was the one that killed Bobby. The fifth and sixth had cleared a three foot section of roof. The seventh round came through the opening with unobstructed force. It struck Bobby at the base of the spine and tunneled upward. One of the 32 caliber buckshot pellets lodged in Bobby's heart.

Jimmy watched his nephew's demise with little emotion. He had noticed the bullets had all come from one spot. Somebody had become overanxious or else they were unable to move. Whatever the reason, Jimmy Pierce was not one to miss an opportunity. He leveled the 30-06 and emptied it into the gymnasium. His aim was good but not fatal. The third round struck the shotgun that Arnett Boswell held. The bullet bounced off the wooden stock and tunneled up Boswell's forearm and lodged underneath the armpit. He could not move his right arm. Every time he moved, he screamed with pain. Neither the rifle or shotgun were within reach. He still retained his service revolver. The problem was, he couldn't shoot for shit with his left hand.

Jimmy knew time was running out for him. He needed to get off the roof. He grabbed two of the smoke grenades from the full sack that Bobby had stolen. His hope was to cause a cover dense enough so as to enable him to sneak down the ladder. He inched toward that side of the roof and looked down. The view was not to his liking. Two officers were on the ground below. A third was inching up the ladder. Jimmy hesitated, and then took aim. He fired two shots. The first knocked the man from the ladder. The second spread his brains across the tarmac. The two remaining officers turned and ran. They dove behind a dumpster.

Jimmy, sensing an operative moment was at hand, lobbed two CS grenades in their general direction. He fired the remaining rounds in the 30-06 at the dumpster. No return fire ensured. Jimmy took a deep breath, exhaled and leaped over the rooftop and placed his boots on the outside of the ladder. He slid down the ladder much like a man sliding down a banister. The act was done on pure adrenaline.

Jimmy's gloves were made of cloth. They were the type purchased at flea markets. Five pairs for three dollars. They quickly turned to tatters. The skin underneath blistered. The ground jumped up and smacked Jimmy hard. His ankle turned beneath him. It hurt like hell.

Jimmy knew he had to get out of there before the gas cleared. He could hear the officers behind the dumpster. He threw the gun at the dumpster when it clicked empty. He regained his feet and limped away. The darkness encircled him like an old friend.

Arnett Boswell noticed smoke coming through the hole in the roof. He had no way of knowing the residue was from a smoke grenade. He knew he did not want to die in a fire. To escape being burned alive, he made a decision. He got on the radio and announced, "The building is on fire. I am trapped. I cannot get out. Do not send anyone after me. I will be dead. Tell Verna, I died a man." He then placed the barrel of this service revolver into his mouth. It was awkward to cock with his left hand. His body would be one of the last found.

CHAPTER THIRTY-FOUR

Brandon had spotted Ellen running out the gate before the first blast. He had fallen in step behind her. "Wait a minute. What's up?"

Ellen, not recognizing the voice had turned and glared at Brandon.

"Oh, it's you."

"Yeah, it's me. What's wrong? Where you going?"

"Oh, it's nothing. Just the same old shit. Some big jock fuck trying to play stud. I hope he gets his ass kicked. Can you take me home?"

"Sure! I sorta got nowhere I gotta be anyway."

"Why? What's happened?"

"Ah! I got into it with my dad. He kicked me out."

"Over me?"

"No, not really. Apparently my father hasn't liked me for some time. You just seem to be one more in a series of my failures."

"Is that what you think?"

"No! Hell no! I didn't mean it like that. Hell, I love you."

A silence ensued. "You love me? Are you sure?"

"Yeah, I guess I am"

Bobby had seen his sister run out the front gate. This cleared any doubt for Bobby. He could now pursue his chosen course of action to whatever end the fates saw fit. He noticed his sister had been running. Having been a victim most of his life, his first instinct had been to look for signs of pursuit. Further investigation led him to his old friend, Vernon.

Bobby, much like his Uncle Jimmy, knew this was his lucky day. Before Bobby could get to his friend Vernon, who seemed to be involved in some kind of fight, two coaches accosted him. Head Coach, Tony C. and Assistant Coach, Big Carl stopped Bobby in mid-stride. Bobby had always hated both men. They represented everything he wasn't. He was weak. They were strong. Carl, the weight training coach caught the first bullet of the night. It slammed into his larynx and out the back of his head. The last words from his mouth were his killer's name. Coach Cobin, Girls Basketball Coach, dove for cover. Bobby fired twice more before finally killing the man. A couple of people had seen what had transpired. They stood in shock, not believing their eyes. Bobby calmly reloaded his pistol and returned his attention to Vernon. We know Bobby's night from that point.

Ellen, meanwhile, had heard the gunshots. She had recognized them for what they were. "That's not good. Somebody's got a gun."

Brandon was quick to reply. "Nah. That's probably fireworks."

"No, those were gunshots. I don't know what's going on, but I'm pretty sure it isn't good."

"Well, let's get outta here."

"Sure. But what if it is gunshots?"

"I don't know what you mean?"

"Are we just going to leave? What if somebody's hurt?"

"I guess they'll bleed or die. I'm not a doctor and you're not a nurse. I personally don't care if the whole damn place goes up in flames and all these useless people with it."

"Oooh, down boy. What's got you so evil with the world?"

More shots were being fired and people were screaming.

"Something is going on, something bad. Let's get while we still can. I think it's about me."

"How so?"

"Vernon Price was trying to get with me and I screamed. A couple of stoners got him off me. I ran away but Vernon's got a lot of friends."

"Did he have a gun or something?"

"No, he didn't. But somebody does."

"Where do you want to go?"

"I don't know. Home, I guess."

"Okay. I'm parked over here."

The couple headed out toward the parking lot. Before they could leave, people started streaming out the gate, screaming.

"Something is going on. Something bad."

A young girl, Ellen knew, came running by. "Karen! Wait up, Karen! What's wrong? What's going down?" She grabbed the girl's arm. The action spun the teenager around.

Recognition replaced terror in the girl's eyes. "You should know. It's your brother. Isn't it?"

"What? My brother, what? What's my brother done?"

"He's killing people! He's got a gun and he's shooting people. I hope they kill him. I used to like him but he was always so creepy. I hope he dies and you too. I hope your entire family rots in hell." Having had her say, the young girl emphasized her feeling by spitting in Ellen's face. She then turned and ran.

Ellen and Brandon stood transfixed. The entire experience was unreal. They could hear more gunshots. A second gun was firing now – the machine gun that belonged to her uncle.

"I know that sound. That's my Uncle Jimmy's gun. He brags about that gun all the time. Oh my God! It's true. Something really fucked up is happening. My asshole, little brother has flipped out. He's got a machine gun and he's killing people.

"No way!"

More people came streaming out the gate. Bullets were going through car windows and ricocheting around the parking lot.

"We got to get out of here. Whoever is shooting is good."

People were falling everywhere. A young boy of about eight years of age stood crying at the gate. His mother lay slouched beside him. He clutched her lifeless hand as he yelled. A bullet smashed through his little chest silencing his bellowing once and for all.

"We got to stop him. They'll kill him. He's my brother. We got to try." Ellen pushed against the crowd. Just as she neared the gate the first explosion roared through the night. A piece of metal that acted as a support arm for the bleachers spun lazily through the air. It stopped suddenly when it slammed into Brandon's back after glancing off Ellen's head.

The girl was knocked unconscious and Brandon had the wind knocked out of him as well. He recovered quickly. The amount of blood pouring from Ellen's head scared him. He decided to take her to the hospital himself. He gathered her in his arms and carried her to his motorcycle. The act of riding would be difficult with the girl's dead body weight but he had to do it. He placed her on the bike in front of him and strapped her arms to the handlebars with a length of bungie cord that he kept on his bike. He did not bother with helmets. No time and he didn't want to risk further injury to Ellen's head.

The couple were two of the first victims of the night to reach the emergency room. Brandon even had the foresight enough to call his father and inform him where he was and why he was there.

News of the explosion had reached the hospital. Someone quickly assessed the damage to Ellen's head as a superficial cut and possible head concussion. A nurse explained to Brandon that they would need all available beds for people in worse shape. She inquired if there was someone home available that could take care of the injured girl.

Brandon called his father. His father had received the news of a second explosion and knew the National Guard had been alerted. All of the emotions from earlier in the night evaporated. "Yes, bring her here. I'll come get you." His father and one of the bodyguards jumped into the care. They were at the hospital in less than ten minutes.

Ellen had regained consciousness and did not seem overly disoriented. She recognized Brandon's father. "What are you doing here?"

"I've come to help. Let's get her to the car."

Ambulances were starting to arrive. They were dumping people, yelling out instructions and turning back for more as quickly as possible. All of the surrounding communities had been alerted. No one knew exactly how many people were injured but the estimate was in the hundreds.

Brandon's father volunteered his house as a makeshift clinic. Some of the less serious cases would be routed to his residence. Many makeshift clinics would be assembled before the night's end.

Jimmy had gotten clear of the gymnasium. The smoke from the grounds had provided cover. He located his van but was not able to leave. Emergency vehicles had him blocked on both sides. He would need to steal a car. That wouldn't be too difficult in all of the confusion. Police officers and fire fighters were trying to clear the area. Jimmy let himself be herded with the rest of the crowd.

A large man in a Massey Ferguson cap recognized him as a Pierce. "There's one of them goddamned Pierce's right there. He's probably in on it. I seen that boy a shooting people like they was dawgs. He's probably done it hisself." The man swung a big right hard that knocked Jimmy onto his ass. The big farmer reached into his pocket and pulled out a folding pocketknife. It was an old case "Sodbuster." He flicked it open with a big callused thumb. "My boy was on that team. He's a probably daid. I'm a thinking maybe you oughta be daid too." The big farmer stabbed Jimmy in the gut and twisted. He pulled the blade out and started to stab him again. An ambulance driver from nearby Prestonville grabbed his arm in midair. He had stopped his arm with his left hand. He used his right to knock the big farmer out. "You're bad hurt buddy but I'm gonna patch

you up. My name is Kyle Salsbury. I'll get you out of here. Helluv'a thing ain't it?
They say some boy no more 'n sixteen years old done caused all this grief. What 'cha
think about that? I don't know. It's like they say, some people's kids, can't take 'm
nowhere."

The hour was drawing late. Jimmy lay in a room with seven other people. The room
had been intended for four boys but the hospital was heavily overloaded due to the night's
events. His wounds had been serious but nowhere near fatal. A young intern had told
him he would be able to leave in the morning.

All in all it had been a good day. He asked the man next to what time he had.
"Eleven, forty-seven," the man replied. Jimmy laid back content. This had truly been a
great day, one of the best he could remember. He wasn't worried about being caught. He
didn't have to worry about being seen. He had been behind cover all night. He didn't
have to worry about fingerprints. The guns were his. The boy had stolen them. Hell, his
injury would even help look innocent. It had been a truly great day. Ellen heard the last
explosion from Brandon's house right at midnight. Bobby's final bomb had went off
exactly as planned. The tanks that he had thought were filled with propane were filled
with liquid oxygen. One side of the hospital complex had evaporated in a massive
fireball. Maxi Pierce and his brother were burned beyond recognition. Their bodies had
been identified by dental records. The final death toll for the day stood at two hundred
and sixty-three. No family in town had escaped unscathed. Brandon and his father had
come the closest. For some reason the day's events had made Brandon's dad stay in town
and try to reopen the wiring plant. Ellen and Maxine were the last of their family to

remain in Pineville. Brandon and Ellen were to be married. Maxine was pregnant and would not name the father of her child. Maybe someday…

THE END

Made in the USA
Coppell, TX
27 March 2021

52481517R00154